I0822762

THE WITCH

AN INTERVIEW WITH THE DEVIL STORY

MICHAEL HARBRON

"The power you unleashed that afternoon was enough to shake the very foundation of Hell, and stir Satan himself out of his crypt to come for you."

— MALLORY

CONTENTS

1

SALEM

1692— A Spring Awakening

Twilight descended upon a layer of thick mist, illuminating the small town of Salem in vivid layers of light perfusing through the air, giving the place a touch of spectrality. No man nor woman was expected to walk the cobbled streets at such a time when even the oil lamps were providing a meager halo of light and no more. The marshlands were responsible for the creeping fog, smuggling their cold and wetness toward the town, eager to reclaim it.

It was the kind of evening where shadows moved of their own volition, and the cries of night birds were muffled and distant. Every breath of wind carried with it the whisper of dread.

And yet, amidst all this, a blonde woman, having done away with the bonnet and coif she was supposed to wear, strutted with staccato steps on the cobblestones, her wavy, luscious hair bobbing with the motion of her gait, a smile bejeweled upon her face. There was a bottle of rum with her name on it in a tavern somewhere, or better yet, a nice cold cider. She would decide when she would reach the tavern, but there was one matter of fact: tonight was for getting drunk, and Lilly was going to make the most out of this otherwise dull night.

All nights were dull nights when you were a woman, but if word of that ever slipped from a woman's tongue, it was seen as heresy. Despite every woman feeling the sentiment at one point or another, no one dared to say it. After all, rebelliousness was seen as the first sign of witchcraft, and given just how obtrusive the atmosphere had become around that word, no one wanted to be misconstrued as a witch or someone sympathetic to the cause of witches.

Not if they wanted to live.

But Lilly would be damned if she was going to let that fear keep her from letting her hair flow freely. It was no ordinary feat, washing her hair and then retaining its luster, and she was not about to tie it all up in a coif and render all her efforts pointless. There was no law that said she couldn't walk around with her hair loose. The Puritans were quick to quote First Corinthians to one another, pointing out that the Apostle Paul emphasized the importance of women covering their heads as a sign of modesty and submission to male authority, but unless they were going to personally drop off buckets of fresh water and bars of soap at Lilly's doorstep, she was not going to ascribe to the teachings of any apostle. They did not have to deal with deterred scalps in such humid weather. She did.

Besides, there was no one out and about at this hour. The farmers had farmed, the bankers had banked, and just about everyone had headed back to their abodes in the village and the town, leaving the streets empty. Mothers had grabbed their children by the collars and yanked them inside in the wake of the mist. Husbands had scolded the unrulier of their wives and told them to bolt the doors and shut the windows lest they wanted the water in the air to ruin the food in the pantry.

Lilly, unencumbered in the sense that she had neither a husband to report to nor a child to take care of, walked freely through the streets, peering into the windows of shops, wondering if it was warm inside.

The Salem Town Hall stood imposingly amongst the brick buildings that adorned the main street. With its two chimneys standing high above its rooftops, its rectangular windows looking like the eyes of some brooding machine, and its steeple at the center of the roof, it was a distinguishable building by all accounts. It was the town's gathering place for all purposes, both religious and civic. Worship, town meetings, court sessions—this was where it all happened, and as such, Lilly had come to loathe this place for the oppressive governmental entity it had become.

It wasn't the town hall she'd come to town for. The twenty-five minutes she'd spent walking from the village to the hall were spent fantasizing about warm company and cool drinks. Such was what she deserved, and such was what she searched for. A perfect way to cap off a tiring day.

Even on days when there was nothing momentous to be done, you had the day's worth of chores to get through. Jonathan, a grump of a man and her elder brother by blood, needed his breakfast before daybreak so that he could get ahead of the day out in the field. Then there was making sure there was enough firewood for the evening, water fetched for cooking and cleaning and washing, animals tended, wool spun, herbs in the garden tended to, clothes washed and mended, and after all of that, preparing dinner.

It was just about hectic enough that her body felt swollen and tired each night, and there remained little in the way of enjoyment other than enjoying a good night's worth of sleep. Even that was a luxury come hard by, as the cattle mooed and bleated in the barn all night.

Not tonight though.

Tonight, Jonathan was away selling the fruits of their labor in Boston, and Lilly had no one to account for other than herself.

A well-deserved break on a rather bleak eve.

But that was the only way she knew how to live. Sneaking little pieces of silent rebellion here and there, packing them with unspoken desires, and surviving in the suffocation that her society imposed upon her. She had heard the rumors. They thought her odd, too quiet, too secretive, and lately they began to think that she was suspicious.

Suspicious on account of her being bold, unmarried, and childless past the age of thirty. If it wasn't enough that this suspicion came from outside, her elder brother, the paragon of puritanical conformity, was the one who eyed her with disdain the most. Could she blame him? He, like her, stemmed from a family that cherished tradition above all else. Her father had been a stern man, a blacksmith who believed in the rigid structures laid down by God and enacted by God-fearing righteous men. Her mother was a quiet woman who bore the weight of her husband's expectations without complaint.

A free spirit from the get-go, Lilly spent most of her time in the woods during her childhood, talking to trees and her imaginary friends and making pretend potions from flowers and plants. As she grew older, her desire for independence clashed with the expectations placed upon her. Her parents pressed her to marry again and again, but Lilly refused every suitor that came her way, much to their dismay. When her mother passed away, the bond between Lilly and her father became much more strained. It got so bad that the two wouldn't speak to each other, and when forced to do so, would only use the bare minimum of syllables to fulfill the obligations of conversation.

After her father passed, it was just her and Jonathan in the house. Instead of letting her move elsewhere and live on her own, he insisted that she live with him for the sake of protection. Lilly knew well enough that it was more about him overseeing her and controlling her behavior than it was about protection. He, being her elder brother, wanted to keep her out of trouble.

Despite her brother's intentions, she felt trapped. The house she shared with Jonathan was stifling, a reminder of the kind of life she was expected to live. Despite his temperamental flaws, was a good man, kind and hardworking. But he was not an understanding man. He refused to acknowledge Lilly's desire for something more than this meager life. Whenever she brought up the issue to him, he dismissed her dreams and told her to quiet down her childish whims of defiance.

No one suspected the depth of her dissatisfaction.

She believed that she was born in the wrong place at the wrong time, and there was nothing much she could do about it other than perhaps change her place. There were cities where liberty was cherished. There had to be. When it came down to it, it was only a matter of finding them. She had heard tales of cities on the coasts where women could walk unaccompanied and no one batted an eye. Where women could talk freely to men and drink according to their heart's desire and work. Sometimes, she figured that such talk was just fantasy woven by gullible women who wished that such a utopia would exist. Other times, she felt it in her bones that there were such places and they were calling out to her.

What about that port city, New York? Or St. Augustine? There was an English settlement she had heard about called Jamestown in Virginia. A Spanish one called Santa Fe. The word was these weren't towns that were settled by Puritans, and as such, did not have such tyrannical structures in place that belabored women like stray bitches in the streets.

Perhaps she would have some semblance of a social life in those cities. Here in Salem, it was nonexistent. And even in that nonexistent state, a state that she likened to the dark before God said, "Let there be light," she frequented taverns that catered to the spritelier folk, folk who weren't too bent on religion. As such, these places were marked with the black stamp as taboo places. Taboo, yet not altogether illegal. Regardless, folk who visited such places were not looked upon with admiration, but with shunning disdain. Lilly could bear the shunning disdain if it meant that she could sit at the bar, enjoy a pint or two of apple cider, and be on her way back home before the night became too quiet.

The town square hosted a barrage of buildings, all of them drab, built of wood and stone, a stark contrast to the brilliant display of overgrowing nature all around the outskirts and beyond Salem. This brilliant display changed colors according to the time of the year, and right now, with spring yawning awake after its deep slumber, nature had taken on colors aplenty. Colors that would have looked beautiful if not veiled by the mist.

One of the buildings that stood out from the rest was an old barn house, a remnant of the time when Salem Town and Salem Village were one and the same. Dilapidated, this old barn house had been converted into a tavern owned and operated by Bridget Bishop. With women unable to own land, Bridget had gotten hold of this barn house under the legal doctrine of coverture. Her husband, Edward Bishop, had bought the place and given it to her, himself retaining the rights to the place. She figured that she didn't need the rights to the place; only the place itself, a place she had turned into a warm and welcoming tavern for all her ilk to come by and drink heartily and avoid the company of those who did nothing other than gossip, fearmonger over smallpox, and feverishly follow the Bible.

As this was the town center, the mist in the streets was thinner. Fearing that someone would see her with her hair flowing loose like that, she took her shawl and covered her wavy blonde hair with it, now looking no more nondescript than any other woman. She knew how to cover herself well. Well enough to pass by.

Lilly approached the heavy barn door and knocked in the pattern she'd learned from someone long ago. You could not be granted entry into the tavern without knowing the right knock. Even then, someone standing on the other side of the door opened a thin sliding panel to ascertain if it was a friend who had knocked or a foe. If it was a friend, then the smaller door affixed to the bigger, heavier barn door would swing open momentarily, and you could step inside. If foe, then foe begone, and come back with a warrant for cause if ye must. Since most people did not bother with the bureaucratic process of procuring warrants, most foes just let the place be, conspiring amongst themselves as to what would be the best way to burn this barn house without being caught.

"Let God himself strike thunder upon this den of debauchery," Lilly once overheard someone say. She laughed, amused at the notion that if there were a God, he was some nobody Puritan's personal thunder deliverer, to strike where commanded. Lilly held the belief that if there was a God, he had taken a leave of absence and had left the world in the hands of insufferable children.

Four raps, then, after a long wait, a fifth, beckoning the door slit to slide open and a pair of green eyes to stare at Lilly and ask, "Hark, who goes there?"

"Clive Robertson, you know better than to ask me that question, don't you?"

"I have to be careful, Lilly," Clive asked. "The answer, if you please."

"A weary tongue and parched lips," Lilly groaned, rolling her eyes hard at the banality of the passphrase.

It did the trick, opening the smaller door. Lilly, knowing that it would close in another ten seconds, quickly stepped inside into the warmth of the bustling tavern. Since she had never seen real bustle, the barely a dozen present within the place, drinking quietly, talking even quieter, and casting each other conservative looks was the equivalent of good bustle for her.

Fire fumed in the fireplace, its broad licking flames making the wood crackle, sparks turning to embers mid-flight. Snow was still thawing out on the pathways in the wake of spring. It had been a rather cold and long winter, and spring, as spring always did in Salem, was slow to come, meaning there was still need aplenty for fires such as these, and just as much need for stronger drinks that set a similar fire down your throat and into your body.

Lilly walked over to the bar, taking off her shawl, her feet crunching sawdust and floor-hay, and sat at a stool at the far side of the bar, waiting for the bartender to come to her. The usual, Thomas McLarty, was not here tonight for some reason. In his place, an aging woman with silver hair stood pouring drinks, looking sharp while she did it.

"And what will you be having, young miss?" she asked without lifting her head up. "Ale, for what ails you, or beer to bear your burden better?"

Her words made Lilly fall into a weak trance, muting the others in the tavern and making her fixate on the woman, everything else dulling in the background. What had she just said, and why did it awaken something in Lilly?

Funny. She wasn't one to indulge herself in nonsense such as limericks and verses, and yet, at this time, it had come out of her almost spontaneously.

The woman laughed, showing a couple missing teeth in the back of her mouth.

"I don't believe we have had the pleasure of meeting each other before," she said, giving Lilly her drink of choice. "I am Bridget. Who may you be?"

As Lilly drank her cider—and verily, it did indeed stoke the fire inside her—she gasped like a thirst-parched person coming across water and then was quickly reminded of her manners. The woman had asked her something.

"Lilly Frost. Err. My name is Lilly Frost," she said, returning the woman's beaming smile. "I actually love this place. I've been here a couple times. It feels homelier and cozier than those two pubs down the street or the one at the left of the town hall, for that matter. Besides, they look at me funny if I'm there alone, as if I'm barging in without permission. No one does that over here."

"That's because this place welcomes strays of all kinds." Bridget raised her hand and waved at the frugal company in the tavern. "And its owner also got tired of being harangued by men in men-owned taverns. This right here's a hundred percent mine."

"I've heard so many things about you," Lilly said. "Somehow, I thought you'd be older. But you don't look a day over forty."

"I'm sixty, kid," Bridget said, "but you're sweet. And for that bit of flattery, your next drink's on me."

"Gee, thanks," Lilly said, gratefully taking the pint of beer from Bridget and setting it in front of herself. She wasn't one to mix drinks, and right now, her tongue was still relishing the distinct flavor of cider upon it.

"Not many people in Salem approve of a woman enjoying a pint on her own," Bridget said, procuring a cloth seemingly out of thin air and wiping a spotless glass with it. "But it's good that you're marching to the beat of your own drum. I always appreciate a woman who does that."

"And I always appreciate a free drink and pleasant company to enjoy it with," Lilly said, lifting her beer.

"Ah, what the hell," Bridget said, then put her glass down and filled it with beer. "I'll drink with ya. Cheers, lady."

They clinked their steins and drank deep, drank away their worries and sorrows, drank till their glasses were empty.

Bridget burped heartily, then laughed loudly, wiping her mouth with the back of her hand. "Lilly Frost, is it? I think you and I might have more in common than either of us realizes."

"Do tell," Lilly said, helping herself to some roasted nuts from a bowl within her hand's reach.

"I don't know how to," Bridget said, busying herself with serving the new customers who'd just turned up at the bar. "You, Lilly Frost, have a touch of destiny about you, and for now, that's all I can say on the matter."

"A touch of destiny?" Lilly asked once the customers had thinned at the bar once more. "I'm in my thirties, Bridget. I'm unmarried. I'm childless. I have never stepped foot outside of this state. If there's a touch of destiny about me, it must be a faint one, because I'm as ordinary as it gets."

Bridget smiled once more, her wrinkles pulled back, her skin seeming translucent with the sweat accumulated on it and the way the lanterns beamed light upon it at just the right angle, making her seem like an ethereal vision. She wiped her hands clean on a dishcloth and came over to Lilly's side again.

"Be that as it may, you cannot deny that all your life you have felt that you were different," Bridget said.

"What would give you that impression?" Lilly felt suspicious of this woman. Was she in cahoots with the townsfolk, eager to get a confession out of Lilly and then have her punished?

"Because I am the same as you," Bridget winked.

"Bridget, people say you're on your third husband nowadays.

You're married. From what I've heard, you've got a daughter, and you're quite vocal about everything and anything on your mind. On top of that, you're operating this tavern. It's no secret that you're one of the richer residents of this town. You and I couldn't be more apart," Lilly said, the heaviness of her statement sinking in her chest. Thirty years had gone by and she had done nothing with them other than bide her time in passivity.

"There are more ways to be similar with someone than marital status, wealth, and children," Bridget said.

"Well, you just named all the major ones, so what's left?" Lilly asked, tapping her stein for another drink. Bridget filled it deftly and handed it back.

"The fire in your heart burns the same as it does in mine!" Bridget leaned in and whispered with her lips close to Lilly's ear.

Lilly did not know what that meant, but she liked the sound of it. It beckoned her to talk about all her aspirations, dreams, and desires with this woman she had never met before. As the night wore on, the tavern began to empty and the lively chatter died down to a low murmur. Lilly and Bridget found themselves alone at the bar, the flickering candlelight casting long shadows on the wooden walls.

"There's been whispers," Bridge said with caution. "There's talk of...strange happenings in town. Things people cannot explain. Have you perchance noticed anything of the sort?"

"Like the cattle suddenly dying? Kids disappearing in the dead of the night? Blood in the wells? Those sorts of things?" Lilly asked.

Bridget was not amused. She shook her head, her mane-like hair whipping back and forth with the intensity of her movement. "Do you believe in the Devil?"

"About as much as I believe in God, which isn't to say a lot."

"Child." Bridget shook her head once more. "When the Devil comes to a town such as Salem, do you think he sows temptation in the hearts of harmless women, or do you think that he instills fear in the hearts of men who can act upon their faulty premonitions? Who would stand to do more harm in such a situation?"

"Well, seeing as how this topic has been thrust upon me out of nowhere, I don't really know because I have never given it much thought," Lilly answered. She was done with drinking for the evening, and from the looks of it, it was getting late. Later than when she was usually out. "Interesting conversation though, I think we'll pick it up later."

No sooner had she gotten up to leave when Bridget shot out her hand and grabbed Lilly's arm, holding her in place.

"Not so fast," the woman said, her eyes narrowing with an emotion that was altogether alien to Lilly. Later, she would learn it by the name of ambition.

"Let me go!" Lilly grunted, wringing her arm free from Bridget's strong grip. "What gives?"

"Are you seriously stupid? A head-in-the-clouds sort of girl? Or are you simply feigning ignorance just so you can get by without trouble?" Bridget asked, severe indignation masked on her face, her nostrils flaring.

"Listen, lady, I just came here to get a drink. I honestly don't know what you're talking about," Lilly said, eager to turn her back and head toward the door. The sooner she could be out of here, the better. She strode fast, crossing the empty tavern, her heart palpitating upon seeing the emptiness inside and the utter dark of the night sky through the rafters. If she were any later, men who roamed around with torches in their hands and bloodhounds on leashes would come across her and ask her all manner of questions in all kinds of mannerless ways. Questions the answers to which would inadvertently land her in trouble.

"Calm down," Bridget said, not from behind the bar, but suddenly, inexplicably, standing before her. "And breathe. It's all right."

Rather than ask her how she got so quickly from one place to the next, Lilly did as the old woman bid and breathed deep. It was not that late, surely, and even if it were, she knew of ways to go back to the village that would avoid the patrolmen. And what was there out in the night to be afraid of? On that note, what was there to be afraid of in here?

Bridget was just a harmless woman and nothing more.

Yet the fear and panic persisted in the form of a layer presiding under her consciousness.

"Witchcraft has made it to Salem," Bridget spoke warily, standing her ground by the gate. "And they're looking for women like us. They are not going to stop until we're out of their way."

"Witchcraft? Who are *they*? What do you mean 'women like us'? I don't know anything about any of that," Lilly replied, her voice shrill.

"Come now, dear. Let's not stand on occasion and lie to one another. I will show you mine if you show me yours." Bridget grinned and lifted her hand, making all the lanterns in the tavern go dim.

"You... You're one of them?" Lilly whispered, eyes growing wide in terror.

Bridget snapped her fingers, making the lanterns go back to their optimal brightness once more. "Well, that was disappointing. I was expecting you'd show me a trick or two of your own, but you're strange. You don't quite know that you're a witch, do you?"

"I'm not a witch," Lilly whispered, looking around. "You are mistaken."

"I've taken a shine to you, dear, and believe me, we of the craft are rarely, if ever, mistaken." Bridget grinned, her face cast in stark shadows in the questionable glow of the lanterns. "But I won't hold you against your will just yet. Go if you must. But should you feel that touch of destiny I was telling you about earlier, you'll know where to find me."

Lilly did not acknowledge Bridget's invitation as she barged through the door and left in the dead of the night, her heart hammering for a handful of reasons, one of which being that a self-proclaimed witch had shown her a magic trick that was too vivid to be an optical illusion; another was the sudden revelation that she, too, was a witch like her.

~

The next morning, there was no sign of the mist anywhere. The sun, in its benevolence, had shone with its brilliant spring fervor, striking darkness in whichever pools it dwelled, doing away with the mist, doing away with the humidity.

The Sunday ritual of church was attended by mostly everyone, but it was missed by one Lilly Frost, who had claimed sickness as her reason for not showing up.

She had not slept all night, tossing and turning in bed in the throes of what she thought was a fever. Why else would she be burning so hot?

When daylight beamed, Lilly got up and dressed in her most conservative clothes to not draw any suspicion, and while most of the townsfolk were busy gathering in the church for the service, she let the compass of her heart guide her to the woman who had awakened something in her.

1666—A Collector Calls

The forest hummed like a living being with the sound of bush crickets and stream water. Every so often, the impermeability of the humidity would be disturbed by a gust of wind, breathing fresh life into this packed grove, making the towering trees whisper ancient secrets to those who dared to venture within. Sunlight filtered through this quiet place of mystery through the dense canopy in soft, dappled patches.

Sentinel-like, the forest, in all its autumnal colors, stood its ground over the fallen leaves, sheltering the fauna within, surreptitiously paving the way for a four-year-old blonde-haired girl to traipse through its twisting paths with her tiny footsteps.

This was not the first time Lilly Frost was making her way through this forest, and in the coming years, she would acquaint herself intimately with every secret that this quiet, almost sacred place held within. Where most kids her age would get scared at the sight of the twirling, fingerlike branches poking out of the dark, Lilly held out her hand to each of them, shaking them as if they were the hands of friends and family members.

"Enough dawdling now, child," a matronly voice boomed deep within her head, but rather than frighten the little girl, the voice served to focus her. "The trees will take you for one of their own if you keep touching them. Do you want that?"

"No, Madam," Lilly giggled. The ludicrousness of the notion of her being adopted by trees rendered Madam's warning inane. Lilly hesitantly let go of a low-hanging pine and carried on her merry way. All ways were merry when you were a child. Merrier if you were a child named Lilly Frost, for instead of the blanket of darkness that had most of the forest still submerged in sleep, she saw the yellow-orange of the maple leaves smattered about the ground as an opportunity to jump upon the crispy leaves and hear their satisfying crunch under her shoes.

A deer poked its head from behind a pine—perturbed, undoubtedly, by this two-legged creature raising a ruckus. When it saw that the child bore no malevolence nor possessed any urgency to leave, the deer retracted its irritated head back behind the thicket, salvaging some more minutes of sleep from its disturbed slumber.

Given that she was only four, she did not possess enough vocabulary to explain her uncanny ability to perceive the world—and more specifically, these woods—with a depth far beyond her years. While most toddlers feared the wilderness that stretched long and dark, teeming with shadows and whispers, Lilly had always felt welcomed here, as if the trees themselves had called her name and beckoned her into their embrace.

It wasn't just about the trees. It was everything that this forest represented. Old stonework covered in moss. Puddles of rainwater in the troughs of the terrain. The mist that weaved in and out of this labyrinth of nature. The birds peering at her from their perches. Animals rearing their heads to acknowledge her. It was by no means a quiet, lifeless place wreathed in foreboding. Not to Lilly. To her, it was as busy and bustling as the town square.

When her mother would be hanging the clothes on the rope, and her father would be administering the routine health check on their family's aging horse, Lilly would climb over the wooden fence. She would make sure that her elder brother, Jonathan, was busy tending to the goats and the chickens, and once affirmed that all three family members were trapped within the wheel of banal routine, she would wander. Her small hands brushing against the bark of cedars and firs, the pulses of their arboreal lives felt in a rhythm on her fingertips, a rhythm that matched her own heartbeat.

Today was no different. Father had been diagnosing some new malaise that was causing the horse to neigh in pain. It had been raining for the past two days, which meant that the pile of clothes Mother had to wash was bigger thanks to two days of missed washings. One of the chickens, having been cooped up for two whole days, had attacked a goat in excitement upon newly securing post-rain freedom, and Jonathan was busy breaking up the scuffle.

She knew she would be back before they'd even noticed she was gone. Such was how she always did it. A child, she had learned rather early on—almost as early as she had learned how to speak well before the other children her age—how to make herself subtle and evade notice of the adults. Barely past their knees, she often eluded their lines of sight.

Her own line of sight granted to her by her two piercing green eyes held wisdom that belied her age. Not only did she use that to discern the nature of things beyond what they seemed, but she also used it to intuitively know things before they happened. It was as if the very earth whispered its secrets to her, and she alone could understand its language.

"You have to walk gently today, Lilly," Madam crooned, a formless presence whose voice resided within Lilly's head. "I sense bears suckling on honeycombs in the woods today. You wouldn't want to get eaten by one of the bears now, would you? What a horrible end that would be for you."

"No!" Lilly giggled, finding the idea hilarious instead of scary.

"Just a little farther, my child."

Lilly did as the ethereal voice bid, her mind realizing but not understanding why Madam was being more insistent, more imposing today. However, the urgency in her guide's voice beckoned Lilly to move past the smaller clearing in the forest and head toward the bigger one, where a small lake lay in somber silence, its miasmatic surface covered with algae and leaves.

All around it were trees of all kinds—oaks, maples, cedars—but the ones that were present the most and pronounced their presence with their imposing branches and leaves and trunks were the firs and pines, their packed vicinity making the area feel cloistered. Here, even the sunlight was sparse. It tried to reflect upon the surface of the lake, but the mist prevailing atop the lake's surface prevented it from doing so.

Lilly was quick to notice the sudden silence that had befallen this clearing. It did not shake her as such an unnatural silence would any other person, because all the while, Madam was accompanying her in her head, telling her to tread ever so gently toward the surface of the lake.

"Where are we going, Madam?" Lilly asked, her big green eyes affecting the area with curiosity. She had never been here before. It was beyond the rolling slopes on the uneven forest surface, and Lilly almost never made it this far. Not on her own. She knew that if she were to wander farther—

"Do you know what scrying is, my dear?" Madam asked.

"Is it what the baby Sarah does and her mother slaps her on her butt for it?"

Madam laughed.

"No, Lilly, don't be absurd. That's crying. Scrying's when you look at the surface of water and see things."

"Like fish?"

"No, child. Not fish. People like you see the world differently, don't you? You can look at the trunk of a tree and see the rot inside it. You can see, can't you? When someone such as you stares at the water, they don't see just fish. They see the future. They see the past. They can see other places. That's what scrying is."

"It's like a game, is it? I scry with my little eyes, tadpoles in the lake water!"

This time around there was no laughter. Whatever Madam wanted her to see warranted graveness.

"Keep looking at the water, and whatever you see, tell me about it when I return," Madam said, her voice absconding, leaving Lilly alone next to the lake, looking around at the tendrils of fog swiping finger-like atop the still lake, grasping the trees as it moved across the clearing, enveloping everything with deliberation.

It was at this moment that Lilly felt all of it, the sudden quietude, the aloofness of this place, and just how dark it was even in daytime. Fear found foothold in her heart, made her breath shallow, and caused her to sniff as tears—brought on by the sense of abandonment—surfaced in her eyes.

"Madam?"

There was no Madam, and it was beginning to dawn upon Lilly that there had never been a Madam to begin with. Just as she had ascribed voices to the rabbits and katydids, so, too, had she ascribed a voice to the forest itself, dubbing it Madam. Of course there was no Madam. There was only her childish voice, teaching her nonsense words such as "scrying."

Before the saner part of her mind could pontificate further, something befell, something far more silent than silence itself. Perhaps it was because she had never seen someone cross the threshold before, or perhaps because no matter how mature her mind was for someone her age, she had yet to come to terms with the concept of dying; Lilly did not recognize this new, alien perfusion in the atmosphere.

It was the stillness of death.

She sighted ripples disturbing the placidity of the water, a gust clearing away a path in the surface mist. She tried to move away from the bank, but she could not. The water spilled past the sandy surface and onto her shoes, wetting them.

As she stood there, stifling her sobs, she saw the presence suspended over the surface of the water. Where it currently floated (making Lilly wonder if you could stand on the surface of the water, and what did that mean about everything that the adults had told her about not going near the water lest she drowned; were they lying?), it was hidden in the remnant mist, its form rendered a silhouette in the dark of the cloister.

And then it began its approach, floating upon the surface of the lake, making its form clearer as it moved from a place of darkness to a place of light. But it was a remarkably draining form of light that shone near the end of the lake where Lilly stood. Not the warm, yellow sunlight she was acquainted with, but a graying light that seemed to fade the rest of the forest away.

Earlier, Lilly had been afraid. Madam had always been her guide whenever she stepped into the forest. It was her voice that turned this otherwise wild place into a serene one, her reassurance that the animals wouldn't harm Lilly, her affirmation that all the paths she saw twisting and turning in the woods would lead her back home. To that effect, Madam would, without fail, guide Lilly back to her back yard whenever she lost her way, and she lost her way every single time.

When Madam's voice left, it made Lilly feel like she was abandoned. That none of the paths would ever lead her back home.

But this presence, this strange creature gently moving across the water, gave off an energy that placated Lilly in a similar manner as Madam. This was no foe that approached her. Whoever, whatever this was, it meant no harm. Lilly no longer felt fear, for whatever bit of alienation and strangeness was left within her mind was now replaced by a sense of familiarity and recognition. As if she had been waiting for this moment her entire life of four years.

The figure, now having run out of lake to float upon, hovered in the air, cloaked in a robe fashioned out of Hessian fabric. She tried to pry underneath with her inquisitive stare, but could make no sense of the thing within. It wasn't until the floating figure extended its arms from its sleeves that she saw its graying, skeletal figure.

There was no flesh covering the bones of this creature, if it could be called a creature.

A decade later, Lilly would come to learn the word "specter," and while her mind, having been made to forget this meeting, would try to place a picture next to the definition of the word, she would come up dry. Just as she was coming up dry right now as she tried to put a word to the sight she beheld.

The Collector beckoned to her, and Lilly stepped forward without hesitation. The air around her grew colder, the colors of the forest fading to muted shades of gray. As she drew closer, the figure began to take shape, its features becoming more defined. It was cloaked in darkness, with eyes that gleamed like polished onyx, and though it did not speak, Lilly understood its message as clearly as if it had whispered in her ear.

The figure before her was a being from beyond the mortal plane, tasked with maintaining the balance between worlds. But this Collector was different from the others. It had not come to mark Lilly for death or to claim her soul—it had been summoned by Madam herself, the Keeper of the Axis Mundi, the ethereal plane that lay between this earth and the next realm.

The Collector was here to protect Lilly from a fate that was still decades away. Madam knew what was to come—she had seen the trials, the fire, the death that awaited Lilly in the distant future. And so, she had enlisted this Collector not as a harbinger of doom, but as a guardian, a shield against the dark forces that would seek to extinguish Lilly's light before her time.

As the Collector reached out, its hand hovered above Lilly's head, and she felt a surge of power unlike anything she had ever known. It was as if the forest itself was pouring its essence into her, filling her with ancient knowledge and a deep, abiding purpose. The world around her faded away, and for a brief moment, Lilly glimpsed something far greater than the woods she had wandered into—a vast, cosmic order in which she was destined to play a crucial part.

The Collector's touch was gentle, almost reverent, as it bestowed upon Lilly a mark of protection, a seal that would bind her to the Axis Mundi and to Madam's watchful care. This mark would ensure that when the flames came, when the townsfolk gathered to cast judgment upon her, Lilly's soul would remain intact, her destiny unfulfilled until the time was right.

And then, just as quickly, the vision was gone. The forest returned to its familiar hues, and Lilly found herself standing alone in the clearing, the Collector vanished without a trace. But something had changed within her, a seed had been planted, and as she made her way back home, Lilly knew that her life would never be the same.

This was the beginning of her awakening, the first step on a path that would lead her to a destiny she could scarcely imagine. The forest had claimed her as its own, and Madam's whispers would follow her for the rest of her days, guiding her toward a future where she would play a pivotal role in the eternal dance between light and darkness.

1692—A Touch of Destiny

"There's a great blockage in your mind," Bridget said, concentrating with her eyes closed and her hand on Lilly's forehead. They had met once again in the tavern, only this time around, it was not in the bleak dark of the night but in the stark light of the day. The scent of spirits lingered in the air, making Lilly's eyes water a little. From outside, they could hear the chatter of townsfolk going back to their homes after the service.

"It's almost as if someone or something is trying to make you forget a part of your life," Bridget summarized, and then retracted her hand from the confused woman's forehead. "You really don't remember anything, do you?"

"The more you mention it, the more frustrating it gets for me, because I don't know what it is you're talking about," Lilly said, crossing her arms. She tried to remember last night and wondered if that little trick Bridget had pulled was real or a trick of the lights. It felt a little embarrassing to ask Bridget for another magic trick to ascertain if she was really a witch or not.

"You think I spew bullshit?" Bridget grimaced. "That I am deliberately wasting your time?"

"The more you speak, the more I do, aye," Lilly said, getting up from the bar stool and grabbing her purse. "And you made me miss church on top of that, so there's that."

"I did not make you miss anything. I did not even call you. You came here of your own volition. Or have you forgotten that?"

"If you did not call me, why were you waiting here for me?" Lilly asked, making Bridget smile slyly.

"Because I wanted to see if you would come. And you have. Which means that you are just as curious about knowing more as you are afraid. I can help you with knowing more, but as far as being afraid goes, you better hold onto that fear for now. Not of me, mind you, but of those who would seek to strip you of the power you hold," Bridget said. Unlike last night, when she had been wearing a loose flowing green gown, today she was dressed in a black gown, as if she was in mourning. The hat she wore was a standard Pilgrim hat contorted to appear crooked and pointy. It suited her, this unorthodox appearance.

"You keep implying that I am something that I am not. What could you possibly know about me?" Lilly asked, the very same skepticism that propelled her to leave this tavern also rooting her to her spot, dispersing uncertainty in the forefront of her mind. What if this woman was right?

"What I do know is that the old world as we know it is dying. Like a diseased elephant on the verge of collapse, our world is swinging back and forth, tusks moving, trunk striking every which way. The men of this old world are not willing to go without a fight. They appear their strongest, traveling past the seven seas to newer continents so they can continue to oppress and stifle what should never have been stifled in the first place. I know that you know that. I can see it in your eyes. Just as I can see that you, Lilly Frost, are not just touched by destiny, but by magic too," Bridget said, holding Lilly's hands in her own and staring into her eyes intensely. "Don't tell me strangeness doesn't have a way of finding you on its own."

"It oddly does," Lilly remarked, thinking back to all the times something inexplicable happened. Such as when just last month, during a winter storm, the roof seemed like it would collapse and crush both her and her brother underneath. Lilly had closed her eyes and prayed, not to any God out there, but to the thrashing wind and the downpour, requesting it to cease its violence. No sooner had the whispered words left her pressed lips than the storm stopped, and the roof that would have caved in had the downpour continued for a couple more minutes stayed on stalwartly.

Bridget's insistence upon strangeness brought to mind something that happened a year ago, when a pack of coyotes had somehow found their way past the fence of their homestead. They were sniffing around the closed barn, eager to get to the cattle and poultry inside.

No! Lilly had ordered, the instruction sharp and adamant in her mind. Each of the coyotes had lifted their heads and looked in her direction as if understanding what she was saying, then whimpered in submission as they walked out of the homestead, their tails between their legs. She had not told this to anyone.

Just as she had not told anyone when one of their aging cows had squirted a copious amount of blood into the pail along with milk, and Lilly, knowing that this would be the only milk they'd get for the next day, somehow, with the motion of her hands, siphoned away the blood, leaving the milk unadulterated. Then she put her hand on the cow's abdomen and wished upon her to get better. Get better the cow did, for after that one time, she never squirted blood from her udder again.

There had been other innocuous occurrences like that in her life, things that could be brushed off as bizarre, things she had forcibly put out of her mind because there was no explanation for them, and to share them with someone would be an invitation to get called mentally unstable.

She remembered those incidents as she stood there, her self-enforced skepticism giving way to fitful belief.

"Have you told anyone?" Bridget asked.

"Not a soul."

"Then keep it that way."

"But what about you? You know," Lilly whispered.

"Child, are you thick in the head? I am not some interrogator out to get you. Just as I know that you are one, so, too, do you know that I am a witch also!"

Lilly guffawed, unable to help herself, and then threw her head back and laughed loudly, clapping her hands as she did so.

"Quiet down!" Bridget said, slapping Lilly on the shoulder.

"Sorry," Lilly chortled, her giggles dying down. "But what exactly am I supposed to do with this information? There hasn't ever been a good thing said about witches. Just that they are agents of the Devil, that they sleep with him, drink of the milk that flows from his loins, and do his bidding as hellish harlots."

"And who has been telling you this? The preacherman who won't stop thumping his Bible?! Or the townsmen who have nothing between their ears other than what the feverishly religious have fed them? The Satan they talk about is a creation of their own minds. As are the witches they fear. Tell me, girl, do you fear it when you walk out into the forest by yourself, touching the dew-kissed leaves and running your fingers through the water of the stream? Do you loathe yourself when nature talks back to you? For that is witchcraft. A gentle and honest attunement with the world around you," Bridget said. "Look at me. Am I doing something profane in this tavern? I serve drinks. I make potent homebrews that people love to drink. Where in my daily life am I calling upon Lucifer?"

"Are there others like us?" Lilly asked. Now no longer pressed by her own anxiety to leave, she went back to the bar and sat down on the same stool she had occupied last night, and Bridget went behind the bar, procuring a bottle of something dark and strong.

"You'd be talking of a coven," Bridget said, pouring rum in two glasses, giving one to Lilly and taking one for herself. "I fear there aren't that many here to warrant the formation of a coven, but then again, two can form a coven, and more can join along the way. It is a matter of putting faith in the right women, finding out if they're witches or not, and if they'd like to join us. But for now, it looks like it's just the two of us."

"I figure it's a gamble every time you corner someone and try to ascertain if they are a witch or not, yes?"

"A gamble that can cost you your life," Bridget said, clinking her glass with Lilly's.

The two downed their drinks in somber silence, looking at each other, a bond of solidarity forming between them.

"Now what?" Lilly asked.

"Now, your tutelage begins," Bridget said.

Unbeknownst to Lilly, Bridget had plans of her own.

Plans that would never come to fruition.

At least not in the way that she wanted.

But about one thing she was right—the old world was dying, and as they died with it, men of this old world thrashed against the dying of the light, hunting whom they thought were the culprits of their downfall.

Over the next couple weeks, the two of them would meet every other day at the tavern, sometimes early in the morning, sometimes late at night after the last of the drinkers had come and gone. To make things seem above board, Lilly took up a job as a barmaid at the tavern.

It did not draw any more heads in her direction other than Jonathan's, who could not for the life of him comprehend why his sister would start working as a lowly barmaid serving other people drinks when she had a whole homestead and adjacent farmland to reap from. He put up a fight, but when Lilly resorted to tears, he gave up on the matter and left the room. Shortly after, Lilly dried her tears and smiled rather satisfactorily to herself.

"Are you a lettered woman?" Bridget asked early on during their meetings. The two of them had brooms in their hands and were cleaning the floor of the tavern after a rather rowdy night.

"Come again?" Lilly asked, unable to focus on the conversation on account of wondering when she'd be actually able to ride a broom and fly.

"Can you read?!" Bridget asked, bonking Lilly's head with the business end of the broom.

"Ow! What's that for?!" Lilly said, rubbing her forehead. "And yes, I can read, no thanks to anybody. I taught myself how to do that."

"Then do us both some good and read this book for me, shall you? I am many things, but I am not a lettered woman," Bridget said, putting her broom down and disappearing into the back of the bar. She came back sometime later with a dusty tome in her hands, leatherbound, girthy in length.

Lilly could not believe that she was holding an actual magic book in her hands. The title said, *Gertrude's Grimoire and Secret Sorceries.*

"Who's Gertrude?" Lilly asked, opening the book and peering inside.

"It says her name, does it?" Bridget asked, a tear coming to her eyes, a tear that Lilly did not notice. It wasn't until Bridget's voice broke that Lilly looked up and closed the book. "Gertude was my matron. Every witch is initiated by a matron figure. This happened before we came to Salem, mind you. I was in London when she initiated me. Tried her darndest to teach me to read. The other witches in the coven learned quickly enough, but I have always had trouble with letters and words and whatnot. But I mimicked what she did and, in doing so, learned my spells and potion work. She would tell me that I was her favorite. I guess that's why she gave me her grimoire."

"I'm sorry. It sounds like something happened to her," Lilly said.

"Motherfuckers found her tending a wounded cat to life in a back alley. They thought they saw light sparkling from her fingers. They cornered her, beat her until they got a confession out of her, and then set her on fire in that very alley. She might have confessed that she was a witch, but she never gave them any names." Bridget sniffed, wiped her eyes, then cleared her throat and said, with authority, "But never you mind that. I want you to look up the spell for levitation. It's one that I never got around to learning. It must be in there somewhere because Madam Gertrude knew how to do it. She taught the other witches how to do it. I...never got the words quite right."

Lilly did as she was bid. "It doesn't just say her name. It has your name on the first page. It says, *For Bridget Bishop, when she learns how to read.*"

Bridget beamed, saying, "Ah, she always had high hopes for me, my Madam."

Lilly searched the table of contents and found the chapter on charms. There was a subchapter that spoke at length about levitation.

"For things to levitate, they must be lifted free of their weight. With your voice no louder than a dormouse's gait, whisper the word 'levicantate,'" Lilly read aloud. To her surprise, the broom she'd just put down on the floor shifted where it lay.

"That's it. That's the word. Try it again, this time with heart. No book will ever tell you this, but witchcraft comes from the heart, Lilly Frost," Bridget said, her eyes brimming with excitement as she watched Lilly read the book.

"Okay, here goes. With my heart then," Lilly said, closing the book, her focus affixed on the broom. "Levicantate!"

This was the first time in her life Lilly Frost performed a spell of her own volition. She watched with widening eyes as the broom slowly rose from the floor and floated up to Lilly's hand, the surge of magic making the wood vibrate.

"I cannot believe it," she whispered, first looking at the broom, then at the book. "Can I ride it just yet?"

"We don't really ride brooms, my dear. There's separate spell-work for flying. One that I wouldn't want you to learn about just now. For now, make mine and your brooms soar across the floor. Let's see magic clean our mess for once," Bridget said, propping herself upon the bar, sleeves folded back, hair flowing loose over her shoulders.

Lilly tried the spell again, this time putting the book down and using both her hands to direct the magic to both brooms. To her joy, the brooms lifted off the floor and moved along the rhythm of her hands, swiping the floor left, swiping the floor right. She laughed, laughed loud, and shouted, "Oh, I could get used to this."

She looked at Bridget for approval, and found the woman beaming. "It's yours."

"I'm sorry?"

"The grimoire. It's yours now. In my passing it to you, I am also passing some of my magical will down to you, just as Gertrude did to me. You shall find that your magic will come to you more frequently now. More powerfully. All I can bid you in that regard is that you use it with caution. Never make the mistake of using it in front of another person. Never cast a spell that draws too much of your power, for I have known women to die whilst casting spells that are too powerful for them to cast by themselves. But you shall find all the warnings for all the spells in the grimoire. Go then, learn it. Memorize the spells by heart. And maybe you can teach this old bitch a few new tricks while you're at it," the silver-haired witch said, getting off the bar, picking the book up off the floor, and handing it to Lilly with both hands.

"Are...are you sure?"

"Yes, child."

"Thank you!" Lilly grabbed the woman and hugged her fiercely, smelling the lavender in her silver hair, feeling the warmth of motherhood in the embrace, an embrace that her own mother had never graced her with.

"Don't thank me yet. There'll be a time when you are more powerful than you can possibly imagine, when the will of men will be yours to mold, when the might of magic courses like lightning in your veins. Thank me then, and not a moment before," Bridget said, patting Lilly's cheek with a tired and withered hand.

"I guess that makes you my Madam, doesn't it?" Lilly asked, stowing the book in her purse.

"No, child. I'm just a mentor. A Madam finds her brood. Grooms her. Empowers her. When it is time, may your Madam come and guide you, though something tells me that she already has. It's the darndest thing, I'll tell you. Reading minds and memories is a specialty of mine, and for some reason, I cannot read a part of your mind that seems to be locked away, the key thrown away."

"I wonder what's in there." Lilly chuckled.

"You and me both." Bridget chuckled back.

That night, when Lilly went back home, she did not sleep. She read the grimoire with great interest, the door of her room bolted from the inside lest Jonathan intrude. Every so often, she would come across a benign spell that she could cast, and cast it she did. She made the curtains dance, the fire flick, and shadows move from one corner of the room to another, her excitement akin to that of a child as she read page after page.

Was this the touch of destiny Bridget had talked about?

If so, it wasn't a destiny she altogether minded pursuing, just as she did not mind that it had taken thirty years for this destiny to be realized.

1692—A Reckoning of Witches

On one sunny morning in July of 1692, three girls by the names of Alice, Mary, and Ann ran after each other in the outskirts of Salem, their energetic and excited steps taking them beyond the oft-trod path and toward the wilderness.

In each of their hands, they held portions of half-eaten rye bread, their mouths still chomping on the loaves, their voices shrill with mirth as they raced past brambles, jumped over streamlets, and gave each other the chase of a lifetime.

"Stop! I'm tired!" Alice called out, both hands on her knees, her lungs burning something fierce.

"Alice! Come on!" Mary yelled from ahead, already disappearing into the forest along with Ann. Their giggles were loud and mischievous, beckoning Alice, the older of the three, to chase after them, despite the burning in her chest not subsiding. She coughed sporadically as she chased after the girls. Beyond this point, the town ended and the village began. As townsfolk, their parents never took them toward the village, which had only resulted in them feeling a sense of awe for what lay beyond the border of Salem town.

Mary and Ann had just about convinced Alice that they had

heard tales of fairies and all sorts of fantastical creatures in the forest. Alice, who was older than both by a year, still believed in the existence of such myths. What would be greater than coming across pixies in the grove and getting to peek at them bathing in the lake? Ann had said that there was a lake somewhere in there. As sickly as she had just begun to feel, Alice still wanted to go and check out the lake. She had never seen one before. The thought of so much water in just one space, and all of it surrounded by trees and greenery, made her push through this sudden bout of unwellness.

The three girls caught up with each other at the start of the woods and wandered in, each of them holding hands.

"Don't let go, okay? If you let go, we get lost," Alice said, trying to be the voice of reason. She coughed loudly, spurting out a glob of undigested bread still clinging to her throat. *Gross*, she thought, looking at that phlegm-covered, semi-chewed piece in the mud. She stomped her foot on it and carried on.

"I...I don't feel so good," Ann said all of a sudden, her grip on Alice's hand growing tighter.

"What's happening? Do you want to go back?" Alice asked.

"No. It's not something outside. It's inside," Ann said, worry smattering over her face as she let go of the other girls' hands and grabbed her stomach. "I think I need to go to the outhouse."

"There are no outhouses here, silly," Mary scolded. "You better wait till we go back ho-ho–" She could not finish her sentence. Instead, she burst into a series of dry coughs and fell to her knees, her hands covering her face. "Oh no."

At this point, understanding started to dawn upon Alice. There was something wrong in these woods. Something powerful—or someone—was trying to stop them from entering. Whoever it was, they were doing it by imposing sickness upon these girls. Alice figured that they could stop and turn around, go back to their homes, or they could show a little bit of defiance and continue down the path. Since they had already come this far, why not a little farther?

Their faces turned pale, sweat embossing upon their foreheads, and all three of them burst into coughs one after the other. They continued walking down the path, following its twists and turns until they could not see where they had come from. They were lost in the maze of the grove, but despite their sudden sickness, they were all fine with it. After all, there were fairies ahead.

Another five minutes of walking, they came upon the majestic lake, the lake that Alice had only heard tales about.

"Wow!" she whispered, letting go of the girls' hands and running toward the water.

"Not so fast, Alice. You can drown!" Mary called.

Alice did not know what that meant. She had yet to gain an understanding of the fact that lakes were not a shallow sheen of water, but quite deep. She learned that lesson in the next second when her over-eager step sank past the surface of the water and kept going inside. She squealed and pulled back just in time, retreating from the lake.

"It's deep," Alice said.

"That's what I was trying to tell you, dummy," Mary said.

"Look," Ann added, picking up a rock and throwing it in the water. "Look how deep that goes? If you go in the water, you can drown."

"And then what happens?" Alice wondered, imagining herself at the bottom of the lake.

"Then you're stuck there forever," someone said, but it was neither Ann nor Mary.

Alarmed, the girls jumped to their feet and looked around for the source of the voice, and upon not finding it, they clung to each other, staring around, looking at the suddenly shifting shapes of the forest, the shadows being cast long and wide even in the middle of the day.

"What are three young children doing so deep in the forest?" the voice carried over the surface of the lake and boomed in their ears menacingly.

As if struck by something invisible, the three of them fell to their knees in agony, their feeble hands holding their writhing bodies as pain shot and bolted from their stomachs and reached the peripheries of their tiny bodies.

Screaming, coughing, rolling over, the three girls looked around with terror-widened eyes, hoping to locate the speaker.

But there was only the forest and all the darkness that was pooled inside it.

"Three little children, so far away from home," the woman's voice chanted as it neared, still unseen, only heard.

Alice, Ann, and Mary convulsed where they lay, their bodies seizing, tremors running through their hands and feet. They screamed at different pitches, unable to comprehend what was happening to them.

Amidst this madness, Alice came to understand something. They had indeed trodden upon the territory of a fantastical creature, it just wasn't pixies or fairies or lake-nymphs.

It was a witch.

She could see it approaching from beyond the cedars, the woman dressed in black garbs, a crooked hat upon her head, her skeletal fingers caressing the trunks of the trees as she approached them.

A snide smile upon her face, the witch cackled as she strode across the path and came upon the squirming children.

"What kind of spell have you put us under?!" Alice cried, her wail resonating with the tenor of the cries of Ann and Mary, their cacophonic symphony of screams ringing through the forest.

"A spell? Oh, nothing of the sort, dears. You appear to be quite sick," the witch said, kneeling down and touching the foreheads of the little girls. "I must tend to thee."

What Ann heard was, "I have a bubbling cauldron for you, you wretched child!"

Inside Mary's head, the witch's voice shrieked, "I punish intruding children like you by tearing their limbs apart!"

But it was in Alice's mind that the witch spoke its most damned secret: "After I have consumed your petite forms and have devoured the stew I'll have made from your meat and sinews, I will throw what remains of your bones in the lake. Your parents will try, but they will never find you!"

The three girls shrieked, blood oozing out from the corners of their eyes and their nostrils, and before the witch could inflict her twisted violence upon them, they passed out, lying unconscious on the forest floor in a puddle of their own making.

THE WORDS to the spell for luminescence lingering on her dry, crusted lips, Lilly could not muster the minimal strength needed to whisper, "Illumis." Instead, she sat slumped in the cold, damp, six-by-six enclosure that was her jailhouse cell. A large window covered in iron bars allowed a thin shaft of moonlight to flit in, casting everything in a much ghastlier light than it really was: a muddy slab of stone that was to be her bed, a grimy pail that was to be her means of answering nature's call, and a general slickness on the surface of the slippery brick floor that made sure she fell every time she tried to get up and walk a step.

On second thought, it was as despicable as the moonlight made it look.

Not having bathed in a week, Lilly stunk to high heaven. Not having eaten a proper meal in three days, hunger growled in her empty stomach. She rubbed away the crusts from her eyes as she heard the sound of boots echoing in the confined space on the other side of the reinforced wooden door.

Guardsmen approaching.

Lilly rose slowly from the floor, making sure to grab onto the wall for support lest she slip again. As weak and will-broken as she was, she could not let the guardsmen see anything other than powerful defiance on her face.

The door swung open and men with passive faces reached in, grabbing her by the arms, the roughness of their grip a taste of the pain the shackles would bring in a moment when they'd be clamped on her wrists.

There they were, clanging in the belts of one of the guards. He took them out and wordlessly locked the tight iron cuffs around her, almost breaking into a smile when she winced in pain. The chains clinked ominously as they pulled her and escorted her out of the prison and to the courthouse adjacent to the town hall.

The brief walk from the jail to the courthouse was enough to give Lilly an idea of just how rabid the townsfolk had become, and that even if she were declared innocent—not that that was happening—she'd never live amongst them the same again. Snarling faces, pointing fingers, wagging tongues hurling insults. The crowd gathered around the courthouse was imposing upon itself, people eagerly climbing over one another to get a better look at the witch who had cursed the children.

She closed her eyes and ears to the sights and sounds, and let the guards take her inside the courthouse. Unfortunately, the courtroom was just as packed within as it was outside, with people spilling out of the benches in anticipation and anger alike.

The guards took her to the stand and bolted the waist-high door once she was inside. They did not release her from her cuffs. She stood there in pain, acknowledging the grim nature of the room with its broad bench with five empty seats. The magistrates would fill them shortly.

Behind her were all the people she'd ever known in her life, all of them wearing hostility upon their faces, cursing her under their breath.

The authoritative raps of Chief Magistrate William Stoughton echoed in the room. A man of stern conviction and unwavering belief in spectral evidence, William Stoughton had garnered a most fearsome reputation even amongst the Puritans. A Harvard graduate, he had been lobbying for witch trials for a long time, and as far and wide as his Puritanical influence would allow him. Word of him was widespread in all adjoining counties and cities. After a decade or so of lobbying, his time had come. A witch trial, the very first one, here, in Salem.

Stoughton bore a deep smugness on his face as he walked over to the bench and placed himself upon the largest chair in the center. The other four magistrates came shortly after and took their seats.

The court clerk, a stout man with a pudgy face standing by the bench, yelled, "All rise for the Honorable Magistrate William Stoughton, Chief Justice of the Court of Oyer and Terminer!"

Everyone in the courtroom stood up, Stoughton looking at them with a mix of patience and passivity. A jury sat on the right side of the room, comprising honorable folk from the county of Salem.

As everyone sat down, the other magistrates approached and sat down on either side of Stoughton.

Stoughton took the gavel and twisted it in his hands, admiring it, weighing the power it held, and then looked at Lilly, as if trying to say her fate was already decided, this was just a formality.

She returned his piercing gaze with a scornful one of her own, telling him that if he thought he'd broken her by putting her in prison for a week without proper food and water, he had another thing coming.

"The court," Magistrate Stoughton cleared his throat and consulted his documents, "will now hear the case against Lilly Frost, charged with the crime of witchcraft."

A low gasp traveled through the crowd in the benches, but it was a deliberate shout that escaped Lilly's indignant lips as she said, "You dare bring me here solely because I was at the wrong place at the wrong time. An unmarried woman in her thirties, having done nothing wrong, and you dare accuse me of heresy, to condemn me of my independence? I scorn you and your false judgments." Her voice was trembling with righteous fury, each word dripping with defiance as she cursed the judge.

Sarah Brooks, Lilly's best friend in Salem and the impromptu attorney who'd defend her in this case, came rushing forward from behind, crossed into the court area, tried to catch her breath, and stood up, adjusting her dress and her coif, doing a little bow at the magistrates' bench.

"I am ever so sorry about the late arrival, your honor," Sarah said, panting. She was no lawyer, but she had a way with words that was akin to witchcraft unto its own. She could sway even the stubborn minds and have people in the trance of her charisma when she needed to. She had offered her smarts to Lilly without hesitation, knowing full well the risk it posed to her own safety, knowing that once the trial was over—for better or for worse—she would have to leave Salem for good.

"Another error of such nature, and you shall be held in contempt of court. Let it be known Sarah Brooks has been fined three shillings for her late arrival." William Stoughton grimaced, his half-moon spectacles on the very edge of his nose. He peered through them at everything and everyone with a unanimous distaste.

"But, Your Honor..."

"Enough. Another word out of you and it will be you on the stand," Stoughton barked. It was evident within the first few minutes of this session that Stoughton was immune to Sarah's charms.

Sarah hushed up very quickly and gave Lilly a brief side-glance, murmuring the words, "I'm sorry."

"It might do you good, Mrs. Brooks, to inform your client that whatever she says can and will be used against her. Her inane ramblings and cursing during this session will be taken into account. Mind her leash," William Stoughton said, and then beckoned quickly with his hand, procuring forth the prosecutor who would be presenting his arguments against Lilly.

Thomas Newton came forth with a file clinging to his chest. He promptly placed it on the table in front of him and consulted the notes he'd scribed. He had a hawkish gaze and a face that seemed to be sculpted in an effigy of sternness. His dark robe swept the floor as he addressed the magistrates, the jury, and the townsfolk, all of whom leaned forward to catch his every word.

"Your Honors, esteemed members of the court, and fellow townspeople, we stand here today to prove that Lilly Frost has engaged in acts of witchcraft, conspired with the Devil to bring harm upon our community, and has inadvertently harmed three little children in her attempts to bring ruin upon Salem. You will hear testimony from those who have suffered at her hands, and we will present evidence that leaves no doubt as to her guilt. We will be calling upon Bridget Bishop, the owner of that accursed tavern, and Jonathan Frost, her brother, as witnesses so they may speak on the matter and tell you how she conspired with the Devil to curse Alice, Mary, and Ann. These innocent children who were possessed for hours at a time, writhing in torment while she reveled in their suffering."

Thomas had commanded the very air of the courtroom into submission with his words, rendering complete silence in the room as the magistrate, jury, and crowd members, one and all, dug their glares into Lilly's flesh.

Sarah cleared her throat, bringing the attention of everyone in the court upon her person and, while doing so, relieving the high tension hanging suspended in the room. She spoke confidently and with much poise. "Esteemed members of the court, ladies, gentlemen. I know all of you, and that is saying something. It's a testament to how close-knit our community is. Salem is our home, and we have worked hard to build a life here. We greet each other in the streets during the day and, after toiling in the sun, gather for a pint of beer and cider, don't we? Our sense of community is strong, wherein one looks out for the other."

Her warmth thawed the ice in the room, making a few jury members acknowledge her with chuckles and nods, their tense expressions easing just a little.

"And today," Sarah continued, her voice growing stronger, "what you are going to hear is that Lilly Frost is not the demonic, devil-worshipping woman that the prosecutor would have you believe. In fact, many of you have known Lilly for most of her thirty years. Have you ever known her to be a troublemaker? Has she ever caused harm to any of you? Absolutely not. Lilly Frost is a quiet, independent woman, decent and kind. She has always been willing to help anyone in need. That is who Lilly Frost truly is, and that, my friends, is what you will hear today."

The jury exchanged glances, some nodding in agreement. The townsfolk behind them shifted, murmurs spreading through the crowd as doubt began to creep in.

Were it the world of women—a world of gentle reasoning—perhaps things would have turned out another way. But in 1692, it was still very much the world of men, men who sought order through violence. Impatient men with their wills guided by fear, not reason.

Thomas Newton was unfazed upon hearing the defender's opening statements. He wasn't one to mince words nor trade them meaninglessly. He beckoned quickly, signaling Alice, the eight-year-old girl, to take the stand. Barely recovered from her ailment, Alice was still pale and weak. Her small frame trembled as she approached the witness box. She climbed the steps with hesitant, teary eyes, and stood overlooking the courtroom, clutching her dolls as if it was the only anchor in a world gone mad.

"Alice Hawkins stands before you, daughter of Thomas and Wilfreda Hawkins. She is one of the three girls who suffered maliciously at the hands of Lilly Frost. As it happens, she is also our first witness. Come, child. Speak to the court. Tell us how old you are," the prosecutor snapped in quick succession, each word impatiently on the heels of the one before it. He spoke with the insensitivity of a man who did not know the way of children.

"E-e-e-ight." Alice struggled with her word, tears spilling out of her eyes as she stood there, feeling as much victim as she did witness.

"Eight," Thomas chewed on the word. "And do you know who this woman is?" His insinuating finger aimed at Lilly, who rolled her eyes, mocking the proceedings of this court, wincing with the pain the shackles inflicted.

Alice shook her head profusely, her eyes nervous as they darted between the prosecutor, the magistrates, and Lilly.

"Do not lie here, for lying has severe consequences, even for children such as yourself. Be truthful. Have you not seen this woman before?"

"I...I have seen her before, but I do not know who she is," Alice said meekly. "That day, I saw her in the woods, but she..."

"She what, child?" Thomas barked.

"She wasn't the only thing I saw in the forest that day. Them other two girls were with me. They can tell you. This woman was not alone!" Alice shuddered with fear as she spoke, and she wasn't the only one to do so. A grim whisper raced through the crowd as they discussed this latest development in hushed silence.

"Silence!" Magistrate Stoughton banged the gavel. "Order in the court!"

That quickly shut everyone up.

"Speak," Thomas said, his gaze peering into Alice's soul as he presided over her. When she did not speak, Thomas accounted for his tone, and added, "My dear, that order was not for you. You can tell me all you have to. I am your friend."

Alice was not buying any of it. Tears continued to stream down her face as she spoke. "Me and my friends went down to the forest. But it was like the forest was bewitched. She was hiding behind every shadow, it seemed. And she spoke from out of nowhere. When she appeared before us, she inflicted much pain, and she cackled as she did so. She wore black, black her hat and black her robes. Her face was most sinister."

"What did she do to you?" the prosecutor, Thomas Newton, asked with impunity, banging his fist on the edge of the witness box.

"She rushed toward us while we lay on the floor. All three of us screamed in pain. She made us see things. Dark and horrible things. She told me that she would tear my meat and sinews and make a stew out of them."

Lilly could not help but laugh out loud in disbelief.

"You know that that's not true. Ask anyone. I was in the woods; about that part, she's right. But I did not haunt them or taunt them. When I came across these kids, they were lying on the floor, half-eaten loaves of rye bread by their feet. They were covered in vomit and reeking of urine. I took them to my home one by one, because they're heavy to carry all at once. And then I alerted the sheriff. That's the first thing I did. I made sure that these girls went back to their homes. I did not terrorize them, as little Alice is making it out to be. It was clear they were sick before I'd even come across them!"

"You shall not speak out of turn again," Magistrate Stoughton yelled, banging his gavel. "Tell your client to speak only when spoken to!" This next bit of admonishment was directed at Sarah.

"Lilly, cut it out!" Sarah whispered.

"Or what? They'll clamp me in irons? They've already done that," Lilly snapped.

"What else happened, child?" the prosecutor continued.

"I don't remember anything after we passed out. But she still comes to me in dreams, telling me that if I open my mouth, she'll pull my tongue out and boil me alive. That day, she walked with the Devil. She was not alone."

"Excuse me!" Lilly interjected. "But what would a little child like you know of the Devil?"

This time, the court did not interrupt her.

"Who was it walking behind you?" Alice whimpered. "With hooves for feet and a black ram's head? I remember seeing it as clear as day. It had red eyes and a forked tongue."

"That was my goat!" Lilly exclaimed. "And it did not have red eyes. I take my animals out into the woods so that they can graze."

"Your Honor," Sarah Brooks quickly interrupted before things could become tense once again, "if I may?"

Magistrate Stoughton nodded briefly.

Sarah approached the witness box and smiled at Alice. "Alice, dear. Do you think that the things you thought you saw in the woods could also have been due to the fear of being alone in the middle of the forest?"

"But I wasn't alone. I was with Ann and Mary and they saw the same thing as me!" Alice retorted.

"It is possible that sometimes when a person gets scared, others around them get scared and become impressionable," Sarah said. She wasn't expecting Alice's response to be this sharp and sudden.

Needless to say, she hoped that reason would prevail over the hysteria that had taken root in Salem. But above that, she hoped that the jury, the public, and the magistrates would see enough sense to trust the word of an eight-year-old, especially when that eight-year-old had been known to lie.

"Alice, dear," Sarah said. "Is it true that you stole loaves of rye bread with your friends, Mary and Ann, and wandered into the woods as you enjoyed the fruits of your thievery?" After failing to present any condemning arguments against the young girl, Sarah had resorted to pulling the one trick she had under her sleeve, perhaps a moment too soon.

"We were going to pay for that bread!" Alice caved in, causing an uproar in the crowd.

"No, you weren't. Mr. Adams, the owner of the bakery cart from where you stole that bread, confronted you while you were on your way to the woods. When confronted, you lied to his face and told him you didn't steal anything."

"That's not true," Alice said.

"Aye, but it is!" Mr. Adams rose from the crowd, a thin wisp of a man with graying hair and a scurvy-marred face. "I thought I saw 'em take three loaves. Now, I's known their fathers and mothers, so I gave 'em the benefit of the doubt, like so. But they straight up said they didn't take 'em. Your Honor, it takes me quite some time and a lot of resources to make my daily bread, as the Lord intended. I need to earn my keep. How can I, when thieves as young and innocent-looking as them go about stealing my bread?"

"Be that as it may," Magistrate Stoughton said, rearing his big head. "You are not on the witness list, nor is this a case of bread theft. Sit back down or be escorted out of the court, Mr. Adams."

Mr. Adams looked enraged as he sat down, but one thing was clear. The jury's view had been swayed by this spontaneous display.

"You are correct, Your Honor. This is not a case of bread theft, but the fact remains that Alice is not a reliable witness. Her testimony does not bear any merit," Sarah said.

"That will be for the court to decide, Mrs. Brooks, and not you, mind you," Thomas Newton stated.

"Nor you, then, mind you," Sarah chided, sarcasm rife in her voice.

A little taken aback by the display of boldness, Thomas Newton struggled with his words for a moment before finding his footing again. "Your Honor, I would like to call my next witness, Alice's father. A man who shares my namesake. Thomas Hawkins."

Thomas Hawkins, a grief-stricken man with a worry-besotted face, rose from the bench and approached the witness box. As he paused there, he patted his daughter's head and gave her a kiss on the forehead before stepping inside and taking her place.

"Thomas, may I?" the prosecutor asked.

"Yes," he replied.

"When your daughter returned from the woods that day, she was frantic, dirty, had vomit on her clothes, and was not quite in her senses. What can you tell us about that day?"

The six-foot-three man burst into profuse tears before beginning his testimony. "I thou... I thought that she had been ravaged by another man. She was passed out when the sheriff delivered her to our home, and when she came to, she writhed and puked and thrashed. We had to tie her arms and legs down before we called the priest."

"The priest?" the prosecutor asked.

"Aye. For it was clear to us that this was the work of the Devil. Father Agnes came at our first beck, and spent the night exorcising the demon out of her."

"And did he succeed?"

"Aye. I should think so. Come morning, she was feeling much better, but she wasn't remembering much of what had happened other than the witch. Kept telling us that a witch gone done sicced the Devil upon my baby daughter!"

The prosecutor stood with his arms behind his back and looked at the jury, possessed of all the confidence in the world.

"This, ladies and gentlemen, is the testimony of a man you all know. A carpenter who has worked for most of you, who you have all enjoyed a pint of beer with in the local tavern. Do you think this man, a man of God, would make up such a lie? Do you think that a man of this stature would be reduced to tears if he did not think the Devil himself had paid a visit to his daughter, Alice?"

It was Sarah's turn to address the witness. She began so earnestly, saying, "It deeply grieves me to hear what befell upon your daughter, Thomas. I have a daughter of my own, Rebeccah, and had something similar happened to her, I would have felt the same agony you have. But let me ask you something, Thomas. Before the bread, has Alice ever stolen anything before? And please remember, you are under oath."

"Well," Thomas said, patting his head, stuttering just a little. "There was that one time she brought home a dog. I asked her about it and she called it a stray."

"But the dog wasn't a stray, was it?"

"Objection, Your Honor. This is very speculative," Thomas Newton cried out.

"Sustained," responded Magistrate Stoughton.

"It is true!" a woman called from the back of the court. "Old Tumnus, my border collie, went missing. And when I asked the girl about it, she lied about it!"

"Remove that woman from the court," Magistrate Stoughton shouted, banging his gavel. "And should anyone speak again out of turn or order, I shall have them arrested for contempt of the court."

While the pleading woman was dragged out of the courtroom, Sarah addressed Alice, saying, "Did you steal the dog from your neighbor's yard? And did you tell your father that it was a stray?"

"Yes," Alice cried, covering her face with her hands. "But I was just playing."

"And is it true that you were so scared of being caught with the stolen bread that you concocted this tall fable about Ms. Frost here, a tale that has no roots in reality?" Sarah asked.

"This is entirely speculative!" the prosecutor yelled.

"Mrs. Brooks, this is your final warning. Another speculative insinuation out of you, and it shall be you sharing the cell with Ms. Frost," Magistrate Stoughton said.

"Speculative, Your Honor? Isn't the entire trial about my client being a witch speculative?" Sarah shot back.

The magistrate smiled slyly and gave a nod to Thomas Newton, whose face was now lit with a malevolence that made Sarah afraid. What were the two of them planning on doing?

"Excuse Mrs. Brooks here, Your Honor. She is not an educated lawyer. If she were, she would know what speculative means. But on that note, Mrs. Brooks, no. This entire case is not speculative. We are only ascertaining something we already know with surety. We thought that this would be a good opportunity for the public to know just how forked the tongues of witches are and how they can warp the beliefs of those around us."

"What are you getting at?" Sarah asked. Then, turning to Lilly, she asked the same question. "What is he getting at?"

Thomas Newton smirked before he raised his hand and beckoned the court clerk to disappear through the side door.

"We are only doing this as a formality, Mrs. Brooks. As it happens, we have irrefutable evidence that Lilly Frost is a bona fide, God-cursed witch practicing black magic in the confines of her home and out in the wilderness of Salem."

Lilly's heart, already a palpitating mess, skipped a couple beats altogether. Bridget was sitting silently on the bench behind her, so she could not very well be the surprise witness. Who, then, was it?

"Be that as it may, your Lordship," Sarah said, not losing her nerve. "I should think that the unbiased nature of this most esteemed institute would allow us a chance to offer our defense as we see fit. Could we have that?"

Stoughton deliberated with his fellow magistrates, all of them whispering in snide, low voices, smiling at each other, laughing at whatever it was they were talking about. After a long time talking to each other, they looked at Sarah, and then at Lilly.

"We have decided that we will allow you to present a defense. After all, despite all our evidence, if two women can think they can sway the view of the entire jury and all the magistrates present in this room, not to mention the views of the townsfolk of Salem, I believe I would very much like to see that happen." Stoughton sneered, adjusting his pose behind the table and banging his gavel. "The court shall reconvene tomorrow at this same time. In the meantime, please escort Ms. Lilly Frost back to her jail cell so that she can think on her life's choices and atone for her sins. Even if she is tried, an atoned soul would be saved the eternal torture of Hell."

Sarah and Lilly shared a desperate look, one in which Sarah was trying to say, *Don't worry and don't you lose faith in me just yet. I will do something about this*, and Lilly was trying to say, *Don't you see, Sarah? They've already made up their minds.*

As the session came to an end, the rough guards grabbed Lilly brutally by each arm and dragged her back to her cell. Lilly was thankful, despite their violent grips, that they were here, because they were the only thing standing between her and the even more violent mob ready to get their hands on her and rip her asunder well before her sentencing. Even from afar, they threw whatever they held in their hands at her, some of those projectiles being blunt rocks that ripped Lilly's clothes and tore her skin open.

She winced, but did not cry. This was expected to happen, and who was she kidding? There was no way she was coming out of this alive.

Once she was thrown back into the desolate cell, she hugged her body and let herself weep from the pain all those things thrown her way had caused. It wasn't just the bodily pain from the blunt collisions; it was that the people throwing those things were people she had called fellow townsfolk, people she had known all her life.

How quickly they turned on her.

After an hour, after going through the whole process of wanting to speak to her client, Sarah came into the prison and spoke to Lilly through the door.

"I don't have a lot of time, Lilly, but we will get through this. Somehow, I know we will."

"I don't think so, Sarah. They've got someone who's going to turn on me come tomorrow. What are you going to do in the meantime? What could you and I possibly do that would absolve me, clear my name?"

"You need to tell me all the details all over again so I can get something, anything," Sarah pleaded. "It looks bleak, I know, but trust me. We'll get through this."

"I don't think we will, but I have come to peace with this. I am one with the earth, with fire, air, and water, and I have made peace in the notion that I must die to be recorded in history, to set the trail for change. I cannot fathom that these accusations can last much longer; surely people are more intelligent than this," Lilly responded.

"Lilly, what do you think was happening in the woods? What were the girls saying or doing when you were there?" Sarah knew she was clutching at straws and her argument was waning thin.

"I really do not know, but they were eating that rye bread when I saw them, so they must have just stolen it from Mr. Adams' cart, that for sure is true," Lilly responded.

They didn't let Sarah sit for long in the prison. Before she could talk any further to Lilly, the guards pulled her out and bid her—rather roughly—to go home, leaving Lilly alone in the cell.

Sarah, disgruntled, began her walk home. As the evening was drawing to a close, the markets on Main Street were coming to an end, selling their wares cheaper than they were during the morning dawn. Included in the cheaper sales was Mr. Adams and his loaves of bread, staler than they were first thing in the morning. Sarah stopped by his cart and took stock of his goods.

"Good evening, Mr. Adams, how are you feeling after that little outburst today?" Sarah greeted him.

"Good evenin', ma'am. I just couldn't control myself, but alas, the truth shall prevail!"

"It shall indeed, what do you have that I can take?" Sarah asked him, hungry, tired, and in need of sustenance. She would have taken anything Mr. Adams could have given her.

"I just sold me last loaf, but I do have some rye bread that's a couple days old, nuthin' wrong with it, just a little stales is all. Tells ya what, for outing that little beggar today you can take a couple loaves for free, they did nuthin' but cause me heartache, they did." Mr. Adams was happy to get rid of his bread and gave Sarah two loaves for free.

As Sarah trudged home, she opened the door to her abode where her husband Tobias greeted her with a warm bowl of venison stew. The bread would serve as a good accompaniment, and Tobias was delighted that Sarah was able to nab a couple loaves for free.

As they sat down for dinner, Sarah was regaling Tobias about her day, talking about the trial and the issues surrounding it. Tobias dunked the hearty rye bread loaf into the venison stew and took large bites, almost obliterating the loaf in a few bites. Upstairs, their three-year-old toddler was crying.

"I'll see to her. Enjoy your dinner, my love, I'll be back in a moment," Sarah told Tobias. A carpenter by day, and Sarah a stay-at-home mother, she was overjoyed that Tobias had allowed her to lend her sharp wit, albeit not today, to Lilly's trial.

Their daughter, Rebeccah, was throwing the tantrum of all tantrums and demanded over an hour of Sarah's time. Her dinner getting cold, she did not want to leave her crying, taking away from Tobias' relaxing evening with his free loaf of bread, and as she descended the stairs once Rebeccah had drifted off to sleep, a howl she had never heard before from her own mouth nearly brought her to her knees.

Tobias was convulsing on the floor, his body spasming, his eyes rolled to the back of his head, mumbling in what seemed a foreign language, foam billing out of his mouth.

"TOBIAS, TOBIAS!" Sarah screamed. He'd been cursed, she thought; the Devil had found his way into their home and possessed her husband.

But Sarah was more astute, and she knew something was very off. As sharp as a tack ninety-nine percent of the time, it didn't take her long to realize that Tobias had eaten rye bread, as had Alice and her friends the day they all convulsed in a similar fashion.

"That fucking bread," she scolded to herself. Sarah knew that since three eight-year-olds had eaten something similar and lived to tell the tale, Tobias would be fine. She covered his mouth with her hand to stifle the screams and rocked him until he became stable. The effects would last well into the evening, but Sarah had work to do.

"Darling, I need you to stay here for one hour, I'll be right back," she told her husband as she dashed out the door.

Dressed in her dark cloak and hood above her head, Sarah rapped on the door of the baker, Mr. Adams. As he frantically opened the door with a look of horror on his face, "Sarah, I had a feeling you would show up."

"Just what the hell do you think you've been doing, Mr. Adams?"

Mrs. Adams took no time in asking what the hell Sarah thought she was doing in their home causing a ruckus at such hours.

"You know very well what is in that rye bread. How long have you known?"

"I...I didn't know for sure, and to be honest, I wouldn't have given you free loaves if I knew for sure. It was a hunch. People don't overly enjoy the rye bread, so it runs bad and I keep it for those who may just have a few extra coins to help me keep my family warm and fed."

"At the expense of people's lives? What is in that bread that is causing this?" Sarah demanded.

"If bread is moldy, a fungi called ergot will grow within it, particularly in rye bread," he responded openly and honestly, but it wasn't enough to curb Sarah or his wife. "I pick the mold out of the bread and I thought it would be fine. People have been eating it for years, and only occasionally would I hear of people getting sick!"

"How could you?" Mrs. Adams responded.

"Sick?" Sarah chimed in. "An innocent woman is about to die because of you. I need you to admit this to the court tomorrow. I'm calling you in as a witness," Sarah demanded again.

"I'm afraid I cannot, Sarah. I would be ruined, my family would be placed in jail, and no doubt I would be hanged."

"My friend is about to be hanged!" Sarah cried. "If you're not in court in the morning, I'll be reporting you to the court myself. I still have one of those loaves and I'll take it myself in front of everyone if I have to."

Sarah slammed the door behind her as she left the Adams' home and returned to her husband. Tobias was slumped on the floor with a bucket by his side, feeling queasy.

Sarah drew water and with a small washcloth soaked it on his head. "It's fine, my love. The bread had mold in it and it poisoned you. This whole hoo-hah about witches is nothing more than mold poisoning. I don't really know how or why yet, but we'll get to the bottom of it."

It was just an hour after Sarah had returned home, comforting Tobias with cold washcloths. She had extinguished the fire and was helping him to bed, but a noise was coming from outside, a noise of chatter and clanking.

"SARAH BROOKS, OPEN THESE DOORS IMMEDIATELY!" a voice rang out outside the Brooks' family home.

As Sarah ran to the front door of her humble abode, she saw the townsfolk outside with sticks ablaze. Leading them was Father Agnes, the local sheriff, the prosecutor on Lilly's case, and one Mr. Adams.

"Sarah Brooks, you have been charged with witchcraft. Now step aside and let us in," the sheriff demanded. The demand wasn't in any sense a request, and both him and Father Agnes barged in to see Tobias slumped in a chair, the convulsions having begun again. Those that could see into the Brooks' home would scream at the sight. "Was this what you witnessed with Alice, Mary, and the third child, Father?"

"The Devil is in this town, and he has taken hold of the soul of Tobias Brooks," Father Agnes cried.

"How COULD you?" Sarah screamed at Mr. Adams. "He is poisoning the entire town. This isn't witchcraft, it's HIM!"

But it was too late; Sarah was shackled and carried to the jail cell, where she sat in a six-by-six brick cell next to Lilly Frost.

THE NEXT EVENING, the trial continued. Stoughton entered a packed courtroom, the night outside dark and full of terrors. He walked slowly to his podium, smirking at Newton and gleaming at Sarah in a beguiled fashion. He began, "I see you are not represented by anyone today, Miss. Frost."

"How can I, when the entire town is against me, when you've had my friend imprisoned?"

Stoughton laughed, showing his yellow teeth. "Ah yes, the other witch."

"Enough with this charade," Lilly said, trying to keep herself strong for the sake of the other two.

"You're right. It is quite enough. We have a very short order to tend to. The witness who has incriminating evidence against you. Something that solidifies your guilt. You are who we say you are, witch."

Lilly did not say a word. Instead, she watched as the door opened and guards escorted someone very familiar inside holding something even more familiar.

She gasped audibly, the life going out of her legs and making her collapse in the stand as the court clerk appeared with Jonathan behind him. Jonathan averted his gaze from Lilly as he went to the witness box and stood there.

"Jonathan?" Lilly addressed him across the court. "What is the meaning of this?"

"You don't have to speak to her if you don't wish to," Thomas Newton said, his hand on Jonathan's arm. "Ladies and gentlemen, I present to you Jonathan Frost, an honest and hardworking man of Salem. He tills and sows and reaps and sells his produce all over the county. He also happens to be Ms. Frost's elder brother. I am sure that he has plenty to say, but the time of the court is valuable, and so is Mr. Jonathan's. So rather than say anything, I would much rather he presented the exhibit for all to see."

Lilly's heart sank even further when she saw the black shawl-draped book Jonathan held inside his coat. He brought it out and presented it to Newton. Thomas carefully held it and stepped into the middle of the court.

"Before I take the cloth off this thing, would you mind sharing with us what you found, Mr. Frost?" Thomas Newton spoke, holding the rapt attention of everyone in the courtroom.

Lilly and Jonathan looked at each other. Lilly shook her head in one last plea, hoping her brother would see some sense. It was still not too late. This betrayal could be overturned. But Jonathan shook his head in response. He was more a Puritan and a Salemite than he was her brother. His allegiance was not to his blood, but to this town and to the beliefs that its people held, him being one of them.

"Honorable Magistrate Stoughton, sir. Jury members. Mr. Newton, what you hold in your hands is the book that I found hidden deep within the recesses of her room, and I can attest that she made sure to hide it well. But this was my father's house. And as a man knows his father's house, so, too, do I know mine. There wasn't a place she could have hidden it in there where I wouldn't have found it. I've had my suspicions for some time. It wasn't until she was caught and imprisoned that I tried to affirm these suspicions by searching her belongings. That what you hold in your hand is as damning as it gets," Jonathan spoke, wiping his brow with his handkerchief. "That item is most cursed."

"Let it be known that the item Mr. Jonathan Frost is talking about is a most heinous book of magic!" Thomas Newton said, revealing Gertrude's grimoire from underneath the black shawl.

People screamed. Some people ran for the door, afraid that being in the same room as such a cursed object would put them under a hex. There was chaos in the courtroom, chaos that no amount of gavel-banging could bring to order.

"ENOUGH!" Magistrate Stoughton stood from his chair and bellowed. "I will have order in my court. It's a book, damn ye all. It's only potent in the hands of a witch. Last I checked, Mr. Thomas Newton was not a witch. Are you now, Mr. Newton?"

"No, Your Honor." Thomas Newton shook his head and placed the book in front of Magistrate Stoughton. "But while Sarah Brooks was fabricating a tale of bread and stray dogs earlier, I would like to know what she has to say about this incriminating evidence here. Oh, wait, she's not in the room, is she?"

"Don't you dare deny that this is your copy!" he said, pointing his finger at Lilly. "Right there, it also implicates another whose name is written on the first page! Bridget Bishop!"

As the court erupted into chaos once again, with orderlies trying to subdue Bridget, and the magistrate banging his gavel, Lilly turned to Jonathan and looked at him with wounded eyes.

"How could you?" she asked.

Jonathan spat in response and turned his face away.

In the meantime, the magistrate rose from his chair once more and boomed loudly through the room. "In light of such stark evidence coming to light, by the authority vested in me by the Commonwealth of Massachusetts Bay Colony, in accordance with the laws of God and man, I find Lilly Frost and her co-conspirators Bridget Bishop and Sarah Brooks guilty of witchcraft! You shall burn at the pyre until the flames have gnawed away at the sins stuck to your blackened souls!"

Lilly did not expect such a betrayal, but what she also did not expect was two more women being convicted in the same proceeding.

And then, with much malice aforethought, they dragged her off the stand and paraded her through the crowd, the hands of the townsfolk striking her as she walked amongst them.

Behind her, she could hear Magistrate Stoughton finishing his remark by saying, "May God have mercy on your souls!"

1692—This Town Will Burn

After the deafening din outside, after all the violent blows her body bore as the deputies escorted her from the courthouse to the prison, the familiar stench and silence of her jail cell were all too welcoming. Here, she could lay and whimper, least till daylight, which would be when they'd hang her.

Except now, she was not alone.

Sarah wailed in the cell next to her. Bridget sat quietly in the next cell over. Both of them bore bruises on their bodies, their skin ripped open where they had been beaten brutally, blood trailing onto their tattered clothes.

It was only a matter of time before Sarah's wails subsided into sobs. Stoic and silent, Bridget sat with her back against the wall. Or so

Lilly imagined. She could not see into any of their cells. She could only sense their presence.

"If I'd...if only I'd known that you were what they said you were... I'd have never made the mistake of representing you," Sarah hiccoughed. "What must my husband and daughter think of me?"

"Will you quit your yammering, you silly girl," Bridget scolded. "It has happened. We are caught. Whether or not you're a witch is irrelevant. They are going to use this as a precedent to round up women such as ourselves all over the colony. Do you think this ends with our sentencing? It's only the beginning."

"Damned be your beginning," Sarah screamed, bursting into wails once more. "And damned be this entire case. I woe the day I met you, Lilly."

"Will you shut her up, or do I have to?" Bridget snapped.

"Let her be," Lilly sighed. She did not want to say what she'd thought of saying next: *It's her last night on this mortal coil. Let her wail all she wants.*

"Fine," Bridget scoffed.

"LET ME SEE MY WIFE!" Tobias, Sarah's husband, shouted from outside the jail cells. "My hand on the good book, my hand to God Almighty, that woman is not a witch. I have known her all my life. She goes to church every Sunday, Arnold. You know this. You've seen us there every week."

Arnold must have been the name of the guard stationed at the gates of the prison, Lilly presumed.

"Be that as it may, Tobias, I cannot let you in."

"SARAH!" Tobias screamed from outside.

"TOBIAS!" Sarah screamed back, making Lilly's ears reverberate with the intensity of her scream.

Her husband found the window to her cell and shot his hand through it. She reached forward and clasped her fingers through the bars, meeting his touch.

"My love, what happens to us?" Tobias wept from outside.

"I don't know, but you must promise that you're going to take care of Rebeccah for the both of us, and if you can, my love, leave this cursed place as fast as you can. I wouldn't want you festering here." Sarah sobbed, holding onto her husband's hand.

"That's quite enough, Tobias! Or do you want to be thrown in the cell next to her?!" Arnold the guard said, dragging a struggling Tobias away from the window.

"I love you," Tobias yelled as he was being dragged away.

"And I you! Kiss Becca for me! And don't come to the town square tomorrow morning," Sarah cried. Once her husband's protests were no longer audible, she slunk back and began to weep with even more fervor than before.

"Sarah," Lilly said. Her throat burned. Out of dryness, her lips had clung to each other fiercely, making it nearly impossible for her to open her mouth. Yet she did as she tried to console her friend. "I did not wish such a dark fate upon you. I am sorry."

"Save your apologies! Had I known you were a witch, I'd never have chosen to represent you. I don't even know who you are!"

"Lilly," Bridget said over Sarah's sobs. "She's right. You need to save your apologies. This isn't your fault. It's mine. I should never have given you that damned book."

"Don't say that," Lilly said, her face pressed to the door so she could hear Bridget better. "You've done for me what no one else in this fucking town has. I will never forget that. You nourished me in a place otherwise so stifling."

"Fat load of good that did us both, huh?" Bridget chuckled. "I cannot complain. I've lived my life. I've made my peace with myself. Tomorrow morning, before the fire can engulf me, I will bewitch myself and fall into blissful slumber. I bid you do the same. You remember the spell for inducing slumber, don't you?"

"Yes," Lilly said. "You taught me well."

"Why don't you try it? Try it on your friend. Otherwise, she'll sob herself to exhaustion."

Lilly closed her eyes and focused on the sound of Sarah's sobs.

"Don't you dare perform any magic on me!" Sarah shouted.

"Somnus!"

Sarah immediately quietened down, indicating that the spell had worked.

"Good. Let her know some rest, at least. And I reckon you should do the same," Bridget said.

"I am scared," Lilly confessed after long last. "I do not want to burn."

"Legend says that when someone possessing of magic is set aflame, they don't just die and disappear as it would seem. They become one with the ether."

"What's the ether?" Lilly asked.

"The ether is the life force of magic. You can feel it on the tips of your fingers in the form of gentle pricks when you perform magic. It's where women like you and me draw our power from. Tomorrow, when I burn, I will become one with the ether. Magic returned to its source. And so shall you."

"But I have yet to live," Lilly said. "There is so much I could have done if I hadn't been foolish."

"Come now. There's always the next lifetime," Bridget joked. "And I don't altogether think that's a lie."

"In the next lifetime, then," Lilly sighed.

There was no sound from the other two cells for a long while, indicating that perhaps Bridget had enchanted herself to sleep.

Lilly allowed herself to weep in the cold and quiet of her dark cell.

It was a biblical sight to behold, as it was meant to be. The magistrates saw this as a fitting opportunity to reenact the crucifixion of Jesus, hoping that such a sight would drive the fervor of religion in the hearts of people, altogether missing the point that in their religion, it was the good people getting crucified by the bad people. But allegory, metaphors, and parallels were often overlooked by these people who took things at face value.

Lilly was hung to the pyre at the center, with Sarah to her left side, and Bridget to her right. The pyres each were built in the shape of crosses. While the women weren't nailed to these crosses, they were tied rather mercilessly with ropes meant for rearing cattle.

Lilly looked upon the crowd of Salemites gathered in front of her. Here was everyone she had ever seen, talked to, known, heard about, or even taken a fancy to. All of them stood with loathing in their eyes, fear on their faces, and readiness in their idle stances. They wanted to watch the witches burn.

Below the cross she was tied to, there was a mound made of dry wood. The deputies were emptying buckets of pig fat atop the dry wood so it would burn better.

Sarah's family stood at the far back of the crowd. Tobias held Rebeccah in his arms, and the two of them wept at the sight of Sarah on the pyre.

"Sarah," Lilly called out, looking at her haggard friend rendered red-eyed anew after watching her family members standing in the crowd. "I am sorry that it came to this."

Sarah ignored her. She kept sniffling and sobbing, her eyes on the deputy holding the torch, approaching the pyre with a frenzy on his face. He really wanted to see women burn today. Smell their burning flesh. Watch sin be purged from the world. Amidst all the thoughts racing through her soon-to-die mind, one stood out. What sin had she done that deserved such a brutal purging? Hers was not a name written in any grimoire. Hers was guilt by association. That hardly qualified her as a witch. If she were a witch, she'd free herself from these ropes.

Lilly looked to Bridget for guidance, but Bridget only grinned, winked, and whispered the sleep spell. It was not like Bridget to give up so easily, Lilly thought. From what she had seen, Bridget was the kind of woman who would fight the world for her rights. What had gotten into her that she'd give up so readily?

"Ah, look here, folks. One of them has gotten so bored that she has fallen asleep. Let's wake her up, shall we?!" the sheriff yelled, grabbing the torch from the deputy and going over to Bridget's pyre.

"Bridget, wake up!" Lilly yelled. "You can't do this!!!"

Lilly watched helplessly as the sheriff cast the torch into the mound of dry wood, setting Bridget's pyre aflame.

So powerful was Bridget's magic that she did not wake as the flames licked her body, seared her flesh, and burned the hair off her head. She got the last laugh, as there was no satisfaction to draw from her burning for anyone in the audience. Not the sheriff, not the magistrates. All they saw was a quiet woman burn, burn without screaming, burn without thrashing. It was not the spectacle they had anticipated.

But Sarah, on the other hand, having just witnessed a woman burn alive, was screaming ear-piercingly, her arms and legs flailing, nearly coming loose of the ropes.

"Enough with you!" the sheriff barked. He took a scorching piece of dry wood and threw it at the base of Lilly's pyre.

It was remarkable how ready she felt to burn now that she had seen Bridget burn. It was Bridget's silent conviction in the ether that made Lilly believe in an all-powerful magical force existing beyond the bounds of one's body. Once the flames were done with her, she would meet Bridget in the ether.

In anticipation of the maddening pain, Lilly closed her eyes. Yet the pain never came.

She opened them again to find everyone standing frozen in the town square. It wasn't just the people who had gone immobile, it was everything. The flames hung suspended. Time itself held its breath. Not a sound. Not a movement. Sarah was not screaming anymore.

What happened just now?

Amidst all the stillness and smoke, Lilly saw the one figure who floated without burden—a gaunt silvery being, robed and hooded, hovering beyond the crowd. Lilly squinted to see it, trying to confirm if this was real. Its aura dulled the very daylight they were all standing in, making the day dark and gray. It looked familiar; she had seen this being before.

It hovered slowly toward Lilly.

"What are you?" Lilly whispered, suddenly remembering her time at the lake. Exhausted, sweaty, and ready to die.

"What do you wish for?" the Collector replied to Lilly.

"What choice do I have?" Lilly asked, tears welling up in her eyes.

"Choice...is the illusion of the mortal. You stand at the threshold between the smoke and the endless dark. Step beyond the veil and follow me into the Axis Mundi...or rise and tether yourself to this realm forever. Beware...for if you stay, you shall wander the earth, eternal. Not as human...but as the keeper of souls...the voice of the forsaken," the Collector whispered back.

Lilly had all but given up on mankind, but a power surged through her and she refocused her gaze. And in that moment, time started up again. The crowds chanting, the smoke billowing, the smell of Bridget's flesh on the tip of her nose.

Lilly's eyes rolled back in her head and she hit the point of almost passing out, but she quickly regained her strength.

"What do you choose?" the Collector asked.

Lilly opened her eyes and fixed her gaze. "I choose to stay," she responded.

"Then let us begin." The Collector's skeletal arms opened wide, reaching farther than Lilly's eyes could see. The entire power of the ether surged through Lilly's body, something the townsfolk could not see, and she let out a howl that they definitely could hear, bringing them to their knees holding their ears.

Lilly flung her arms outward, freeing herself from the pyre.

A sonic boom accompanied by a white cloud belted out in a radius so intensely, it put out the fires and blew everyone that was still standing to the ground.

The crowd was silent, their hands clenching their ears. As they slowly raised their heads, they looked up in amazement at Lilly, now floating above the pyre. This time, she could fly. Her arms lay by her side, her dress flowed freely, and her blonde, wavy hair brushed against the wind. The sky above remained gray, darkening even further as Lilly's body, cloaked in darkness, hovered over them.

Lilly turned her head to look at Sarah, who was in shock, breathing heavily and staring back at her.

The Collector was gone, leaving her imbued with all the power it had promised. Looking down at her palms, she saw the cosmic strength of the Axis Mundi coursing through her. This would be the first true test of her power because, as of yet, Lilly was not bound by good or evil.

She was the in between, the balance, part of the Axis Mundi.

Lilly noticed a man scurrying to get out of the crowd. It was Stoughton.

"You," Lilly spoke, her voice demonic, a grinding, grunting vocal sound that even she didn't recognize.

She pointed in his direction and the judge was set ablaze. Screaming and thrashing, he begged for mercy. But mercy had long since abandoned this town. The townsfolk that took part in the burnings attempted to flee, horrified by what they'd just witnessed, but Lilly wasn't ready to let them go.

The townsfolk who had gathered to watch her burn, the ones who had cast the first stones and called for her death, turned in terror. They tried to scatter like frightened animals, desperate to flee the horror they had unleashed.

Lilly held out her hands, and the very earth beneath rumbled. The buildings around the town square trembled as if in fear, their wooden beams and stone walls groaning in protest. The terrified screams of the townsfolk echoed as the structures they once called home began to buckle and collapse. Roofs caved in, walls crumbled, and the ground shook with a force that brought everyone to their knees, unable to move across the quaking of the earth.

Her eyes burned with a cold fury as she watched the chaos unfold. The townsfolks' cries for mercy went unheard. With each wave of her hand, she directed the rubble, bending it to her will. The ruins of the shops and homes were dragged across the square, crashing into one another, stacking upon themselves with brutal precision. Timber and stone formed an unyielding barricade, surrounding the square like a cage. There would be no escape.

Dust and ash filled the air as the last building collapsed, sealing the barricade shut and trapping those who had sought to escape.

Silence, for a moment.

The square was now a prison, the once-familiar structures twisted into a fortress of ruin, with no way in or out. The crowd huddled together in the center, their faces pale with horror, knowing that this was no longer their town—it belonged to her now.

Then, the screams. The fact that they were trapped had dawned on them, and their fate was sealed.

Horrid, bloody screams. Children shrieked, and babies wailed in the arms of their mothers.

Lilly's long, wavy blonde hair was flowing, hovering in the air. She raised the town's sheriff off the ground with her hand, and he clenched his throat; he was choking without Lilly even having to touch him.

Slowly, she removed one eyeball from its socket, and then the other, his screams charging louder and louder until she ripped his tongue from his mouth and set him alight, throwing his body on top of the pyres.

"TOBIAS, REBECCAH!" Sarah screamed.

Lilly turned back slowly, looking at Sarah. Sarah, for a moment thinking she was owed the same fate, started screaming, pleading with Lilly, who was now floating toward her.

"Please, please, don't kill me," Sarah pleaded further.

Lilly didn't respond. Her eyes were the whitest of whites, glowing, with no pupils or detail visible. She removed the ropes that had tied Sarah down, and with a wave of her palm, Sarah started to float away from the pyre toward Tobias and Rebeccah.

With the wave of her other palm, she lifted Tobias and Rebeccah from the ground, and the family joined each other in midair. Too scared and shocked to even speak anymore, they embraced each other twenty feet off the ground. She then gently moved them beyond the barricade, dropping the family two feet from the air, and as they fell to the ground, they could only hear the screams from the townsfolk, their attempts to scale the barricade only to be dragged back by Lilly's invisible force and set alight, their flesh burning, their hair singeing.

Sarah and Tobias then saw smaller figures rising from the barricade. The children of Salem were spared and moved from harm's way, set down beside the Brookses, including Alice and her two friends, their parents burning for the accusations they had made.

The whole ordeal took less than thirty minutes. The barricade acted as a dark barrier; inside, it looked like the gates to Hell. Red and orange fire, smoke, and the dark shadows of arms and faces clambering to get out. And when Lilly was done, all that remained was smoke billowing from inside. Ash and soot covered her face as she hovered above the dead bodies.

Those who had been spared, those hiding in their homes, and those in Bridget's tavern unwilling to take part in the witch hunt, looked on in terror. As the dark sky beyond started to form thick gray clouds, the heavens opened, and rain started to pour down.

"This town will rise again," Lilly's voice echoed over the remaining living people, who started to scatter and scream. But that was alright, for Lilly did not expect them to understand. She expected them to think that it was her that poisoned and cursed the town. As the square cleared of any living folk, she started to chant while looking up into the sky.

The earth trembled beneath her feet, responding to Lilly's silent command as the air around her seemed to hum with raw power. The ground cracked and groaned, as if awakening from a long, dark slumber. The debris, the blackened timbers and shattered stones of the fallen buildings, began to stir, shaking off the ashes of the fire she had birthed. Slowly, the rubble moved, shifting and floating as if guided by unseen hands. The barricade she had erected—once a twisted mass of destruction meant to trap her tormentors—began to unravel, piece by piece, returning to its origins.

The bricks slid back into place like a puzzle coming together, walls rising where none had stood moments before. Charred wood groaned, stretching, reshaping itself into beams and doorways, homes reappearing brick by brick, plank by plank. Storefronts and houses, taverns and churches—each rebuilt, each restored to the way they were, yet with a dark and unnatural perfection. The windows gleamed as though they had never known soot or flame, the walls stood straight and tall as though untouched by the horrors of the night.

But beneath the beauty lay the truth, hidden deep within the foundations. The bodies of those who had wronged her—the townspeople who had screamed for her death—sank into the earth with each rising wall. Their bones settled into the ground, woven into the very fabric of the new Salem. Some were entombed within the walls, their twisted forms forever watching over the town they had once claimed, their presence a silent, eternal witness to the cruelty they had inflicted. Others lay beneath the streets, buried deep in the soil, where every footstep would tread on their forgotten graves.

Those who would come to rebuild Salem would never know what lay beneath.

After she had rebuilt the town square, Lilly slowly returned to the soil, touching down with her bare foot. Cracking her neck to one side, she looked at her hands and danced a pirouette in the middle of the square before looking over at Bishop's tavern.

She smiled to herself as she walked slowly over to the saloon doors, opening them to a quiet, empty bar. Walking to the bar top, she saw that the whiskeys, beer taps, and ciders were intact, ready to serve the living. She walked behind the bar and poured herself a handsome pint of cider, setting it atop the bar in front of her and then walking back to the other side, where she would sit as a patron.

As she slowly brought the cider to her ashy face, she closed her eyes and took a long deep swig of her favorite beverage.

There remained one final score to settle. One who had not shown up at the town square today, perhaps out of shame or an urgency to leave the town. She would catch up with him. Look him in the eyes and extract the truth from him. Ask him why he would betray his own sister.

And then she would wring his neck, till he croaked.

2

BRIDGEWATER

Salem's Little Sister

The radio hummed in the background, playing Eric Clapton's "Tears in Heaven," and Lilly Frost drove her Range Rover along a road littered with crisp, maroon fall foliage. Sugar maples, red maples, white oaks, and the odd American beech stood guardianlike along the road that led to Bridgewater. Even in the evening, the canopy of red, yellow, golden, and bronze was visible, and it was a sight that she could never get enough of.

It did her witch-heart some good, being out in all this nature, away from the concrete coldness of the Big Apple. Lifeless buildings—although filled with life within—you could touch and get nothing other than a faint whisper of cement mixers and construction workers cursing each other and catcalling women while they worked. Everything contained memory, whether it was something as unremarkable as a rock or something as fascinating as the fallen crown of a king, preserved behind glass. But trees—a single touch and they spilled their secrets in a second. Even passing them by with the window of her Rover rolled down, she could hear their whispers and make sense of all the deciduous mutiny brewing in the air.

She smiled to herself, knowing that around every corner in this small town, things whispered to her in welcome of her arrival.

After all, she owned this place.

She put her foot on the gas, speeding up on the empty road, the whiffs of wildlife invigorating her. Birds chirping, deer peeking from behind their hideouts, eager to cross the roads without getting caught in highlights, and squirrels zooming from one branch to another, undecided on what they wanted to do.

Ahead, the town began and the roads got a little convoluted, as towns often do. But Lilly Thurman did not need her car's built-in GPS or her iPhone's guidance to show her the way. She had been coming to this town since long before either of those things were anything but distant dreams in the minds of crazed entrepreneurs.

Driving through Main Street shot a bolt of nostalgia through her heart and made it ache in the bittersweet way only a mother feels when she watches her offspring all grown up, no longer a child (the bitter part) but a grown, strong adult (the sweet bit). She did not need to drive down Main Street in order to get to her home on the hill. But she couldn't help but take a look at all the shopfronts with their awnings and quaint glass windows displaying trinkets, knickknacks, and antiques alike. Small box stores with decals derived straight from the fifties. Bakeries, gift shops, boutiques.

Over the centuries, Lilly had closely watched Bridgewater evolve from a modest settlement into the thriving community it had become. Though she didn't cater much to the affluent few, she played a crucial role in shielding the town from external influences. It remained a small bubble, a sanctuary where she could retreat and find solace away from the madness.

And it was all madness. Everything that had happened since her trial in Salem had been nothing but madness. She knew that another age was on the brink, and she knew that if she had to learn to live in that age, she had to get with the times, but she was in no way prepared for the Industrial Revolution, the advent of technology, and how quickly the world had outgrown its magical roots and turned to something soulless and convenient in its lieu.

Thankfully, Bridgewater was still a little free of that. Here, nature and civilization existed in the fine balance you saw on postcards from Vermont or artistic depictions of Massachusetts in paintings. Here was harmony, or so Lilly thought.

She flicked on the blinker of her car and turned right. There were no cars on the road, and this flicking of the blinker was not as much an indication to any car behind her as much as it was a rite of passage. She always did this when she turned right to Alameda Avenue. The engine of her car caught the attention of the seven women dressed in black.

She observed the women passively, watching their heads turn and their mouths open for gossip as she drove by them. They were all of a kind, surmised Lilly, this similarity evident in the top-of-the-line cars they'd parked on the street, in the attire they wore, in the way their hair was done, and most importantly, in the ghost-like aura they all emanated.

Lilly deduced that perhaps the reason the town looked so forlorn was the same reason why all these women were dressed in black. Someone notable had died recently, and their funeral must have been held today. Probably where everyone else was too.

She continued driving, reminding herself that there would be plenty of time to indulge in the town's business and get to know what happened in her long absence. For now, she had to get to her home atop the hill.

Alameda Avenue was not a cul-de-sac. It gave itself the appearance of one, but the HOA couldn't ignore the broad asphalt road at the end of the avenue, the road that stretched along Lake Nip and reached up the hill. No amount of zoning coaxing could get anyone to budge the road and turn the avenue into the cul-de-sac that they dreamt of. They argued that no one lived on the ancient (yet serenely maintained) home atop the hill, and that the road was not used by anyone. But the home on the hill and the road that led to it were as much a fixture of Bridgewater as the lake, the woods, and the quaintness of the town itself.

She could feel the gazes of the seven women following her as she exited Alameda Avenue and embarked upon the gentle slope of the road that led to her home. The house on the top of the hill bore the signs of Bridgewater: aged, strong, and independent. It had for centuries been her home away from home. It was her home when she needed to escape the massacre of Salem a few hundred years earlier. And it was her home now, when she was escaping Manhattan, the Devil, and Joseph Banbury, for a short while.

Joe Banbury had made it certain in their last meeting that he wanted nothing to do with her and that the journey he was on did not require the services of Lilly Thurman. Well, guess what, Joseph? Here, in Bridgewater, she was not Lilly Thurman anymore. She'd hot-swapped her last name back to her original one for the duration of her stay in Bridgewater.

She pushed all thoughts of the madness of New York out of her mind as she crested the hill, fixating her gaze on her home. It was the oldest building in Bridgewater—the oldest in terms of still standing upright and being inhabitable—and as such, was deemed an unofficial historical site, of sorts. No walking tours though. Someone actually lived here. People often tried to conclude as to who this elusive personality was who visited so very infrequently and came and went as they pleased, but that was all people did.

Speculate, speculate, speculate.

Atop this verdant hill surrounded by lush forestry, the house sat alone commandingly, its isolation lending it an aura of quiet grandeur. Manor-like elegance dripped from the aged walls, its architecture retaining its 18th-century Georgian roots but with the poise and presence of a grand estate. She had, of course, rebuilt parts of the home over the centuries.

There was a tall wrought-iron fence encircling the property, its black metal bars weathered by time and overgrowing vines alike, and yet still standing strong. This Gothic fence separated the house and its surrounding lawn from the unkempt overgrowth of the hill. The lawn and the flowerbeds had been meticulously maintained in anticipation of the arrival of the house's master.

With a stately façade—a central doorway that was flanked by

slender columns and framed by the signature fanlight window, and a heavy oak door with an ornate brass knocker—the front of the house imposed upon the senses of anyone who dared to stand and gawk.

Above, the steeply pitched roof with its wooden shingles still held firm, a black chimney rising defiantly into the sky. A remnant of another era, this house. It had a wraparound porch that offered views of the landscape beyond the hill—namely the lake, the town, and the wilderness beyond it.

But to Lilly Frost, aka Lilly Thurman, this was home.

Once past the outer gate, Lilly drove around the house, parking her car in the back, while at the same time taking in the astonishing view of Lake Nip in the evening, a view that she never got tired of.

But this was it for the view for now. She had been on the road for the entire day, taking a much-needed detour from New York to Salem and then to Bridgewater. As it was, she was beat, and she could do with a nice, long bath and some homely food.

The key slid into its lock rather familiarly, and as Lilly opened the door, she was greeted by the sudden display of all the lights in the house coming alive. She had bewitched this place during a time when her magic had been surging through her. It still surged from time to time, but lately, she had to keep things under check. Lilly Frost might be a witch, but Lilly Thurman was a klutzy literary agent who always forgot where her glasses were.

"Easy now," she called out to the house, watching as the lights turned off, leaving only the hallway dimly lit. This was much better. The overhead lights were harsh. She needed the right ambience if she was going to relax. A feeling of relief swept over her as she walked down the hallway. Her next order of business awaited her in the master bathroom.

She made a detour to the kitchen, studying the housekeeper's work as she walked in. The place was spotless, and there we go, the fridge was stocked with food. A quick look in the freezer, and all the meats that she'd instructed the housekeeper to get were there, frozen in their packets. A good thawing was in order for the wagyu tonight.

While she could conjure food at will whenever she wanted, it was not her forte. It wasn't as easy as one would think. Witches in Europe predominantly focused on conjuring feasts for their families in the olden days, but it often came with setbacks. Meat ended up tasting like leather. Alcohol tasted like fumes. Vegetables tasted like flavorless paper. It took a damn good witch to be able to conjure up a feast that would taste as intended.

But in times of rationing, poverty, and death, conjuring up meager morsels of bread did the job just as well.

The reason conjuring food wasn't Lilly's forte was because she had invested most of her efforts in the subcategory of magic that dealt with intelligence. She was no stranger to having to survive in tough situations. After the Collector in Salem gifted her with immortality, she knew that she would have to survive on another scale altogether.

In Europe, Lilly had met witches who survived on a day-to-day basis. They would kill, conjure fake currency, and use their powers to alter the minds of people to allay suspicion and escape notice. This only went so far before people started to get wise to the fact, and witches learned the hard way that despite their magic, they could still be killed.

She grabbed a bottle of wine and a glass and walked out of the kitchen. It wasn't hunger that her body immediately alerted her of; it was sobriety that was begging to be extinguished.

She took off her shoes before stepping into the bedroom, her bare soles coming in contact with the cool hardwood floor and her silk rug, a rug that stood the test of time. Lilly's clothes effortlessly slipped off before she walked into the bathroom.

She prepared her moment of relaxation by drawing a bath, the wine and its glass sitting next to the tub. The lights turned off and candles came to life of their own volition.

She stepped into the water, the heat doing her body good, and sank in, settling her back against the tub. She wished for rose petals and found them on the surface of the water when she opened her eyes. A resting board for the bottle and the glass, and in another blink, it was there.

The house cared for her.

Her magic cared for her more.

The smell of lavender perfused through the candlelit bathroom, mixing with the faint aroma of rose petals, taking Lilly somewhere back in time, reminding her of a tall, handsome, oak-scented man wrapping his arms around her as the two of them stood in a flower-riddled meadow. Whoever he was, however long gone he was, his memory was as sanguine as it was poignant, forcing Lilly to open her eyes and focus on her immediate surroundings.

Whatever that was, it was a long time ago.

This next bit she did not employ any magic in doing. She uncorked the wine bottle and poured it heartily into the glass, then brought the glass to her nose, taking in the earthy notes, the sweet ones, and the sour tinge that lingered around the corner. This was what good pinot grigio smelled like. She brought the glass to her lips and tasted everything all at once. The crushed gravel, the citrus, the floral notes, and the gentle undertone of apple and peach.

She let the wine do its bit to elevate her mood, and the hot water its part in extracting the tiredness from her bones.

She looked around at the dark bathroom, its decadence matching the rest of the house. Gold sconces upon the wall with red damask-embossed wallpaper complementing them. A deep green chest of drawers commanded the corner where her oils, creams, lotions, and potions sat center stage, ready for Lilly to use post-cleanse.

Living forever had its advantages, but it did not mean that her skin didn't get dry after a thorough wash.

"How long has it been?" she asked aloud, expecting the sconces to answer her. But the house, in its grandeur, remained silent. It was a feeling like nothing else, having no one around her, but at the same time, she could not deny that it was a lonely feeling.

It had been a decade since she had last been to Bridgewater, or so she thought. There were stories of an evil witch who lived up on the hill. There were stories of all kinds. And more than the wrought-iron fence and the aloofness of the house, it was these stories that made sure that no one ever went inside the house. The gardener with his malevolent eye—he would show up every week out of nowhere with his haggard white hair and his patchy stubble. He would mow the lawn and trim the hedges and give the flowerbeds the fertilizer they so desired. He would never speak to anyone. As strangely as he'd arrive, he'd leave just as strangely. There was the housekeeper, a woman with a stern blonde bun on her head which stretched her skin. She did not speak a word of English. At least, not any English that the people would understand. She, like the gardener, arrived every so often to ensure that the house was clean, stocked, and its aura unadulterated.

If these two eccentric personalities were not enough to keep away inquisitive onlookers and passersby, it was the police. Lilly had a great rapport with the police in this town, just as she did with the old shopkeepers who had been around long before the turn of the century. These old-timers and lawmen knew one secret that most of the other townsfolk were unaware of.

Lilly Frost owned Salem's Little Sister.

Every last acre of Bridgewater was hers in a deal done centuries earlier. It was through this level of respect and understanding, along with a rather subtle bit of magic known as mind veiling that Lilly was able to visit her hometown frequently without disturbance.

Mind veiling, like conjuration, jinxing, hexing, scrying, charming, and cursing, was a powerful aspect of magic in her repertoire of spells and sundries. With her mere will, she could alter a person's mind for hours or eternity, depending upon the complexity of the situation. A delicate art, this required a lot of focus to work to its full potential.

For one, she had to know how to navigate the mind subjected to her magic. On rare occasions, she could implant a permanent memory. One that had people thinking that they had experienced something they hadn't, or to instill a familiar feeling to help them calm their nerves.

The bath had done Lilly good. Refreshed, hair wrapped in a towel, she walked out of the master bathroom, out of the bedroom, and down the staircase with the bottle of wine and glass still in her hands. She could do with a little more of that drink in her. Lilly stepped out onto the left side of the wraparound porch and propped herself on the bench. She admired the view of the lake. The way it stretched out into the horizon, it looked like it was swallowing the sun.

She could look at that view for hours, fall asleep to it as a matter of fact, but right now she wished for some company. Not a human's, per se, but company nonetheless.

It was then that her diary, her oldest companion, subtly floated from the bookshelf in the living room and out onto the porch.

"Why, hello there, old friend." Lilly beamed at it. After all this time, her attunement to it was still as effortless and intuitive as ever. She'd only thought of perusing the diary and reading up on the centuries that she'd experienced, and here it was, already in her hand. If it could smile, it would, but it only opened itself and fell in her lap.

"That far back, huh?" Lilly looked at the date of her entry.

December 11th, 1692.

The diary, like everything else in this house, was enchanted. On the surface, it seemed that it had no more than three hundred and sixty-five pages, no more than your average diary. But there wasn't a limit to this bewitched book. She could write in it for eternity and it would store her words without showing signs of fullness.

She poured herself another glass of wine, willed the lamp overhead to turn on, and then sat down in the dusk, reading the entry her diary had procured for her.

It was as good a welcome home as any.

Reminiscence

11th December, 1692

Diary,

Dear does not befit you yet, for I have no bond with you. I only bought you today from a very dubious-looking bookseller who asked me five times why I, a woman, needed a diary. It wasn't until I clarified that I was looking to purchase one on the behest of my master did he give it to me, and not without stiffing me on the amount of money I paid.

So, in the meantime, you're just a diary. A rather expensive one. An ordinary, expensive diary bound in leather, and... Christ, I cannot believe that I'm rambling about your inane nature when I have so many things to write. But there's only so much that I can write in you. Unless I find some manner of magic to bewitch you. And then, then I will be able to write in you for as long as I want, and seeing as how I am immortal, I might write till the world ends. You'll have earned the "dear" by then.

In the meantime, Diary. Just Diary.

How many days has it been since the events of Salem? If it has been days, that is. I don't remember how long of a time has passed since the events, but I've been on the run for so long. You tend to lose track of time. You tend to lose track of yourself.

But one thing that I never lost track of was the trappings that come with being a woman in this cursed day and age. I have scried the future and I know what is coming. This age of man is not going away anytime soon. Guess what, Bridget? You were wrong. It's going to be a man's world for a long time, and I must do what it takes to survive in such a world.

This festering year comes to an end, and—I remember now. It's winter as I write this, so it has been a few months since I have self-ousted myself from Salem. What, was I going to live there forever after the massacre I conducted in the town square? Those who survived, Sarah and her family among them, had already started to look at me with eyes wide with horror. Of course I wasn't going to live there.

I had a vendetta to settle. I had Jonathan to find and Jonathan to kill.

I believe that I was justified in doing so.

I found Jonathan hiding in a decrepit hotel in Boston. He had no answer for why he betrayed me, only fear in his eyes.

But his death was deserved. It was only fair that he, too, had to die for the lives that had been lost as a result of his betrayal.

But I could not kill my own blood. I gave him a hell of a bruise on his face, one that I doubt he's going to forget for as long as he lives. As I delivered the punch, so did I deliver a warning that if he were to ever get in my way again, he would truly feel the wrath that I held within.

I've since then not tracked what he's been doing or where he is. Sometimes, while scrying on the surface of water, his face will intrude and I will—without any control—see what my brother is doing. He's been abandoned by the very men who promised him a small fortune in exchange for giving up his witch of a sister. Poverty-stricken, he roams the streets of Boston with a metal cup in hand asking for alms and warning people of witches. No one listens to the rants of this haggard madman, but every so often they do spare a coin or two.

My thoughts, much like my sanity and my soul, are everywhere.

I try to remember Salem, try to come to terms with all the people who were enveloped in flames as a result of my... What would you call it? Being unleashed? Yes, let's call it that. Hell hath known no fury like a woman scorned. And the people suffered for it. The very people who did not do anything to fight for me, the very people who threw things at me and cast their blameful fingers in my direction. All those eyes, all too eager to see me burn.

Fuck 'em. And fuck Salem.

Above everything else, the thing that I miss most is not a person, but the book of spells that Bridget gave me. Without it, I feel naked. I can still channel magic at will whenever I want, but without the right spells, I'm still under-equipped to deal with a world that's out to get me.

Ever since the pyre, ever since the fire, I have not heard from the Collector who offered me power and immortality. My memories unlocked, I do remember Madam, but I haven't heard from her either. It feels like all the forces of the universe, whether it's God, the Devil, or the Axis Mundi, have abandoned me.

Where are those who kept me company in the forest when I was a child and knew not where to walk?

Where is the hooded figure who saved me from my fate of flames?

I am maimed and hurt and alone and so forlorn that I am spilling my heart and my words and my tears for no one else but my diary to hear, and now I'm rhyming, so now I'm two cursed things as opposed to one—a poetess and a witch. There are no prospects for either in civilized towns such as these.

I am dreading what happens to me in Bridgewater. So far no one has recognized me here. And I have found a quaint little inn that I can call home for a night. I shall sleep, and see what awaits me in the day.

~

12TH DECEMBER, 1692

Dear Diary,

I rested well and after a long while I have awoken in a warm bed in a heated room. It's been snowing outside all day, but inside this inn, it's quite cozy. My mind is rested, and I can think much more clearly now.

For starters, let's document what I did yesterday.

After a long spell of meditative aloofness in the woods, I finally decided to reintegrate into society. This happened three days ago, by the way. I washed myself in the lake, dried my clothes, did my hair in a bun, and used what magic I remembered to bewitch my face to look different.

Then I walked back into Salem, the scene of the crime.

It baffled me as to how quickly the town had gotten back onto its feet. People were living their lives as per the usual.

It didn't break my heart.

It only bred apathy in it.

There was no memorial for those who had passed. There was nothing in the way of any remembrance for the woman who had been burned to death.

I snuck into Bridget's tavern, the same one where she and I had practiced magic. Bridget had shown me her plans, shared her desires of a utopian city for people like us. People who were otherwise scorned by the rest of the world. Rich wife of several husbands that she was, she had amassed a sizeable fortune hidden in the basement of her tavern.

And then she had bewitched this fortune so none other than a witch could find it. The tavern was no longer functional; it was boarded up, and a For Sale *sign was plastered on the face of the building, but I snuck in and found my way down to the basement. Amidst the barrels of wine and ale, I found it.*

Bridget's fortune.

In her absence, she had made it clear that it was to be mine.

It did not guilt my heart (remember, it's apathetic now) as I took that fortune and made away with it, looking back at Salem one last time.

Seriously. Fuck that town.

And as I stood looking at Salem and its people, magic burst forth from within me, magic that did not come by way of spell words or wand work. It just came from within, a willing, as I call it. I willed the people of Salem to forget all about me. Forget that I ever existed, had ever been made to stand trial, or had been tied up on the pyre.

Now, when they record the history of Salem, they will do so without any mention of Lilly Frost, the witch they couldn't burn. Bridget, however, knowing that she meant for this to be a woman's world, they would remember her, and what Stoughton did to her.

And then the rest, as you already know, is me traveling fifty miles away, far from Salem, and finding my way to Bridgewater. Fifteen hours by carriage, and I reached this nondescript place just last evening with my spirit broken and confused.

It's not broken and confused now.

Now, I can only sense possibility.

See you soon, Diary.

~

15TH DECEMBER, 1692

Hello there, Diary!

Oh, yes, today I'm quite lively. You'll be fascinated to learn that a woman with a trunk of money and a handful of magic can prove to be quite resourceful if she's not sulking in bed. It was a choice I had to make. Lay around wallowing in the puddle of my own pity or go out there and do something.

Can you guess what I did?

I went around, shopped for clothes, bought myself some much-needed adornments and a nice pair of shoes! Several of the handsome, eligible bachelors cast looks of admiration my way, and I can't say that I didn't enjoy them!

I even unbuttoned my top just a little to let them stare. Oh, you can relax, I am only jesting.

I actually scoped the place. I found out everything I could about Bridgewater from the mouths of babes and housewives alike, and a little bit of intrepidness actually paid off in dividends. I found out who owns this town.

A Mr. Samuel Smith. An enterprising fellow who arrived on the Mayflower from Plymouth, England, with a group of other enterprising men. And when I mean enterprising, you should know that I mean drunk off their rockers.

One meek woman buying carrots and peas at the farmer's market told me tall tales of how the generous owner of this town had acquired this land after a brave battle with the Natives. A little digging around and I found that there was no battle. There had been a simple transaction twenty years ago, a transaction that resulted in the Native Americans selling this place, the lake, the hill, and the wilderness around it to Samuel Smith and Co.

Since finding out about this, I've looked around for these men and have learned of the tavern where they all sit, play pool, drink, and talk each other up in the throes of inebriation. They liken themselves to liberators and great thinkers, people who are someday going to make this place great.

They're money-loving, gin-swilling, leering, jeering men who are only interested in making money out of more money.

I have seen dreams, Diary. I have seen great dreams where men like Smith and his fellows penetrate the earth and make black gold sprout from it. I have seen dreams where they peddle coal and gold alike and turn into gods. Very mortal gods who can be killed with something as simple as consumption, but very rich gods nonetheless.

Tonight, I will see to it that they are steered elsewhere.

Whether it's golden gold or black, I will somehow steer them away from this place and claim it as my own.

The many thousands of pounds I have thanks to Bridget's fortune will be enough for me to acquire this place, and acquire it I shall. I have no interest in owning a small shop or a small bakery.

I am not nifty.

I am not quaint. I am someone who dares to dream big, and I dream to own this town. Never again shall a man rip me from my home against my will, and never again will I be duped, waylaid, betrayed, or burned.

LILLY SIPPED ON HER WINE, and did not need to read any further to remember what had happened after that. She could reminisce about it just fine on her own. Immortality was just as much a curse as it was a blessing. You could remember each day you'd ever lived as if it was just yesterday—that was the blessing. But the curse of it was, you blinked and looked around and all the people you'd ever befriended and come to love were gone, leaving you stranded on the crashing waves of endless time.

It drove great bitterness in her heart if she let herself be carried away with the thoughts of everything and everyone she had lost over the years, but this evening had such a spell to it that even if she wanted to feel bitter, she discovered that she couldn't.

Wine-drunk and bath-soothed, she could only smile and look at the lake, using its reflective surface to look back at the memories of that day. No one had actually taught her this, but scrying could also be used to look at your own past, and also, you didn't need to be right up along the edge of the water to scry.

If you were a powerful enough witch, you could do it from as far back as you liked.

Scrying Into the Past

Something about today's date drove a sense of rejuvenation into Lilly's heart as she woke up. The 15th of December, 1692. Half the month had flown by, and this meant the year was just as soon to come to a close. She could not be more ready to step into 1693 and leave this year's nonsense behind.

Her blanket was warm and heavy, and any other day she would

have submitted to its comfort, but not today. Not even while it was snowing outside and the town felt like it was covered in coconut shavings.

She sprang out of bed, her bones bursting with electricity, and looked out the window. The morning haze somehow traveled through the glass window of her room and infiltrated her nostrils with the smell of the cold city with all its people, carriages, carts, and livestock. A lively town, and yet small enough that she could see most of it from her window.

She hurriedly dressed and rushed downstairs to the inn's dining room. In the daytime, it served a diverse assortment of breakfast ranging from different types of breads and cheese to fresh fruit from the market. Lilly filled her plate up with everything that struck her fancy, filled a large mug with coffee, and headed over to a booth where the window gave a wide view of the snow-covered street outside.

She ravenously filled herself up, emptying the contents of her plate and her mug, and then went back to get another helping, ignoring the looks of the innkeeper and the patrons as they observed this very unladylike behavior. A family of four sat at the table next over: a boy and a girl and their parents. The wife wore a modest dress covering everything besides her face and hands. She looked at Lilly with fantasy and disdain. To see a woman out in the open doing as she willed, eating with her hands as opposed to the fork and knife, eating large bites as opposed to small, feminine ones. The woman sighed as she looked at Lilly, and then her husband grunted his disproval, making her look away.

"Er..." The innkeeper, Sean, came over, apron covering his front, a small towel hanging from his shoulder. "Ma'am? We's around here was wondering what you got going today."

"Good day to you," Lilly said, giving her empty mug to the innkeeper. "Another cup, please and thank you."

Perplexed, the innkeeper went to fetch a fresh cup of coffee. He put it back rather timidly. This woman, whoever she was, had paid the entire price of her stay upfront and had given a generous tip for his discretion and compliance. The least he could do was be polite to her. She looked like she came from old money. The way she wore her embroidered dress and had her hair decorated in an elaborate bun, there was no way this woman was a commoner. "Ma'am, are you traveling alone?" he asked. It took him quite a lot of courage to ask this question, but it was a question that begged asking. Not many women traveled alone. At least none that he'd ever seen.

"What interest is that to you?" Lilly asked, taking a deep swig from her scalding coffee. Ever since the pyre, she had taken to hot things. She drew comfort from them, knowing they would not burn her. If that blazing fire hadn't, nothing could. Not even the Devil and all his Hell, she thought rather overconfidently.

"It's just... I was curious, ma'am, as to how long you would stay and such. Have to account for hospitality, bedding, and such," he said, covering his suspicion rather deftly.

"I'm here on official government business, Mr. Deschaine," Lilly said.

The innkeeper was surprised to see that she had remembered his last name. Transients barely even knew his first name. There was something about this woman that he could not put a finger to.

"What business would that be?"

"Never you mind that. I have a question of my own. You happen to know Mr. Samuel Smith rather well, don't you?" Lilly asked.

"Who doesn't know Mr. Smith around these parts, ma'am? The man owns Bridgewater. A well-to-do businessman, he is," the innkeeper said, puffing his chest proudly. Pride by association was the worst kind of pride, Lilly mused, but she did not let that dampen her mood.

"I tried to meet him yesterday at the tavern across town, but I had no luck," Lilly said.

"Oh, Alberto's Tavern," Sean said, spite shadowing his face. "Yes. He's often found there. But sometimes he comes here too. For dinner with the family, and that sort of thing. In fact..." Sean stopped, fearing he had spoken too soon and too much in front of this stranger.

Lilly could have coaxed it out of him another way, but she did not have time. She needed to be prepared for the meeting that she had planned, and she could not be waylaid by a distrustful innkeeper.

Under the table, she twirled her fingers and focused her raw will on Sean's mind, veiling it in the process. *Do not worry. It is completely fine. You shall not worry and you are not going to get into trouble. Just tell me where I can find him.*

Sean's eyes went cloudy, his face becoming vacant as he spoke. "Of course, he's going to be at my inn tonight. He made a reservation in advance. He's going to be here with his family tonight, yes, yes. But if you've got some urgent business, you can always find Mr. Smith down by the river at the old grist mill."

"Why, thank you. You've been especially helpful," Lilly said, trying her best not to smirk and not to call him a chump at the end of her sentence.

"He might not take too kindly to strangers showing up at his door. It's just a bit odd, don't you think? Coming up to someone's door," the innkeeper said. Lilly did not have as strong a hold over her wild magic as she thought she did, and in bewitching this innkeeper's mind, she had also made him quite frank and oversharing. "If someone were to show up at my door, and if it were a woman, I'd be damn scared. My wife would ask me, 'Why's there a woman at your door?' It's strange, isn't it? Not that I wouldn't have welcomed a woman at my door if I were unmarried and if the woman happened to look like you, mind you, but I am a married man."

She unclenched her grasp on his mind just a little bit so that he would stop rambling, and then asked, "So, where do you think I should meet him?"

"I think it would be just as strange if you were to impose upon his family time. Tell you what, if you do want to meet him, and that too with certainty, you can come around after."

"After?" Lilly asked.

"Yes," Sean grinned, revealing a mouth with several missing teeth. They did not befit a man as young as Sean. "You see, the dinner with the family's just a customary thing. A mandatory thing. For the sake of appearances. Once his kids and his wife have gone home in the carriage, he stays here till dawn, drinking away our reserves with his friends."

"I see what you mean." Lilly smiled back.

"Come then, and you'll find him in much more of a placated mood to conduct any business, government or otherwise," Sean said, winking at her.

Done with her breakfast, armed with this new information, and with a whole day to kill, Lilly set out and walked around town, taking in its sights in a way that she hadn't gotten the chance to do before. She sat for a long time by the edge of the lake, just admiring its crystal surface, feeling herself at one with the flora and fauna all around it, even though it was December.

When she was sure that no one was around and no one was looking, she allowed herself to slide across the frozen surface of the lake by bewitching her shoes to act as blades.

Next, she went to the top of the hill and stood there, admiring the view of the wilderness juxtaposed with civilization. A thought occurred to her as she studied the plateaued top of the hill. She could build a house here. Live as a queen.

As fanciful as this thought was, she first needed to buy the town. And she wasn't sure if it would happen without a fuss. Men in power were always quick to make fusses, whether it was in the form of dubbing them witches or giving them trouble handing over deeds to the land.

And how immense this land was. Hundreds upon hundreds of acres, and if she'd understood correctly, all of it belonging to Samuel Smith.

"I'll come back later," she told the hill and bade it farewell around evening. As much as she wanted to stay here, in tune with the natural power coursing through this place, she had business to tend to.

THAT NIGHT, Lilly stepped into the inn, ready to meet Samuel Smith. She made her way to the bar and studied the room and all the people within. It was late, and as Sean had said, Smith's family had left, leaving him in the company of his friends and their libations.

The crackling fire in the stone hearth cast a warm, flickering light across the rough-hewn tables and chairs scattered throughout the inn's main room. The air was thick with the scent of roasting meat and the smoky aroma of burning wood. The chatter of patrons, the clinking of tankards, and the occasional burst of laughter created a lively atmosphere, yet there was an undercurrent of tension in the air.

Lilly Frost, her demeanor calm and composed, moved through the room with purpose. Her presence, though unassuming, commanded attention. The patrons of the inn turned their heads in her direction as she single-mindedly approached the table where Smith sat with his friends.

Having taken the care to change her clothes, she was now draped in a modest cloak that hid her wavy hair and the intricacies of her features. Her eyes gleamed with a confidence that few women in these parts possessed. No amount of modest clothing could take away that gleam.

At a table near the hearth, a group of men sat hunched over their drinks, discussing the latest developments in the town. They were the leaders of the settlers, the men who made decisions about land, trade, and the future of Bridgewater. They spoke in low tones, their faces serious as they considered the challenges and opportunities that lay ahead.

Lilly approached their table with deliberate slowness, her steps measured, ensuring that each man noticed her before she spoke. She stood silently for a moment, letting her presence be felt, before finally speaking in a voice that was soft yet carried an undeniable authority.

"Gentlemen," she began, her voice cutting through their conversation like a knife through butter. The men did not look at her at once, but when she did not budge, they cast loathing looks in her direction, looks that said, *Who is this wench who can't let us drink in peace?*

But she wasn't in any mood to reel back. She kept her eyes affixed on the group of seven men, her gaze traveling across the table, making them confused and surprised at the same time. There would be time for magic, but it was not now. For now, her charisma and the element of surprise worked well in her favor. It was not often that a woman, especially one whom they did not know from Adam, would interrupt their discussions.

Lilly bore a similar loathing in her heart for them. *Discussions.* They thought their inebriated ramblings were discussions. She had tried to listen to what they were saying, but it was all a string of dirty jokes, political pondering, and complaining about their wives and children.

"I apologize for the intrusion. I am sure that you fine fellows were having a splendid time on your own, but I believe that I can contribute to you having a better time," she said, "for I have an offer that none of you would want to turn down."

Her eyes scanned the group, lingering on each man for just a moment, reading their faces, their thoughts. She could sense their skepticism, but she also sensed their intrigue. These were men who valued opportunity and were always on the lookout for the next advantage.

The leader of the group, whom she identified as Samuel, was a hideous man with a pockmarked face and the irredeemable aura of sin smattered on his bearing. He leaned back into his chair, crossing his arms over his chest, and eyed Lilly with a mix of suspicion and interest. "And what makes you think that we'd be interested in anything you have to say, miss?" His eyes sized her up, traveling up and down her body, lingering at her breasts and her bottom. He licked his lips and bit them in a most depraved manner, making his fellows grin just as lecherously.

Lilly allowed herself a small smile. "Because I am offering you something far beyond what you can imagine. A chance to secure your futures, and the future of Bridgewater, in a way that will bring wealth and prosperity beyond your current means."

The men exchanged glances, their interest piqued despite themselves. The leader narrowed his eyes, leaning forward slightly as some of the other men were laughing. "Go on, then. What is this proposal of yours?"

Lilly placed a delicate hand on the edge of the table, her fingers lightly tapping the worn wood. "I wish to purchase the entire town of Bridgewater, all the land that surrounds it, and all the future rights to its resources."

There was a moment of stunned silence, followed by a roar of laughter from the men. The leader's amusement was evident as he shook his head. "And how exactly do you plan to do that? Bridgewater is no small plot of land, and we've been here for years. What could you possibly offer us that would make us consider selling?"

Lilly's smile widened, and she reached into the folds of her cloak, pulling out a small, heavy pouch. She dropped it on the table with a soft thud. The men's laughter died away as they stared at the pouch, their curiosity overtaking their skepticism. The leader hesitated for a moment before reaching out and loosening the drawstring. He poured the contents onto the table, and his eyes widened as coins, more than any of them had seen in one place from a random stranger, spilled out.

"And where did ya steal that?" one of the men chortled back, inviting another roar of laughter from the group.

"SILENCE!" Lilly snapped back. As she did so, a clap of her hands turned the inn dark; all the other patrons in the room vanished into thin air, and all that appeared around them was a black fog. At the center of this fog stood Lilly. As she slowly walked around the men, running her fingers along the backs of their necks, she continued her story.

"This is but a fraction of what I am offering," Lilly said calmly. "Four thousand, seven hundred pounds, to be exact. Enough to secure your futures, to expand your ventures elsewhere, and to live comfortably for the rest of your lives. In exchange, I ask for ownership of Bridgewater and all that it entails. I have seen the future: there is an oil rush happening four hundred miles west as the crow flies."

As Lilly paused, a cloud appeared in front of the men and showed them what she had prophesied. They saw it for themselves, and it was as real as them being there. They enjoyed riches untold, mansions, land, and generations of wealth. The room snapped back into the present and fell silent as the men stared at the pile of coins, their minds and hearts racing. This was an offer they had never expected, one that was almost too good to be true. But as they looked up at Lilly, they saw no hint of deceit in her eyes, only a quiet confidence that made them believe she could indeed make good on her promise.

The leader cleared his throat, his voice gruff, scared out of his wits; he had never witnessed anything like it. "And why should we trust you? What sorcery is this, witch?"

Lilly met his gaze steadily. "My interests are aligned with yours, gentlemen. I wish to see Bridgewater thrive, to see it become a bastion of prosperity. And with me as its owner, I can assure you that it will. Decline, and I will ensure this town and everything in it rots."

The men exchanged looks, weighing their options. Now was the time for magic. Not a moment before, not a moment after. Lilly flicked her fingers behind her dress, imposing her will upon each of the men who represented Smith and Co., veiling their minds, making them amenable.

She knew all too well what a group of men could do to someone they feared was a witch and she wasn't about to take any chances again.

Being a sorceress was a new thing to her, and she was still mastering her skills. The explosion at Salem was born from fear and being pushed over the edge; right now, she wasn't being tested, she wasn't in danger, and she did not yet fully comprehend her power.

The men, however, were more educated than most, they were practical men, and the revelation in front of them was real, tangible. The future of Bridgewater was uncertain—nothing had changed since they landed in the town some twenty years prior, and the offer on the table was more than generous.

Finally, the leader nodded slowly. "It seems we have much to discuss. But I'm willing to hear you out, Miss...?"

"Frost," Lilly replied smoothly. "Lilly Frost."

"Come to the old mill tomorrow, and we'll talk more about what you have to offer," Samuel responded.

The deal, she knew, was as good as done.

THE NEXT MORNING, she went to Samuel Smith. They talked and negotiated all day, ending it with an agreement that would hand over the entire town for the sum Lilly had promised. The effect of her mind-veiling fluctuated just a little when it was Samuel's turn to sign, but she concentrated harder, taming her wild magic and, in doing so, Samuel.

Once the deal was made and she was the proud owner of an entire town, Lilly began walking home, thinking she had sealed her future differently. Bridgewater was not yet tainted by the madness of Salem and now it belonged to her.

All for the cost of four thousand, seven hundred pounds.

A fortune, but in truth, it was nothing compared to the wealth she'd amass in this town in the coming years. Timber, trade, shipping, all ripe for the taking. The men who sold her this town only saw the coins and bills she gave them. But she could see the life that she would end up building here.

Happy with herself, Lilly went back to the top of the hill instead of the inn. She had made the hill a promise, and now that promise was one step closer to fulfillment.

They did not know who I am, what I am, thought Lilly. They did not know that they had sold their land to a woman who had danced with flames, who had spoken with spirits older than this earth. They did not know that they were now tenants in a town owned by a witch.

I remained in the shadows for the time being, content to let them believe they still held the reins, she continued to ponder. *But in time, they will learn that Bridgewater is mine—its people, its land, its future.*

For now, she was going to enjoy the peace this place offered. The inn was quiet, and the townsfolk were simple, unknowing. But she could feel the land beneath her feet pulsing with life, with energy. It recognized her as its true master, the energy of the earth connecting with the soles of her feet.

Tonight, she thought, *as I close my eyes, I won't dream of flames. I'll dream of what is to come. Of a future where I'm no longer hunted or haunted, but revered. A future where I will not be an outcast, but the queen of this small, unassuming town.*

Once on the hill, Lilly rested her mind, putting a stop to her thoughts and focusing on the view from it. It was a pleasant and rare sunny day in December, thawing away the ice everywhere as far as she could see. It was as if her very mood was affecting the atmosphere around her.

"Lilly."

So severe and sudden was the voice that Lilly lost her footing and fell back. Fortunately, she was not on any slope. The grass and the melting snow broke her fall.

"Who's there?" It was a stupid question to ask, but it seemed pertinent to ask it in the wake of the sudden dark clouds that had gathered all around. Not rain clouds—storm clouds.

"'Tis I, child."

"Madam?"

"Who else?"

Tears furiously streaked down her face upon hearing the voice of Madam after decades. Sorrow mixed with bitterness and relief made for a heavy cocktail that drowned Lilly's senses, forcing her to scream, "Why are you here now?! After all that has happened?!"

"My child, I was never away from you for longer than a moment," Madam spoke.

"You lie! You've never been anything but a voice in my head and you've never been there for me. Not when I was put on trial. Not when I was about to burn! Not when I cast myself into the forest and lived there like a madwoman!" Lilly screamed. "And you come here, upon my moment of victory, claiming that you are really here?! Lies!"

A bright light shone from between the dark gathering clouds and fell upon the patch of hill next to Lilly. When she blinked because of the severity of the luminescence, she saw a woman standing before her. An ageless woman with curly black hair reaching down the length of her embroidered maroon robes. Her face was slim with high cheekbones. Red lips, pale face, and golden eyes—this woman did not look like she belonged in the realm of humans.

She opened her arms, and Lilly, unable to control herself, allowed herself to be embraced by this benevolent being.

"Madam?"

"'Tis I, my girl," she said, hugging Lilly fiercely. "And never think that I have abandoned you for a moment. Ever so proud of you, I am. Ever present in your every vein, I am. My silence does not mean absence."

"You're real," Lilly said. "At times, I thought you were nothing more than a figment of my imagination."

Madam laughed. "Who, then, sent the Collector, dear?"

"What even is it, by the way?" Lilly followed Madam. The embodiment of magic, this ethereal woman stood at the brink of the hilltop, studying the town below.

"An agent of cause in this realm. There are many such as it. And all of them are my children," Madam said. "As are all those who are touched by magic."

"You say all that, and I still don't understand what you are," Lilly whispered, awestruck by the grandeur of this woman. "Are you God?"

Madam scoffed, her back still to Lilly. "No, nor do I share any kinship with Lucifer."

"Lucifer's not real. He's just a made-up monster who—" Lilly could not finish her sentence, for in a moment, Madam was upon her, staring intensely at her.

"Am I real?" Madam asked.

"Yes," Lilly stuttered, taking a few steps back, afraid of what might happen next.

"Then make note that God and the Devil both are real. And neither of them are as they seem. God is not all-benevolent. The Devil is not all evil. But I must warn you, child. Each of them is dangerous in their own way. Make no mistake of their existence, for it may cost you dearly," Madam said.

"It already cost me dearly, or did you not see what men of God did to me in Salem?" Lilly grimaced, remembering that cursed night.

"That is precisely what I mean," Madam said. "One imposes great penalties upon sinners and the other whispers and tempts to sin. It's a rigged game they play, a sick one."

"And what role is yours in this rigged game?"

Madam smiled at Lilly, touching her cheek with her palm.

"I am not confined to such foolish roles. This they do not tell in their little churches and temples, but there are other forces than God's divinity and the Devil's wickedness. I happen to be the overseer of one such force in this universe, as designed by someone higher in authority than God or the Devil."

"What you're saying doesn't make sense to me," Lilly confessed. "Are you the goddess of magic?"

"Goddess is such a limiting term, my girl. I am magic," Madam said with a wide smile and raised arms, channeling raw power from all around her. "And so are you. And as the Collectors play their role in the balance between life and death, so, too, do you have a role in the great order of the Axis Mundi, should you choose to accept it."

"And what role is that?" Lilly asked.

Madam told her, breaking down Lilly's perception about everything she thought she knew.

"I shall keep in touch with you, Lilly," Madam said, and planted a kiss upon her forehead as they parted ways. "Call out to me whenever you wish to seek my counsel, and I shall answer."

In another blink, the day had returned back to its sunshiny disposition, leaving Lilly standing alone atop the hilltop, utterly shaken, her meeting with Madam overshadowing her personal victory of becoming a town-owner.

~

THE MOONLIGHT WANED upon the arrival of clouds, and Lilly was drained from scrying continuously for hours. Tomorrow would be a new day, and tomorrow, she would begin fulfilling the duties of the role Madam had given her all those centuries ago.

After all, she had said yes, hadn't she?

Immortality came at a price. In Lilly's case, it was a lifetime of servitude to the cause of Madam and the Axis Mundi.

To the cause of magic.

In Our Midst

In every American town, there is bound to be a neighborhood harboring trophy wives of the too-rich-to-need-dual-income variety. Whether they married rich or came from rich families themselves was irrelevant. What mattered was that women of such nature flocked to each other, being the birds of a feather that they were. Their habits—ranging from day-drinking to spending ludicrous amounts of money on shopping—were one of a kind, and therefore they, too, were one of a kind. It manifested itself in the clothes these women wore, the top-of-the-line vehicles they drove around town in a devil-may-care fashion, and in the way that they went above and beyond to hide the fact that despite all the money, luxury, and charm, they were living lives of quiet sadness.

In the case of Bridgewater, the small town that it was, it was Alameda Avenue where such women lived. Seven well-developed homes, grand but not too grand, graced this picturesque street.

Bridgewater was a place where the past and present intertwined, where unexplained phenomena were just another thread in the fabric of daily life. People had become so used to the odd happening in their midst that when something ordinary happened, it was perceived as the exception to the rule rather than the rule itself. People called it the Bridgewater Triangle, but the folk who had been around for long knew that it was not love that had born that nick-name. It was a name that had been birthed from a feeling often described as a pricking of thumbs. The residents of this quiet little town were all too accustomed to the strange, the inexplicable, living their lives in the shadows of legends and ghost stories that had been passed down through generations.

It wasn't for everybody, this town. You were either cut out for it or you weren't, and if you were a tad bit normal, well, then head on down to Pittsburgh or Boston, why don't you? And if you fancied yourself a connoisseur of all things slightly skewed, then welcome, by all means, to Bridgewater.

Such strange little places were peppered all over America, whether it was New England or Washington. Teeming with memories of past centuries. Festering with oddities. Populated by those of the left-hand path, both human and otherwise. The people of Bridgewater had made their peace with the fact that all of God's green earth was not, in fact, God's or green. Some of it was black as sin, and so were its denizens.

Now, back to Alameda Avenue and what was happening there. This picturesque embodiment of suburban tranquility found said tranquility disturbed when Jennifer Newington pulled the curtains of her bedroom and observed fresh tire tracks winding up the road exiting Alameda Avenue, a road that she pretended for most of her life didn't exist. Hers was the last of the seven quintessential suburban American houses on the street, and it would have been something perfect if she could have closed off the street so that it'd look like she was the unofficial queen bee of this exclusive colony, but when that hadn't come to pass, she just took to pretending that the house on top of the hill didn't exist and neither did the road leading up to it.

Jennifer stepped onto her balcony in nothing but her silk robe and a cup of coffee. It was seven-thirty in the morning, her hawk-like eyes fixated on the light coming from within the house on the hill.

She grabbed the cup in her hand so hard that her palm became hot with the temperature, forcing her to put it down on the railing and rub her palm against the smooth silk covering her lithe body. Lithe and fragile and just turned forty-four, though if anyone asked,

Jennifer wasn't a day over thirty-six. She could show you her ID card if you so doubted.

"No way," she whispered, observing the golden glow coming from within the house. The first thought that crossed her mind was, *The actual queen's arrived.* This made her blood boil, knowing that no amount of money she'd come to amass in this lifetime would ever make her the owner of that house, and that there was someone in this sordid little town who was more blessed in terms of bounties than her!

Her fingers instinctively found her phone in the pocket of her robe, and she texted Linda to call her. Linda's was the house right across from her, and Jennifer wouldn't have it any other way. In their little group, Linda was the richest of them all, but that did not bother Jennifer as much—Linda was old money, and no matter how many eight-figure deals your husband closed with tech firms across the country, you could never be old-money rich. Jennifer had made her peace with the fact with much difficulty, citing ethical reasons to her troubled consciousness. Who knew how Linda's family had amassed such wealth?

Who cared?

Right now, Jennifer had bigger problems on her hands. Linda called back almost immediately.

"You know Larry, our real estate agent, told me something just last month," Linda began without so much as a hello, how do you do. "He told me that the house's estimated value is over a mill. Can you believe that? A million for something that old and disconnected from the rest of the town?" Her tone was dripping with contempt; a staunch Christian, she was the epitome of house Devil, street Angel. The facade of a "woman of God" suited her when she needed it, but should the need ever arise, she would bury a body and help people look for it.

"It's probably the location. You know many hilltop houses that have been around forever?"

"Just this bitch's," Linda answered. "And who even is she, driving around like she's a baroness or something?"

Jennifer and Linda enjoyed wallowing in each other's misery, or gossip for that matter.

"Did Larry also tell you who lives there? Because for the life of me, I haven't been able to..."

"Find out? Edward wasn't able to get his hands on any of the files either. That's strange, isn't it? You'd expect city hall to have a record of everyone and everything, and yet when Edward demanded to see the files, they said that they were not within the purview of public perusal! How absurd!"

"You wanna know something crazy, Linds?"

"Don't call me Linds. It sounds like a disease you'd get in your bowels."

"Oh, I'm sorry. Would you rather I called you hemorrhoids?"

"Crass, Jennifer. Real crass."

"Oh, get off your high horse, Linds. Do you wanna know the crazy thing or not?"

"Tell."

"My right hand to God, I've seen this woman drive up the hill three times before in my life. Once when I was ten, once when I was twenty, and once when I was thirty. You get what I mean? This was the fourth."

"And?"

"And what?" Jennifer scoffed, wondering why she'd texted Linda in the first place. Linda was insufferable with her ostentatiousness. She'd have been better off calling Evelyn or Maggie or even Nora. Nora with her hot head and her sailor's mouth. Even Sophia, although she'd probably be having sex. She could have called Charlotte, whom she knew was always up for gossip, but no.

"And what's your point, Jen?"

"My point is, what kind of serum is she injecting in her face so that she looks the same each time I've seen her?"

"Has it occurred to you," Linda began, condescension thick in her tone, "that it might not be the same person? It could very well be that the one you saw in your childhood was the mother, and now this, this strapping young woman with the Range Rover, is the daughter. Where does your head go, Jennifer?"

"Argh," Jennifer groaned. "As per the usual, Linda Fairhurst comes in clutch with a dose of common sense."

"Where would you be without Linda?"

"I suppose I'd have gotten used to drinking alone. God knows I feel like I haven't seen my husband in forever."

"I think every gal on this street feels the same. But come now. There's always the others."

It was Jennifer's turn to laugh. "The others. Don't kid me, lady. We're the glue that holds them together. Without us, there's no others."

"Maggie's practically a hick with a wifebeater for a husband," Linda said, deriving great pleasure from insulting the other women of their group behind their backs.

"And Nora's a guinea basket case," Jennifer piled on.

"Tsk. Tsk. We're not supposed to be using that word anymore. What, are you wanting to get canceled?"

"What, guinea? I don't think any wop's gonna cancel me for calling 'em like I see 'em," Jennifer scoffed. "Canceled, my ass."

"Easy there, tiger. How many Ambiens have you taken?" Linda asked with just a touch of concern.

"Two. Why?"

"You get pretty racist when you're on Ambien, I'm not sure Mr. Christ would approve."

"How d'you know? Have you taken any Ambien?"

"I'm a Valium girl through and through. Don't get me to jump ships."

"And what is with this damn fog, Linds?" Jennifer commented, her head swiveling slowly, taking in just how drab the otherwise lush surroundings had turned in the wake of this impermeable mist.

"A little too soon for seasonal affective depression," Linda stated impatiently. "Besides, if it's the fog, it'll go away as it always does."

"Something's different about this one," Jennifer said, commenting on the deep chill this veil of gray set in her bones, the sullen aloofness it made her feel. And empty. So empty. As if there was some of that psyops chemical suspended within the fog itself, obscuring her view of the rest of the city and simultaneously making her lethargic, depressed.

Jennifer stood staring for the longest time, wondering about the kind of light that was lit inside the house atop the hill. Must be those high-intensity gas lamps if they were burning so incandescently that their light was penetrating this dull gray fog.

In the afternoon, Jennifer would ensure that the seven ladies of Alameda stuck to their schedule, and promptly so, for Jennifer did not enjoy a tardy libation. She knew that secretly the ladies enjoyed her imposed structure. Their lives had become such an embodiment of order that even the lunchtime drink had to be enjoyed under the same principles. And not for nothing, it gave them all an opportunity to get together and dish.

The seven women considered this avenue their sanctuary and more or less supported each other like singers in a dysfunctional band. They hadn't ventured into town since Mr. Cowell's funeral, and by the looks of it, they weren't going to be venturing into town anytime soon. Not until the fog lifted. The curse of having expensive cars was that the insurance guys made sure to find loopholes so that they could get out of paying for any damage to the car. Fog would be an amazing precedent for them to get out of paying for dented fenders.

But Jennifer, like the other women, didn't worry about not being able to go into town. Their homes seemed to hold a never-ending supply of sundries and groceries, and their back yards had all but been turned into mini-farms, growing vegetables of any variety that could grow in such parts.

~

As Jennifer made her way to Linda's house on a Wednesday afternoon, she had donned her favorite yellow polka dot dress. A large brown belt hugged her slim waist tightly, synching her hips and accentuating an hourglass figure. Her hair was akin to a 70s spy film and held in place with a large white satin headband. Her eyelashes big and fake, her breasts too, no doubt.

As she confidently walked over to Linda's abode, she carried with her a tote. Inside the tote was a generous bottle of Aviation gin. One could never be seen in public carrying alcohol unless it was a bottle of red wine.

Jennifer had her nuances. "Liquor, liquor, never been sicker. Red wine, red wine, always so fine," she would whisper to herself. Wine, or at least red wine, was the epitome of class to her and was the only acceptable bottle of alcohol that could be seen without the necessities of an expensive tote to hide such earthly pleasures. A bottle of gin, on the other hand, spelled lunchtime whore. Jennifer was the type to judge anyone who did something similar to her but dared to do it in plain sight.

That's why she and Linda were closer than the rest. Jennifer adored Linda's prideful nature; she dressed to the nines almost daily and had a subtle arrogance that surrounded her. Jenn disguised her jealousy through confidence. If you could fake it till you made it, then who would know? The pride that coursed through Linda's veins kept Jenn attached to her hip. She felt the others were somewhat beneath her, yet she needed them for her daily routines. Linda could care less. She thought she was above the group anyway, and it showed.

The door knocker looked brand new, and as Jenn rapped thrice, it took almost no time for Linda to open the red solid wood door.

"Come on, silly goose, you never need to knock."

"Well, manners maketh the woman, Mrs. Fairhurst." Jenn was occasionally knocked back by Linda's devil-may-care attitude and always returned exchanges with age-old adages that were above her. It made her feel important.

Linda's house, while architecturally the same as the others on the street, was impeccable in terms of interior décor. A medium-sized staircase stood to the right of the hallway, with a tight balcony running atop the hallway from right to left. Crucifixes adorned the walls. The dining room was through the opening to the right and the sitting room to the left. The house was almost permanently staged and looked brand new, as if no one had ever lived in it. It would have been a realtor's dream.

Jennifer walked into the kitchen and set her tote down on the table.

"I brought libations." She smirked.

While Linda was unofficially in charge (Jenn being the official title holder), she never scoffed at free booze. The trappings of Alameda meant the women needed their outlets, and since no one was coming in nor out of the avenue, who was to care if the seven women got blind drunk every lunchtime?

Shortly after, the other women entered Linda's home, and fast, as they did not want to upset either Queen Bee.

Occasionally, they would forgo their daily Sunday best and take to the Nip for a lunchtime boating. Nora had a small boat, and since the entrance to the lake was just a stroll beyond Alameda it was one of the more accessible daytime pleasures. The fog rarely blocked the entrance to the lake from the woods. The small road was usually heated up by a dense layer of wood which trapped the heat from the sun, or so Linda would tell everyone. Either way, it was like a secret that the women enjoyed. A clear shot to the lake, which, while still foggy, was easier to navigate than the foggy roads.

Inside number 6 Alameda, the ladies sat with their deck of cards and a stiff martini, talking of the old newcomer who'd made herself comfortable in the house on the hill.

"Technically, that'd make it house 8 Alameda?" Maggie asked in a droopy tone.

"Shut it, Mags, we've been here before!" Jennifer said with a pinch of deep anger. This statement had perforated her delusion that Alameda only had seven houses. And it stung bad.

"Yeah, shut it, Mags," Evelyn chirped. "It's not like we don't have enough shit to deal with that we've got to think about the woman who's perched up there. And speaking of nasty things to deal with!" She waved her hand at the street, drawing the attention of the ladies to the sudden and strange phenomenon taking place before their eyes. The afternoon sun filtered through the fog occasionally, casting dappled shadows on the street.

The last time Evelyn had seen fog of the sort was when she'd made the mistake of traveling to New York with her husband and bearing witness to the suffocating smog slowly poisoning the city. Then, too, the sun had been out and about, penetrating the smog with its indifferent rays. Just like this unnaturalness taking place before her eyes, poking away at her heart with the icepick of fear. What if she was never to escape this street again, never visit her favorite shops and buy her favorite things?

"Darling, what's with the expletives?" Charlotte asked, taking a bite out of a glazed donut and wiping her mouth clean with the back of her hand. "Are you experiencing some kind of bloat?"

"No, Charlotte, that would be your thing," Evelyn said cruelly, and earned the laughter of the others in the group. Charlotte didn't laugh. She looked mournfully at the half-eaten donut in her hand and placed it on the plate. A plate that she'd all but picked clean by herself. "I'm suffocated is what I am."

"What I'd give to be suffocated," Sophia sighed quietly, her face flushing red as her eyes became unfocused and she escaped into the dimension of her fantasies.

The women had a very East Coast attitude to one another; it bordered on masculine, ribbing each other every chance they could, poking fun and not letting one another get away with airs and pretense unless, of course, they were seen in public together.

"What's with the both of you being weird today?" Nora, unable to help her Italian temper, hit her palm on the table.

"What's with you being so angry?" Maggie asked, her tone that of an apprehensive dormouse.

"Never you mind," Nora said, "and we don't use the word angry anymore."

"Err, that would only be toward me, and you do sound kinda angry!" Maggie chimed in.

"Ladies!" Jennifer said dominantly, making them all quiet down. She observed Linda's approval from the corner of her eye and carried on. "I think it's about time we address the mystery of the house on the hill. I propose that we make the first move to go up there and say hello to the Wicked Witch of the East. Introduce ourselves."

Sophia laughed. Maggie clapped her hands. Charlotte, taking advantage of the diversion, grabbed the half-eaten donut and wolfed it down. Evelyn, Linda, and Nora looked uncomfortably at each other before deferring to Linda's judgment.

Linda nodded, and that put a stamp of approval on the matter.

"I think we need to assess the danger, if any," she said. Impeccably dressed, composed, and with an air of authority about her, Linda prided herself on her reputation and social status, often at the expense of genuine connections. Despite her polite exterior, she couldn't stand any of the women. This was not something that she made evident in her behavior with them; it was a deep part of her that came out when she was with one or the other. From time to time, she had bad-mouthed all of them to each other, usually by diplomatically cornering them and having them say ugly things about each other. It sated her pride to know that each of them thought the other was just as imperfect as the next. Try as she did, she could not outright indulge in such verbal debauchery, for she was a staunch conservative, and such things went against her deep-seated religious beliefs. Linda was of the opinion that the Church and State should be one, and that anyone not following Christ was damning themselves to an eternity in Hell. Quite the contradiction.

"Assess the danger? Do you hear yourself? Let's just go up and say hi," Maggie stated. Her life was one of comfort and routine, a life that avoided change or effort, even if it meant staying in unhappy situations. Such as the situation with her husband, a pathological domestic abuser. She often came to their gatherings bearing the marks of great beatings upon her body. It wasn't out of solidarity as much as pity that the others let her hang with them. She was thankful that her brown skin was able to hide such bruises without having to cover up using makeup.

"Yes, Mags. Danger. We need to make sure that this woman is not one of those brazen New Age weirdos who will renounce the Lord and align themselves with all sorts of pagan nonsense," Linda said. There was no pretense in her voice; she genuinely believed what she was saying. "There might be a witch of the east in our midst indeed."

"Pfft," Sophia reacted. "Witches don't exist. You know where the concept of witches riding brooms came from? There were no sex toys back in those days, and they had to make do with what they had." She was always one to seek passion and excitement, and when she couldn't find it in her marriage, she took to other means. These days, she was teetering on the edge of infidelity, not quite there, but getting closer with each passing day. Sophia had always mistaken physical connection for the depth that she had always craved in her life.

"And I suppose you would know all about that coming from riding brooms, wouldn't you?" Evelyn jumped in.

"Bite me," Sophia jeered.

"And you'd like that, I bet," Evelyn responded. She, for one, wanted to explore the mysterious house on the hill. Perhaps there would be something so singular in terms of its value that it would finally sate her need once and for all. A woman could dream. The ladies all started to chuckle.

"Calm down, all of you," Charlotte chirped in. "What in the heck is going on today? We're meant to be friends." Everyone around the table cast Charlotte a startled look. If there was someone who could overpower them in terms of pure physicality, it was Charlotte. No taller than five foot and five inches, she weighed two hundred and thirty pounds. "As for the house, I'm game. Could be fun."

"We should mark our territory. Face whoever lives there head-on," Nora said warningly. She was quick to anger and held onto grudges. Her deep-seated fears and her insecurities were often masked by her temper. Her eyes had defaulted to staying in a perpetual scowl. As such, she was always eager for a confrontation.

"Then it's settled," Jennifer said at long last.

The women fell into a contemplative silence, weighing the proposal, their inner desires clashing with their fears. Their collective gazes fell upon the house on the hill with its ominous presence. Long had it been a source of speculation and whispered tales.

Now it beckoned them, offering the promise of answers—or perhaps something dangerous.

Once Bitten, Twice Shy

It was not the first lesson, but one of the most important ones for sure, in her almanac, was to make friends first, enemies later. Whether it was enterprising antichrists or eldritch gods, you couldn't afford to make a foe out of them. Not if you wanted to live. She might be immortal, but she could very well die if someone more powerful than her deemed so.

Better to err on the side of caution than be trapped in a cell for decades, forced to eat the rats that found their way through the sewers. Better to be amicable than have an angry mob try to torch you and wonder why you wouldn't catch flames.

On a long enough timeline, these things tend to happen to you because you're not always careful. After all, it's impossible to always be careful. Lilly knew all too well that on a long enough timeline, everything that could happen to you would.

Sometimes she wondered if she would have been better off letting the townsfolk of Salem kill her. That would have been pain followed by death once. Afterward, it would have all ended in the black mist that awaits all those who die. But no, she had to choose immortality and experience the pain of a hundred deaths over the course of the next few centuries. And not just her death. Loved ones, family, friends.

She remembered it clear as day when she'd walked up to Jonathan's sickbed in Boston General Hospital. Jonathan, dosed up on meds, unable to open his eyes, lay there withered and wrinkled, a spitting image of their father in his old age. He did not open his eyes when Lilly walked up to him and put her hand in his. He did not register it when she brought her lips next to his ears and said, "If it helps for an easier passage to the next life, brother mine, I forgive you."

Her tears had spilled onto his frail skin. Jonathan had not moved.

She'd felt the life slip out of him while her hand was still in his. It was as if for years upon years he had been waiting, trapped in this state between life and death, for her to come forgive him, and now that she had, he could die.

A lifetime of lifetimes, all those lifetimes filled with bitterness of loss and grief—and yet here she was, ever subservient to the Axis Mundi, to Madam. At least there was Madam, undying, as immortal as she was, or perhaps more.

But she could not call upon Madam as a friend, family member, or even lover. And love was something that she had sought all her life. Casual affairs were all she could muster, enjoying the honeymoon period of three to six months before calling things quits. This was based on another of her rules—don't stick around the same place for longer than fifteen years. After more than that, people around her began to grow suspicious. To her, fifteen years was no more than fifteen hours, and as such, all relationships felt fleeting, no matter how long.

When she met the Devil's prophet, Joseph Banbury, a man whom she'd discovered was going to be as immortal as her, she thought that her prospects might shift. That she could share a love with Joseph, a love that would have allowed her at long last to develop a lasting bond. She yearned for that love despite knowing that what Joe was about to do would change the course of mankind forever, but did it really have to be that way? She had tried to steer him away from the grand design of things, hoping he would have chosen a quieter life. A life with her. A life in which they'd have savored their love for each other for millennia to come.

But how did that pan out? It didn't. She'd made an enemy out of him, despite her best attempts.

She'd wondered often, *Why not marry another witch?* But then the answer provided itself. Sure, there'd be another witch out there just like her, someone who'd been braving it out for many centuries thanks to Madam's gift of immortality, but witches, when it came down to it, were a strange breed. Hippies with powers. Constantly whoring themselves around the planet because they could, or dedicating themselves to a life of solitude or covens. She was not one to swing either way.

Witches had enormous amounts of recourse, from simply eradicating all signs of sexually transmitted diseases from their bodies with a snap of their fingers to wiping the memories of others. It allowed them to be reckless. And frankly, it caused a lot of them to be burned at the stake.

Silly witches, Lilly often thought to herself. Those who lived a paycheck-to-paycheck lifestyle ran out of fuel—overdosed, committed suicide, died by living a life of excess, or sought situations where another witch killed them.

Paycheck to paycheck meant a thieving witch, one who did not have to work or contribute to society. It was a life of constant silly uphill battles, from renting high-scale homes on the private market to liquidating ancient reserves of cash they had on hand.

In the old days, it was simple. You could conjure fake pounds and there was no way to tell if it was real or not. You couldn't conjure fake currency in today's world. Conjuring fake currency in the modern day came with extra work. Depositing cash directly into a bank would require a witch to walk right up to a bank clerk and hand over the many thousands in cash to deposit.

When the cash reader would be alarmed that the money was fake, a silly witch would throw a mind veil over the teller and advise that he or she place the money directly in the cash tray and avoid all other nuances. Should the police ever be called? They would be mind-altered too. While somewhat easy, the rigamarole of mind-veiling people on a daily basis was exhausting. But some witches loved it. Eventually, however, they would be found out.

One must learn to be a tricky witch, not a silly witch, and that is why Lilly had the foresight to buy Bridgewater.

Alas, to date, she hadn't met one witch that matched her energy, male or female. Not that females attracted her sexually, but spending so much time alone, the comfort of any human being would suffice.

She started her day the same way she always had for centuries: with a piping hot cup of coffee. It had to be scalding. The coffee was a morning comfort, one that she could wrap her hands around, especially in this foggy weather. It brought a moment of meditation, ten minutes or so that were hers and hers alone before the ravages of the day would come forth. It was the same in Salem, and it was no different now.

"Friends first, enemies later, or was it the other way around?" Lilly asked the diary. The diary promptly turned over to the page where the rule was written down, reminding her that the difference between friend and enemy could mean life or death.

"Right, right," Lilly said. "Sometimes I'm just being rhetorical, Jane."

During the course of the couple hundred years, Lilly had breathed sentience into the diary. And like all sentient things, the diary had come to develop a unique personality of her own. Based on the things that Lilly wrote into her, the diary had become an assistant, a confidante, more than just a binding with paper between it. Once Lilly had asked her what she wanted to be called, and the diary had written one solitary word:

Jane.

Jane the diary flapped her pages and flopped lifelessly on the coffee table on the porch.

Lilly watched everything unfold before her. She could see the two women standing on their porches on Alameda Avenue, and if she so wished, she could hear what they were talking about, but she was in no mood to do so. It was too early in the day to dip her beak in other people's bullshit, and besides, she was going to meet them in the afternoon anyway.

She hadn't come empty-handed. There would be gifts to give and introductions to be made. She had been watching these women for some time now and knew all of them, although they themselves did not know her beyond their wild speculations. Today, though, they would.

She saw the tendrils of the mist wind themselves around the tree trunks, slide across the surface of the lake, and envelop the houses. It crawled up the hill but did not cross the boundary of her house. The enchantments put upon the house ensured that the place remained warm and untouched by environmental calamities, even if such calamities were as innocuous as a thick fog.

"Jane," Lilly said. The diary rifled through its pages onto a blank one. "No, darling. You aren't to write something. This is just for your ears. Things, I believe, are now in motion that cannot be stopped even if I tried. And you have a role to play in all this. You must do exactly as I say, okay?"

The diary's leather binding creased as if nodding.

"Good. Then here's what you're going to do." Lilly spilled the beans on her plan, making Jane her accomplice in what was to come.

IT WAS AFTERNOON NOW, and as thick as the fog was, Lilly couldn't have the weather be this drab. She needed the sun and, knowing the spell for it, willed it to shine despite the curtains of gray. It wasn't as if her house was affected by the fog. Sunshine beamed upon her home, bathing it in warm light. She watched with amusement as some of the sunlight escaped and fell upon the street and the houses submerged in the murk. She found it hilarious knowing that people in those houses might be wondering what on earth was happening with the weather.

Armed with her basketful of gifts, she traveled down the hill not in her car, but on foot. The women had moved to the porch with their libations, and as much as she had resisted the urge to listen to what they had been talking about, that resistance only lasted so long, and eventually she learned they were talking about her.

Dressed in a plain white dress that spoke of long-forgotten elegance, wearing a hat that cemented her identity as a socialite of means, and wearing jewelry from different centuries, the witch walked with her basket in tow, a faint smile on her face. And these gifts that she had, specifically suited for each of the seven, would ensure that they'd become her friends. Her plan depended on it.

This was a separate personality of hers entirely. This was not Lilly Thurman of New York. This was Lilly Frost, charming, confident, and commanding an aura of mystery about her.

She knocked confidently on the door to Linda's house, knowing that all the women were huddled inside. What she didn't know was that the women, after a much more intense bout of discussion within the house, had made up their minds to come meet her at her abode. When the door was answered, it was to the sight of seven women, all of them dressed for the brisk weather that awaited them.

"Hello," Lilly said pleasantly, giving them a smile.

"Er..." Jennifer was lost for words. They hadn't computed the possibility that the woman on the hill might want to meet them too. "Hi."

"I'm Lilly, I live up there on the hill."

Familiarity flashed across Jennifer's eyes as the memory of decades came into sharp clarity. She *had* seen this woman before, and more than once. She was certain of it now.

"I...I... Well, hello," Jennifer stuttered. Behind her, the six women stared, scowled, lifted their brows, and gaped at Lilly, just as confused. Some were afraid. Others were curious. But they were all caught off-guard. "I'm Jennifer. I live right across the street. And would you believe it, we were just talking amongst ourselves about coming to visit you."

"It's altogether very good that I've decided to visit you then. It's better that one walks up to seven than seven walks up to one, don't you think? More courteous." Lilly gleamed.

"Well? Jenn? Are we going to invite our guest inside or have her stand in that dreadful mist all day!" Linda's voice had gone high-pitched, a tone that indicated the rapid onset of her anxiety.

"Please, come in." Jennifer waved her arm, signaling her to come in.

"If I was a vampire, I wouldn't have been able to until just now," Lilly joked. The women laughed nervously, realizing that they'd all been raised up on their fair share of pop-culture vampirisms to know exactly what she meant, and yet all of them were rendered somewhat uncomfortable that this would be the first thing she'd mention to them. Perhaps she was a vampire.

"You aren't, are you?" Linda asked, picking her glass from the table and bringing it to her lips.

"A vampire? Well, I don't drink blood," Lilly joked as she stepped inside the house.

"How about a martini then?" Sophia asked, handing Lilly a martini before she had a chance to take her shoes off or put the basket down. Lilly gracefully accepted the drink and walked inside the foyer. The foyer stretched seamlessly into the living room, where the women had been gathering.

The house was impeccably minimalistic, drawing great perception of size from the lack of things within. And whatever there was was so seamlessly integrated with the architecture that it did not look out of place. Such as the eighty-inch TV embedded in the wall, looking like a black window more than a TV. Or the furniture, all of it marvelous, all of it in its prescribed place, creating a delicate feng shui flow. Beneath the TV was an electrical fire dancing away behind a pane of glass. It didn't do much to warm the room as much as it was for show. The cedarwood floor was gray and luxurious to walk upon.

Led by Linda, she walked over to the dining table by the largest window in the living room. It was a wall-to-wall window, giving an immensely satisfying view of the wilderness beyond the house: the pines in their great assembly; the oaks and birches in their silent conferences. One side of the window even gave a decent view of the hill and the lake.

Lilly set her basket down and sat at the table, with the other women around her. There was a charcuterie board on the table, populated with grapes, cheeses, meats, and crackers. Jennifer politely pushed one toward Lilly.

"Those carrots are from my own garden," Jennifer said.

"And the cheese, you have to try the cheese. It's to die for," Linda said hurriedly, not wanting to be left behind. “My husband, among many things, owns a cheesery in Wisconsin. We have it in wheels.”

“My, my,” Lilly said, putting some cheese on a cracker and taking a bite. It was okay. These women were laying it on thick with the pretense, but she was fine with it. Then she tried the carrots. Again, nothing to write home about. Slightly stale, if you could call it that.

“It’s uncanny,” Sophia said, her fascinated gaze not wavering from Lilly. The very sight of this woman had awakened something deep and carnal inside her, something that was making her picture the both of them alone in a room, doing unspeakable things to each other. She shook her head and opened her eyes. “I meant...it’s uncanny that we were just talking about you, and you just happened to show up, and too well prepared at that!”

“I must have a long life,” Lilly joked, and all the women laughed heartily in the wake of her statement. It was a common superstition that if someone you mentioned showed up shortly afterward, they’d have a long life. A superstition with its roots deep in this part of the country. An inside joke.

“Or, or, or...you’re the Devil.” Nora laughed, but no one joined. Everyone looked at her awkwardly, until Lilly giggled just a little bit.

“If I was the Devil, you’d know,” she added. “But I’m just a woman.”

“A woman bearing a lot of gifts,” Evelyn said, looking with wide eyes at the basket at the center of the table, wondering if there was something inside that would sate her need. The basket was attached to a set of wheels and a long rod which made carrying the thing easier, not that Lilly needed help in that department.

“Do you want something other than a martini, Lilly?” Linda asked, standing by her cabinet of vintage wines and whiskeys.

“I see you have the ’32 Macallan. You know how rare that is?” Lilly asked.

“Of course I know how rare it is,” Linda said, eying her prized possession. “My father gave it to me, and I’ve never opened it.”

“Well, how about you open it now?” Lilly asked, matching her gaze with Linda’s.

"Excuse me?" Linda could not believe the words coming out of this woman's mouth.

"Oh, I should make myself clear." Lilly chuckled and brought her basket close to her. "I meant, it's honestly so refreshing to see a woman of such cultivated taste. Would you believe I brought you the same thing?"

She lifted the satin off the basket, revealing a splendid selection of the finest and most expensive things that the women had ever seen. She brought forth a bottle of 1932 Macallan from within the basket and gave it to Linda.

"Here. Now you have one that you can actually enjoy," Lilly said.

The rest of the women gasped at the sheer value and spectacularity of the gift. Their own curiosities were now burning like cinders in their chests. If this was what she had in store for just one of them, what did she have for the rest?

"I'm not done," Lilly said, putting her hand in her basket and pulling out a block of pule cheese. "This'll go nicely, I believe, with a red vintage."

"Jesus Christ." Charlotte gasped, looking at the cheese. She'd only ever eaten it a couple times and knew it to be the tastiest cheese she'd ever had. "Lady, are you for real?"

"Y–y–you're very gracious," Linda said, holding the cheese in one hand and the whiskey bottle in the other. She sat down at the head of the table, her gaze affixed at the bottle. "You do realize that this bottle's around two thousand dollars, right?"

"I have a couple more of them lying around my place," Lilly shrugged.

"I simply can't," Linda said. And yet her firm grip on the bottle said otherwise.

"It's bad manners to return gifts, Linds," Jennifer said. "And you're holding the line. Say thank you so the rest of us can be bequeathed!"

Linda looked up at Lilly, managed a faint smile. "I don't even know you."

"I'm Lilly Frost, and I come bearing gifts. I live in the house on the hill. And you're Linda Fairhurst, resident of this fine house. Now we know each other."

"How do you know who I am?" Linda asked, putting both things down on the table.

"You're the richest woman in this town. Who doesn't know you?" Lilly said, placating Linda. A brief smile flashed across the woman's face as her pride was stoked.

"Clearly I'm not the richest if you're saying that you've got a couple more of these at your place. You must have us over sometime," Linda said. "And thank you. You don't even know how much this means to me."

"You're very welcome." Lilly smiled, then moved on to the next item she procured from her basket. "And you'll be surprised to learn that while these are the first of my gifts, they are hardly the last."

"Why?" Evelyn asked. Unable to hold herself, she ditched all her manners and straight-up asked the blunt question that was on everyone's minds.

"Why what?"

"What's with the gift giving?"

"You must be..."

"Evelyn. Evelyn Parker," she said. "And in all my life, I've never heard of people giving each other gifts that would set them in a different tax bracket. What's up with you?"

Now that this question had been put forth, all the women leaned in and stared at Lilly with an intensity any normal woman would have found intimidating. But Lilly only smiled and said, "My dear. Do you even know who I am?"

"Other than the fact that you don't live here and only come around every so often, no. I don't think I do."

"My family built this town. We practically own all of it," Lilly said. The white lie had to come first. The truth could wait. "If I am giving these gifts, it's to women whom I know deserve them. I'm not setting Linda into another tax bracket. The woman's already a millionaire. And so are you. And so is Jennifer. You're not nobodies. I've read up on all of you from the news. Five of you have Wikipedia pages written about you. The other two are not doing too shabby either; looking at you, Maggie and Nora. You're the most well-to-do women in an ordinary town. And guess what? So am I."

That shut Evelyn up for a bit. Lilly took out the next gift, an ornate platinum ring with a humongous ruby at its center. She gave it to Jennifer. "This is the last ruby mined in medieval Persia. It's also said to possess magical powers. Those Sufis were on to something back in those days. You could get it appraised, but no one alive today is capable enough to truly appreciate just how grand this thing is. You can even see the Arabic inscriptions upon the platinum if you peer close."

"Holy shit," Jennifer whispered, looking at the ring, then promptly putting it on her finger. "I'm not even gonna ask how expensive this thing is, but I'm grateful that we have a very benevolent sugar mommy in our midst all of a sudden. Thank you, Lilly."

"Hey, who are you calling sugar mommy? I'm the same age as you," Lilly joked.

Somehow, Jennifer knew that wasn't true. No one really knew Jennifer's actual age, and so Lilly could claim whatever; she just knew that this woman was not forty-four.

Lilly went around the table, baffling the rest of the women with their gifts. And baffled they were, for it was probably one of the rarest and oddest things in the world for a stranger to come bearing such expensive gifts. But these women weren't ordinary women, they could easily be bought.

She gave Maggie the first edition of *Harry Potter* and a pouch of Kopi Luwak coffee, aged and fermented to perfection. She gave Evelyn a pair of heavy gold bracelets from the Mughal era. For Nora, she had a bottle of 1964 First Fjord old vintage wine from Sweden. For Sophia, she had a Japanese fragrance that was rare.

"Hey, what do I get?" Charlotte laughed at long last when all the women had been given their gifts and were staring at them awestruck.

"You get the rest of the basket," Lilly said, sliding it toward her. It was a sizeable basket, one that had taken Lilly quite a lot of strength to pull as she descended the hill with it.

Charlotte groped the basket and pulled it close, her eyes becoming bigger and bigger as she stared at the contents within. There was a jar of Italian truffle honey, its contents shimmering in the light, the scent of truffles intoxicating her. Nestled behind the jar was a tin of Osetra caviar.

"Mother of God," Charlotte whispered, her mouth drooling upon the sight of it.

"Lady," Evelyn whispered, holding the gold in her hand and weighing it. "Just who in the world are you, really?"

"I'm just a woman of means, eager to share said means with other women like me," Lilly said, her warm smile reflecting on the faces of all the women, all of them smiling, all of them with emotions welling up in their hearts of stone.

"We feel quite awkward," Maggie said. "We don't have anything to give you."

"Well, as it happens, you all do have something to give me. I get quite lonely up there. And it's not fun to be alone, if you catch my drift. Dare I presume that my humble gifts qualify me to be a part of this amazing group you've got going?"

"Humble?!" Jennifer threw her head back and laughed. In the brief time since she'd been gifted the ring, she had googled it and was all too satisfied knowing that what she had on her finger was as expensive as the whiskey that Linda had been gifted.

"Listen," Lilly said, waving her hand modestly. "When you've been around as much as I have, and when you've done as much as I have, things start to lose their inherent value. I don't mean it as a slight to any of you who find meaning in the gifts that I've given you. I wanted you to find meaning in it. Fine women as you all are, it'd be criminal if I gave you anything less. You all deserve more. And I offer you a chance to get more, if you'll have me."

"Girl, are you for real?" Maggie, who was sitting right beside Lilly, wound her arm around the witch and gave her a tight squeeze. "Of course we'll have you!"

The others smiled.

"I think that Maggie has rather candidly captured the sentiment we all harbor," Linda said. "We would surely love to have you. In fact, why don't you stay? We're having lunch in an hour. Have lunch with us."

"Please," Jennifer said. "It's the least we can do."

"All right," Lilly said. "That sounds like a plan. What are we cooking?"

"Have you ever had pheasant?" Nora asked. "My husband was off game-hunting and he's been away for another month. Guess who raided his pantry and got a hold of six fat pheasants?"

"You did?" Lilly grinned.

"Bet your sweet ass we did, and now we're going to grill 'em on the patio. You wanna join?" Charlotte asked.

"I'd love to."

"Great!" Linda chirped. "And afterward, we might open this bottle and toast to a newfound friendship."

The women all left their gifts at the table and adjourned to the patio. Given that it was her first time with them, Lilly held her own remarkably well, but after being alive for hundreds of years, one knew how to mingle with any crowd.

They cooked, talked, and ate on the patio, watching the fog weave in and out of the forest behind Linda's house. Each with a glass of whiskey in their hands, they sat and talked freely, words flowing well thanks to the whiskey inebriation and the warm feeling of full stomachs.

"You're the biggest Bridgewater oddity we've encountered so far," Jennifer said. "Hand to God."

"Oh yeah? And what are some others?"

"Oh, you know, there's the usual," Evelyn piped in. "There's the Hockomock Swamp in the middle of Bridgewater Triangle. That's a big one. People have reported seeing cryptids in there. Phantom lights. Unexplained disappearances. All that urban myth and legend."

"And then there's the Freetown-Fall River State Forest!" Nora added excitedly. "In the 80s, there were a lot of Satanic rituals going on down there, or so I heard. It must have been the Satanic Panic, but you know, there's other things down there too. Like murder. Some attribute the violence to the ghosts that linger in that forest!"

"And if you're speaking about the mysterious and sinister, you can't not mention Dighton Rock. It's also there inside the Triangle. The carvings on that rock are a mystery for modern-day archeologists. Some say that the Vikings, when they came to America five hundred or so years ago, left those markings. Others say it was witches," Maggie said.

"At this point, you might ask what's not haunted? Bridgewater State University, Anawan Rock, the Taunton State Hospital—these are just some of the places where people have reported seeing the odd and inexplicable. Trust me, sis, our entire town is a clusterfuck of weird and strange, and you're just the latest addition to it," Charlotte said.

"Not to mention the lone house on top of Bridgewater Hill. That's you, by the way," Linda said. "We've heard stories ever since we were kids. A witch lives in that house. An ancient and immortal force to be reckoned with. Oh, you know, it's the stuff kids tell each other around campfires. Much like we're doing now, even though we're not kids and this patio's not a campfire."

"If that's not odd enough, look at this fog. We've had fog before, but never like this. It's almost like this cloud has a mind of its own and it won't go. Despite the sunlight earlier in the day, I can't even make the drive to Erewhon," Sophia said.

"I can't believe it," Lilly said.

"I know, right?!" Sophia's voice went shrill.

"No. I mean I cannot believe you guys have an Erewhon here now!"

"Girl, that place is popping up everywhere," Linda said, topping off Lilly's glass for the third time. Lilly knew what Linda was doing but let her do it anyway. A simple spell cast within her mind would make her sober. But oh, this whiskey was so damn delicious that Lilly resisted the temptation. "And speaking of popping, where did you pop out from? We haven't seen you around here. Like ever."

"I mean, that's not true. I did mention that I saw her a couple times, but that can't be possible. You look the same as you did when I saw you drive up the hill ten years ago. And then ten years before that," Jennifer said.

"That must have been my mother. People tell me I'm her spitting image," Lilly said. Again, the white lie had to do for now. As warmed up as these women were, they were still not ready for the truth. Despite how much they tried to inebriate her, she didn't want to veil them just yet.

"Oh. Is she around?" Jennifer asked.

"She's been dead for some time," Lilly said, not lying this time around.

"I'm sorry to hear that," Maggie spoke softly.

"Where are you from though?" Linda asked, a blunt question that did not hide behind pretext or subtext.

"Here," Lilly said, waving around. "I'm assuming you're talking about my family. We came here with the Puritans back in the 1600s."

"Oooh," Linda said. "Do tell."

And Lilly did. She told them the exact story of her family, how they came to Salem, and what happened there. She just conveniently skipped all mention of herself from this abridged and altered version of the story. It was a far cry from the Australian story and the *G'day, mate* she threw in Banbury's direction.

There would come a time to share the correct version. It just wasn't the right time now.

Another hour passed and the afternoon gave way to evening. Lilly, quite drunk, bade all the women farewell, and asked them to come over to her house the next day for lunch.

"I don't think that I can outdo the pheasant you grilled, but I might have something that strikes y'all's fancy," Lilly said, her speech a little slurred.

"Need help getting home?" Maggie asked.

"That's all right, dear. I can manage," Lilly said, placing her hand upon Maggie's shoulder for support as she put on her shoes.

"Bye, Lil." Linda waved her hand, as did the rest of them.

"Goodbye, you guys. And thank you for a good time," Lilly said.

"You kidding? Thank you for the gifts! I don't think any of us can ever repay you," Jennifer stated.

They watched as Lilly walked down the steps of the house and headed into the mist, disappearing from view as her shadow embarked upon the road up the hill.

Once she was deep in the fog, Lilly whispered, "Sobrietatem Redde."

All intoxication trailed away from her nervous system upon the utterance of those two words, and Lilly Frost walked back to her house with a satisfied grin on her face.

She'd made the first move. Planted the seed.

Now the ball, as they said, was in seven different courts at the same time.

3

THE INTRODUCTION

1852— A Disruption in Quietude

Each waking day brought forth with it the realization that this town, nurtured and raised by her, had grown up so fast. In the time since she had purchased it from Samuel Smith, Lilly had lived two whole lifetimes. And healthy lifetimes, if she were being specific. It wasn't everyone who was lucky enough to reach eighty years old. And, of course, absolutely nobody was reaching one hundred and sixty.

Somehow, she had. What she'd first thought of as a lie too good to be true was, in fact, unfortunately true. She couldn't die. A hundred and sixty years after the events of Salem (by which time she was already thirty), she was still here. Almost two hundred years old.

Wishing for death but not knowing how to go about achieving it. After a hundred years of trying to end her existence, nothing in particular came to mind. Throwing herself off the tallest mountain, hoping that the rocks would tear her body as she'd descend uncontrollably? She'd done that thrice now, and it'd always be her getting up and brushing the ice and dirt off her clothes and walking away as if nothing had ever happened. Drowning by trapping herself at the bottom of a lake, or worse yet, a sea? Suffocation without the promise of death at the end was just torture and nothing more. She did not need to relive the horrors of anchoring herself at the base of Lake Nip and hoping that she'd just cross the threshold. Upon the advent of muskets, she covertly got her hands on one and tried to blow her brains out in her bathtub. It gave her a headache like nothing else, and after a long enduring match with her own life, she finally came to the conclusion that she was immortal.

The bitter irony imbued in every part of her body was that she did not want to be immortal any longer.

Not after what had happened to Christoph. And David.

The names, if she let them, escaped her tongue like the loose flow of a drunken poet. Sarah, her friend whom she had saved from the fire. Her kids. Her husband. She had attended every single one's funeral. Samuel Smith, the reprehensible man from whom she had bought the land. What a reformed guy he'd become before his demise. A saintly beard on his face and alms slipping from his fingers into the bowls of the poor—all on account of having found God. The innkeeper. What was his name? Sean? The poor fucker had died of lung cancer, spitting blood on his sickbed when Lilly saw him last.

It got so that she became envious of every dying person she ever saw, overlooking their fatal pain, wishing to be in their position so she'd get a taste of what death felt like and what lay in wait beyond the realm of the living. For fifty whole years after Christoph and David's demise, she became addicted to attending funerals and hospices just so she could get in close proximity to the one who had promised to evade her on the orders of Madam—Death.

And while all this was happening, Bridgewater was turning from this quiet little settlement into something industrialized, brick and mortar factories with their billowing chimneys and the smell of sweat and coal rife in the air around them. The iron trade. The construction of the local dam.

She was not so humble that she wasn't going to take credit for her contribution. Bridgewater's transition from one century to the next was all thanks to Lilly's direction. Her ability to think into the future and take life by the balls was only amplified after her spring awakening. Or, for lack of a better term, after she realized that she was a witch.

The town, as much as it was a child (or the closest thing to a child after David), was also a provider for Lilly. A haven where she could survive quietly for centuries, if not thousands of years to come, given that she kept to the straight and narrow and stayed out of trouble. This town was not a glamorous place, and it had steered itself clear of the gold rush and the oil trade. Lilly knew that if it stayed the industrial town that it was, it would allow her to quietly enjoy the fruits of her labor. She needed money, not fame.

Her home, ever a representation of class and resplendence to the people of Bridgewater, was now beginning to retain a sense of lived history within its walls and without. Ivy and age, weather and wear. "A house as old as time," they called it these days. A hundred and fifty years ago, she had commissioned local engineers to build her this grand abode. Because while it would have helped her cause of clandestineness, Lilly could not change the fact that she was not a modest witch. If she was to lead this town and herself into the future, she would need to do it from comfortable beginnings. The house was far enough from town that she wouldn't be bothered, but close enough that she could keep a sharp eye on things.

And she needed to. People were still brash in their ways. Fights broke out between brokers and contractors more often than not. A small price to pay for industrialization. She'd promptly do her mind veils and watch the people turn amicable in mere moments. When she walked into town, she did so wearing an enchantment of invisibility so that she could observe without interference. The silent matron deity of Bridgewater. The reason why no child went to bed on an empty stomach. The cause of the abundance in crops and livestock. The keeper of calm.

Even on days when she was not able to descend upon the town, she watched from afar with her magic-keened eyes and maintained her resolute domain over it. The faint flicker of lights from the candles behind the windows of each house. Gas lamps and lanterns alike in the grasp of the old and young as they walked in the quiet of the night. Glows from the edges of cigarettes and cigars. Bonfires when the crowd wanted merriment. She could see it all just as well as she could see the reflection of the moon on the surface of Lake Nip.

Tonight was no different than the rest of the nights. And as she lay in her bedroom with a glass of warm milk—or something stronger—on the bedside table and her diary on her lap, she wrote rather candidly. Something she hadn't done in years.

Home. This is what the place means to me, Jane. Or would you rather I call you Dear Diary again for old time's sake?

It's the 29th of July, 1852, and I don't know what happens next. Isn't that strange? I just don't know what happens next because I have exhausted all avenues of adventure and monotony alike.

I have ensured the future of Bridgewater as its unofficial baroness of sorts and will make sure that this place thrives in the future to come. But I don't know what happens next. Were I still biblically inclined, I'd have been awaiting the breaking of the seals and the arrival of the horsemen. But I don't abide by that scripture, even though Madam's told me time and again that God and the Devil exist. As does everything that you could possibly imagine. Fairies and dragons. Elves and dwarves. Djinns. Ghouls. Creatures born from magic. You shall not ever know they are there unless you possess the sight. One would have thought that after a century and a half, I'd have gotten the sight, but it's not the sort of gift you get from time and effort. It's something that Madam gifts you, regardless of your stature. So, while I know now that these manners of creatures exist somewhere out there, I can't see them. Just like I can't see God. Or the Devil. Or Madam these days, for that matter.

Fuck.

No more seals and Armageddons.

No thinking about dragons and firedrakes.

All that noise is ill-fit for my enterprising mind. I focus instead on what I can do and who I can be. I can scry, and in doing so, have seen the death and destruction that will plague this country—and this planet, by exten-

sion—in the upcoming century. Wars will be fought. Lands will divide. The enslaved shall be freed. It boggles my mind to see that they aren't already, but I know that it won't be long before an amendment is passed and a president outlaws slavery. I know this because I have seen it.

Do you know what it does to a person when they are able to scry into the future? It makes them careful. It also makes them afraid, knowing what they know. For instance, I know that I have to hide the town and its people under the veil of conservation. I must protect it as discreetly as I can so that I don't change the future of this country and the world in unimaginable ways.

It's hard, Jane. It's hard because I could do things that would make the people of this world kneel in front of me. My power is at its peak. I can now do things that the wildest of poets can't even imagine. Authors write of sorcerers and dervishes, and when I read their dainty little accounts, I laugh. For what they think is power is truly so meek. I could do it all and then some.

And then some more after that.

And yet I shouldn't.

Madam says I have to be secretive.

Madam doesn't talk to me as much as she did when I was a child, but she does keep a check on what I do by visiting me in my dreams or speaking in my head in the middle of the day. She says that she's really busy with something big, and that I cannot ask her questions about it. She's always saying that she's busy with something big. I wonder what it is.

Armageddon?

I worry.

I worry because there's a slight increase in her lot visiting me.

The Collectors. I see them from the corner of my eye. Their presence is akin to the crawl of tarantulas upon the skin of my neck. They mean me no harm. They are just watching. And yet, why are they watching?

Does Madam think something bad will happen?

Or has it already happened?

Was what happened with Chris and David the "something bad," and now Madam's worried that I'll lose control of my power and wreak havoc upon Bridgewater in my anger and desperation?

Does she think me a child?

Then again, Jane, there is another presence that I cannot understand or perceive, and it's been visiting my vicinities with some ill intent. I can feel the darkness of that presence lingering long after it's come and gone.

I'm not sure who or what it is.

It's usually after that dark presence that I see the Collectors lurking about, almost as if they're cleaning up after a mess of someone else's making.

Ha!

Look at me prattling on. That's what immortality will do to you. It's gonna leave you crazy with your sole friend being a binding of sentient paper.

Ouch! Don't bite me!

Lilly stopped writing in her diary. There was blood on the edge of the page. She identified the source of the pain on the tip of her index finger and then, upon seeing the slit the paper cut had caused to appear, looked indignantly at her diary and snapped, "You should know better than to spill a witch's blood. Nothing good ever comes of it."

Putting the diary on the bed, she sat upright, noticing an inexplicable phenomenon taking place within her house. A candle flickered and danced against the wall. Outside, the moon shone as it should, illuminating the lake.

A creak sounded in the hallway.

She looked around, and stared at the door, closed.

Creaks were normal, she thought. But something was different this time, for she could not sense what was on the other side of the door.

Creak.

Lilly took the candle and walked toward the door. Her mind was racing with thoughts—curious thoughts, trepidation, for usually, her thoughts would be placed for her. As her powers had developed, she had also developed less of a conscience for the eerie and unexplained. After all, should anything potentially be there to harm her, she would be able to fend off whatever that thing may be. And Lilly feared the living more than the dead, except tonight.

Reaching for the brass knob, she clasped it with one hand, the burning candle in the other. The door was a cream color and looked aged; the knob turned in her hands and creaked like the noise outside.

"Hello?" Lilly asked in the hallway. Candles decorated the sconces that adorned the long hallway until the point of darkness. The end of the hallway was pitch black, a small glimmer of a stair railing in the distance.

Creak.

"Who is there? Announce yourself at once," Lilly stated.

But nothing and no one replied.

The candle that she was holding flickered harder, and she held it close. In normal circumstances, it would be floating beside or behind her while she kept both hands busy doing other chores. But right now she wanted all of her powers available to her, if any were.

She walked toward the end of the hallway, the darkness palpable, the candles on the wall flickering as if a breeze was blowing through them. Then, a bang. And another bang, followed by another, almost in perfect symphony.

Lilly jolted back; this was new territory, and she was afraid. Her conscience was returning.

She had reached the blackness at the end of the hallway and looked over the balcony into the lobby below. The front door was open and banging against the wall outside.

The moon cast the shadow of an animal onto the porch.

Relief.

It was obviously her horses that had broken out of their stable.

She tried to light every candle in the house with a snap of her fingers, but the snap didn't work. Then came the smell of rotten eggs or something rotting. One thing was clear: something was wrong, something was very wrong.

Madam, if you are here right now, something is not quite right, she said to her inner mind.

Holding the railing tight, she descended the stairs and watched the shadow move away.

"Bella, Bella, my love, stay where you are," she nervously called out to her favorite horse, the majestic thoroughbred that stood tall, a deep shade of brown, muscular and veiny. It spoke to Lilly in a language they both understood, but Bella did not call back.

As she walked to the front door, the shadow was no longer to be seen. Instead, hoof marks from the dirt on the ground wrapped around the porch. But this wasn't Bella. There were only two hoof marks of whatever animal had been waiting at the door, indicating that the animal was standing on its hind legs.

Lilly's heart stopped and her stomach jumped into her throat. At this point she felt blind, as if she was without her ability for the first time. She felt alone and scared. As she stepped out onto the porch, a gust of wind behind her blew the front door shut. Startled, she immediately opened the door and stepped back inside, eager to lock the door and ensure it was bolted. She may be a witch, but like any other witch, she was only immortal until someone, or something, found a way to kill her.

As her breathing intensified, she noticed the moon shining through the window and into the lobby; it was the only light allowed right now in a house of darkness.

Stomp, stomp.

The noise of hooves treading on the wooden porch were enough to send her into shock.

Stomp. Stomp. Stomp. Stomp.

And then, sudden silence.

The animal had come to a halt, and rational thinking was taking over Lilly's brain. In a world of witches and magic, rational thinking was usually the last thing on her mind in situations like this, but with no aid, she turned to the explainable. She peered her head around the corner of the wall and into the dining room, immediately seeing the shadowy figure move past the window as if she either just caught wind of it, or it was hiding from her. She walked in, slowly, and the candle in her hand blew out.

Lilly shrieked and dropped it.

Now lightning accompanied the moon and offered mere seconds of visuals in the otherwise pitch-blackness of her home. The rain came down hard and fast and rattled against the wood of the house, and the lightning soon was accompanied by thunder. Odd, she thought, as it was usually the other way around.

She continued her slow footsteps to the dining room, head cocked to one side as she tried to make sense of what was happening around her. The animal was nowhere to be seen, and as the lightning came crashing down, it illuminated the walls and objects around her and, from behind, the beast that was following her into the dining room.

Something had come for her.

Lilly didn't know what to do. Over fifty years of living as a witch, manipulating people's minds and steering the town in her direction had only gone to ill prepare her for something ethereal. Not for any moment had she considered that the very darkness that created witches could also come back to destroy her. For this, she had not planned.

Her horses started screaming, and she heard the barn gates adjacent to the home break free. Running to the window, she saw Bella bolting down the dirt path to the gated entrance of her estate.

Then, in the cloud above as the lightning flashed, she saw the face of a demon sneering at her.

Thunder clapped the landscape.

"Madam, Collector, is anyone there that can help me?" Lilly screamed. The onslaught of unexplained happenings had come hard and fast.

The beast was no longer in the same room; instead, it stood one hundred feet away from the porch and was staring directly at Lilly, pointing its menacing claw toward her, its two eyes piercing red.

"To hell with this," Lilly proclaimed. This wasn't the woman who brought an entire town to rubble and rebuilt it with the sheer thought of her mind. The woman who melted dozens of people who tried to kill her, and who dragged a tiny village into the iron industry.

Ripping open the front door, she strode out to the porch, the rain belting against her body, soaking her hair, her face. Tears streaming from the anguish, she dropped to her knees and began a chant, any chant, anything that would protect her from evil.

And as quickly as it appeared, the storm vanished. The candles restored themselves and Lilly found herself dry, bone-dry, as if nothing had happened. Her horse stables were intact, there was no demon on the lawn, and her power reappeared as quickly as it had waned.

Mallory

The morning rays shone through her windows, the sun stalwart above the trees and over the lake, ensuring that there would be no darkness, natural or otherwise, while it held watch. Lilly awoke with a sense of relief and a lot of questions on her mind. But those would have to wait.

A cup of coffee was in order.

She could brew one herself, and it would take her no time at all, but she needed to be around people after last night's events. The Railway Hotel in town had become well known for serving one of Massachusetts' best breakfasts. She made up her mind to head down there immediately.

The streets were bustling with people, people chattered away about their work and their wives, wives bought fresh produce from the marketplace, and the marketplace looked fresh and plentiful in the wake of the summer sun, the sun giving a warmth that was pleasant but not too hot. Lilly sat in the window booth, sipping away at her coffee, not touching the breakfast plate in front of her, pondering over the events of last night. That was another reason why she was so eager to come to town. The happenings of last night had made her too petrified to go back up to the house. The chant she had spoken had helped, but in doing so, had drained her.

Perhaps she could concoct another one, a protection spell that wouldn't make her pass out.

She was sorely disappointed that neither Madam nor one of her Collectors had shown up for help or even some aftercare. Lilly had always venerated Madam, but after last night, she was feeling brash enough to hold an impromptu meeting with her. She knew a trick or two that could get Madam to come down and meet her face to face.

The order of business for today was to have coffee (done), ride Bella around the ranch (to pacify her), and then attempt a conversation with Madam.

Now that she'd all but drunk her third cup, she headed back to the house, her ears perked to hear any mention of strange lightning sighted in the night. Not many people talked of the strange phenomenon they observed at night, and those who did brushed it off as nothing more than strange weather.

Which meant that she didn't have to veil their minds. Thank the eldritch gods for that, because she was depleted as it was already.

After ensuring that all was well in town, Lilly went to her ranch behind the hill and took Bella out of her enclosure. She rode her around, talked some calm into the boisterous horse, and then, after an hour's worth of riding that made her feel like she was a free spirit on the back of the wind itself rather than a horse, a very tired Lilly went into the kitchen to prepare some tea for herself. Nothing like some good chamomile to drain away the pain and lull her into a nice nap.

While she was removing her kettle from the fire, a knock at the front door startled her. Her power was still there, and she could sense the woman on the other side of the door.

"Hello there," Lilly answered as she opened the door.

"Why, hi," the woman responded. She was less than five feet tall and wore an ivory silk organza dress with a delicate floral print. She was a tubby older black lady, her hair pulled back with tinted yellow sunglasses. One would generally use such a tint for eye problems, but this lady simply used them to reduce the glare of the sun.

"Can I help you, missus?" Lilly responded.

"Well, perhaps you can. Y'see, my name is Mallory, and I come on the recommendation of Madam," the lady responded, bowing her head slightly with a warming smile.

Lilly was taken aback. Had she muttered something under her breath in town that she hadn't realized? Had she spoken in a dream or had an out-of-body experience? The past twenty-four hours were a blur, and at this point, she really wasn't sure.

"Now, don't be alarmed. I know that a lot has been happening at this home, more than you care to admit, but I'm here to talk to ya and fill ya in on a few things. Now, may I come in?" Mallory was gentle, her voice had a Southern charm, and she seemed anything but dangerous.

"Well, Miss Mallory, now how do you know about Madam?" Lilly chirped back.

"Ya know what, honey? I'm gonna sit ma'self down on this porch right here on this ol' rockin chair, and you go fetch us some of that chamomile tea ya got brewin' in there. The handle on your ol' kettle 'bout to fall off, so be careful when you pick it up next."

Mallory knew that Lilly was feeling scared from the events of the night before, so to make things easier, she decided to wait outside and let Lilly come to her. Mentioning the handle that was inevitably about to disembark from the kettle pot was a slight nod to a common ownership in powers, and that left Lilly feeling easier and somewhat comforted.

The afternoon was your typical Bridgewater noon: the green hills rolled for miles, and the serenity of Lilly's land offered something not everyone in these parts could afford. It was quiet, relaxing, and simply perfect. Mallory could not help but admit it, looking around from the perch of Lilly's porch, but she was quite jealous of Lilly.

"Quite the spread ya got ya self here, huh?" She smiled as she rocked back and forth, her legs hanging off the ground.

"Well, I've done great things for this town, and I'm a fan of stopping to smell the roses, shall we say." Lilly smiled back.

"Hmmm, a phrase they'll learn to use a lot more in the future, no doubt. Now tell me, miss, do you know why I'm here?" Mallory leaned in to grab her cup of tea from Lilly.

"Well, you said you know Madam, but I guess I should start by saying no."

"Honey, I'm not gonna beat about any bush, but I'm here on the order of Madam. Well now, I say order," Mallory laughed, "but in any sense of the word, I'm here on a favor. Madam is quite busy in another realm right now, and so I cometh in the name of her for ya protection."

Lilly looked alarmed as she held the cup of tea close to her lips. *Protection from what? Is this another vision from last night? Is this woman here to kill me? I cannot read her mind.*

Mallory smirked back. "Ma darlin', if I wanted to do ya any damage, I wouldn't have come to introduce myself first. I don't like playin' with ma food."

"I'm...I'm sorry, I must say I was incredibly lost last eve, I have never experienced anything like it. I saw things I'd never seen before, even when traversing the Axis. Miss Mallory, can I tell you that I felt afraid for the first time in nearly fifty years. I shouldn't have let my guard down." Lilly looked worried and accepted the comfort that Mallory was offering.

"Ma darlin', you gon' be just fine. But I do need to talk to ya and give ya a warnin'."

The two ladies set down their cups, and Mallory moved Lilly closer with the brush of her hand. If Lilly was in the slightest mind of doubt, it was eradicated when Miss Mallory moved her with the power of telekinesis.

"I'm gonna be straight up with ya, witch to witch, do ya understand?" Mallory had an intense voice that jumped out on certain words.

Lilly nodded.

"You have lived as a witch primarily untouched and safe from the Hells on Earth, you've chosen to live your life out of any spotlight and in isolation, which has done you well. It's kept other witches from wanting to interfere with ya, and allowed you to live a relatively normal life." Mallory was delivering her speech with kindness and a gentle voice. "Byyyy God, I'm jealous of ya," she finished.

"I'm not really in this for the theatrics of it all, I simply want to use my power for good," Lilly responded.

"Hmm, I see that, although it doesn't account for what you did to the people of Salem, ma dear. Events such as those follow you through life, and I'm afraid some of it has followed you here. You remember the events as a child when Madam and the Collector would follow you around the forest, yes?" The question wasn't so much a question but a statement. "You have been buildin' up this gift inside ya for almost all your life, and when you needed your power the most, you unleashed a force that no witch on this planet had been able to accomplish in their first few years as a witch, let alone the awakenin'."

"Yes, yes, I can see that now," Lilly responded.

"Now, hold onto yourself." Mallory's tone changed and became serious, her lips puckered up. "I can't see that far into the future with you, but I can tell ya that you are on a path for something a lot greater than all of us, you're part of a story that will change the course of this entire universe we live in. You won't know it yet, but in a couple hundred years, you're gonna be part of something cosmic. Does any of this make sense to ya?"

Lilly shook her head.

"A terrible entity came here last night. I've seen it before in the form of its many servants, but I've never known it to appear itself." Mallory's face turned to one of compassion for Lilly; she knew that she wasn't quite comprehending what was being told to her.

"What...what do you mean, *it*?" Lilly responded worryingly.

"Honey, when a witch has her awakening, it is only a matter of time before the Devil introduces himself. And he usually doesn't come up here to do his own bidding; he sends his fucking creatures to do it for him, and follow his orders they often don't do, not without torturing their victim first. Darlin', you are being courted by Satan himself, and the visit last night was the first of his introductions."

"Satan? But Satan isn't real," Lilly laughed.

"Oh, I assure you he is, and God is too, that benevolent bitch."

"Bitch?"

"*Bitch*!" Mallory stated again. "Okay, honey, hold on to ya self once more, because ya need to hear this. This narcissistic asshole," she stated confidently. "Well, let's just say the power you unleashed that afternoon was enough to shake the very foundation of Hell and stir Satan himself out of his crypt to come for you. It will try to recruit you, trick you, and likely disguise itself to get to you. Chances are, he's visited you long before now." Mallory's voice turned deeper, darker, and more serious. "Be very careful around it. The demon will lie to you, it will tell you things that only you understand and will present itself in any manner of ways." Mallory turned slowly to Bella, who was ominously standing at the front porch, staring at them both.

"Oh, Miss Mallory, now come along. Bella?" Lilly looked horrified that her dear love, Bella, could be swayed by Satan. "I don't really recall any other time that something like this would have happened," Lilly resourced.

"No one really does, but he will get to you, and it comes hard and fast. Satan is anything but patient, despite him wandering this earth for millennia; once his mind is set on something, he will start tormenting you. Last night may have been the first real visit, but he's likely to come again tonight and the following night until you parlay with him. Breakin' the seal, so they say. It's weird, I've never, ever, ever known him to come up here and do his own bidding." Mallory ended the sentence on a frustrated and confused tone.

Lilly looked terrified. "Well, what should I do? I lost all my power last night, and I'm afraid if it happens again, will I be dragged into Hell?"

"Honey, Satan ain't murderin' no witch. He knows better than that, he'd have Madam to answer to and she trumps that son of a bitch. The Absolute put her there."

"The *who*?"

"Never mind for now. Listen, your powers will be reduced when he is around, but you are not completely useless. Your chant banished him back to Hell where he fucking belongs; perform a few of those this evening before he comes again and be ready to talk to him. Get it the fuck outta the way. The annoying thing about the

Devil or that bastard Azazel is that their tormenting is real. It brings the worst out in you, and if I see that fucking goat one more time, I'm gonna lose my god damn mind!"

"Have you parlayed with him, or it?" Lilly quizzed.

"I did with one of his djinns; that fucker nearly took me out. We're under no obligation to work with him, but I must say he does make it sound attractive. He can offer things with the snap of a finger that we're unable to perform ourselves or, for instance, build on. You, ma' love, plan to build out this town for centuries to come. Ol' Satan himself coulda give it to you without you having to do a damn thing. Regardless, there's a reason he's coming here himself: you have something he wants."

The realness of the situation had set in, and Lilly looked on to her pastures as Mallory continued.

"Like I said, I can't see that far into the future, I don't foretell well, but with you there is an energy I can't pin down. But mark my words, dear, when Lucifer comes knockin', hold your ground, pay it no mind, and tell it what you will and won't do. But whatever you do, do NOT agree with it."

"Well, I guess..." And as Lilly started to accept her fate, she looked at the place where Mallory had been sitting a second ago, and to her surprise, the woman wasn't there anymore.

"Real crafty," Lilly said, noticing the rocking chair still rocking, and the smudge of lipstick lining the rim of the cup she held in her hands. Her attention went to the table, where she noticed a small parchment inscribed with a spell. Upon reading it, she realized that it was the spell Mallory was talking about.

She had half a mind to cast it right now and sleep through the evening, but she was too frail. An afternoon nap was in order.

Dancing With the Devil

The reason she knew it was a dream was the exact reason why she did not want to wake up from it. And why would she? As a witch, she had some power over the realm of dreams, could make herself lucid during them, and could walk about a dreamscape as if it was reality itself. Better than reality, because all the good things happened there.

David was by her legs. He always had a habit of doing this, even when both parents snugly tucked him between themselves. At night, he would crawl to the bottom of the bed and cling to his mother's leg.

She loved it.

She loved the weight of two more people on the bed. She loved the lack of space on it. She loved the warmth in the cold of winter. She had promised herself that somehow, she would find a way to weave some magic into the lives of her husband and child and make them immortal too, so that all three of them could do as they pleased. She had made up her mind that she would ask Madam for some leniency in this regard.

But for now, she was all too happy sleeping with her man, his arm over her breasts, and her five-year-old son clinging to her leg. Every day, Lilly woke up with a wide smile on her face. Every morning, she was the first to rush out of the bedroom, look at herself in the mirror, and remind herself that this was real. She'd prop David up and put him in her place, tuck him under the blanket, and kiss her husband to let him know that the day had begun and she was going to the kitchen to make breakfast. If they could sleep for another hour, that was fine with her. Her boys needed their rest.

After fixing breakfast, she would wake up Christoph, and the two would exchange pleasantries and compete in terms of loving sentiments along the lines of, "I love you more," and, "No, I love you more." It always ended up in a tie. This handsome hunk of a man would lug himself out of bed after ruffling his son's hair and head over to the washroom to freshen up. He'd often do that wearing nothing on his torso, driving Lilly crazy with the sight of his broad stature. If David was asleep, she wouldn't mind the breakfast going cold in exchange for a few minutes of some much needed hot and heaviness with the husband within the confines of her luxurious washroom.

After the three of them had their breakfast, Christoph would go down to Bridgewater and indulge in a day's worth of honest business.

David would go to the makeshift institute where other five-year-olds like him assembled, playing under the charge of a matron overseeing them, and learning about the ways of the world and the ways of words alike.

This would give Lilly some free time to make supper, tend to the ranch animals, and tidy up the house. She loved being a housewife after having lived a century as a lone woman.

She could not believe her luck that she'd met someone like Christoph. He with his long hair and slightly unkempt stubble, always with that blue-eyed smile on his face and the latest jokes on the tip of his tongue.

"Lilly, what do you call a guy who's lost the will to question things?" he'd ask.

"What?" she'd ask, intrigued, already smiling knowing that the answer would be something ludicrous.

"A gu."

Sometimes, the jokes would go over her head, and she'd go, "Huh?"

"A gu. Because he lost his Y. His why, get it?" And then Christoph would roll on the floor, laughing at the hilarity of his serendipitous humor. Then it would dawn upon her, and she would join him in laughter.

"Where do you keep coming up with these, one after the other?" she'd ask, lying on top of him. She was tall for a woman, but he was taller and broader and could handle his wife lying on top of him on the kitchen floor. He would wrap his hands around her bottom and give it a loving squeeze.

"You have your magic. I have mine," he'd say, kissing her lips.

It was easy for her to tell him she was an immortal witch. How effortless it was for him to get down on one knee and propose, saying that he'd share his one lifetime with her. And just how natural it was that mere months after their honeymoon, she got pregnant, not through spells and sorceries, but by all-natural conception.

And when their child was born, he looked like both of them.

Blond hair, blue eyes, all the world's bliss wrapped in that innocent smile.

And just how quickly it was all taken from her.

One day, when the matron nanny was supposed to return David, she came empty-handed bearing the grimmest of news. Someone had abducted their son. As the unofficial baroness of this town, she spared no expense in trying to find him, but to no avail. There came no ransom letter. There came nothing.

And just as quickly as the happy life she'd built for herself, she lost it all.

First David.

And a year after that, driven by grief, maddened by sorrow, her husband, who could not handle knowing that his son was taken from him, and that his witch of a wife could do nothing about it despite all her magic.

She found him in the ivory bathtub, the bathwater drawn, red with blood from his slit wrists, his face no longer tan but ghastly white, his body dead for a good while. She could not fathom what had happened. Why none of her spells worked. Why she couldn't resurrect Christoph. Why she could not locate David.

First, it drove her mad, her grief. Then it rendered her numb.

And finally, when enough time had passed, there remained only faint and painful memories of her two loved ones, the people she had boldly dared to call her family.

So surreptitiously taken from her, by a human.

Lilly had finished her chanting. Testing her powers every few seconds, she was taking no chances on waiting for Lucifer to show. The sky was blue beyond twilight, but not quite black. She took a bottle of whiskey out on the porch with her and sucked straight from it. Tonight, she wore a loose, flowery dress, a hat, and her cowboy boots. One boot resting on the chair, the other slowly rocking herself back and forth, sipping the whiskey with a stern, pissed look on her face. The wind was blowing and howling, and Lilly had prepared to meet the Devil himself.

The candles on the porch started to flicker, and as Lilly tried to lift one of them off the ground using her mind, it stuttered, and she knew he was coming.

"Get the fuck up here, Lucifer," she said under her breath.

Lightning hit the lawn in front of her, once, twice, six times, and then nothing. Silence for a moment.

The porch creaked to her left. "Y'know, there is an easier way to introduce yourself, and it doesn't include these theatrics," Lilly mouthed, not moving out of her seat. Heavy breathing, grunts, and hoof noises were making their way closer to Lilly, and for a moment, she was terrified. The thing, whatever it was, was beside her face, snorting at her.

She stopped rocking in fear.

The porch to her right then creaked, and the animal disappeared.

A large dark figure, dressed in a black suit and a top hat, appeared in Lilly's peripheral vision from the right. She dared not even look at it. It walked in front of her and stopped, Lilly's face staring at its crotch as it heaved in front of her, as if to intimidate. She didn't look up at its face.

Take a seat, she said in her head.

The beast moved to her side and sat in the rocking chair, its frame seeming to be less that of a ten-foot-tall beast and more of a normal, slender-looking man shrouded in black. Lilly still did not look, but in the corner of her left eye, she could see it. The darkness, the misery, the anguish; it was emanating from the Devil as he sat next to her. His face held no features, just a dark abyss of evil.

"Wiiiiitch," it hissed.

Lilly paid the demon no mind, and it only seemed to excite him further, although he knew the cause of Lilly's ignorance: it was simply fear. It seemed to move closer.

"Lonellllly witttttch," it hissed once more. "I can show you where he is."

Lilly closed her eyes and took a deep breath. He can't, he can't.

"Do you know who I am?" Satan whispered.

"You hide behind this facade; I know what you really look like," Lilly said, focusing on the land in front of her and not Lucifer. "A red-skinned being with horns and hooves. A pointed tail—"

"And...let me finish it for you. A forked tongue? Oh! How pathetic," he taunted, his voice that of an older, croakier-sounding woman that occasionally fell into a hissing noise, versus some God-type, commanding voice. "You buy into the lie the people of your Christ pervaded. I look nothing like their ghastly conjuring, and Hell is not all fire, but I can understand why you would feel that. Seeing as how you've been lied to all your life. What a long life to have been lied to."

"I have burned away any lies that were spoken to me. I see you, the real you, with my third eye. You are not this dashing persona with an air of cavalier about you. I sense the seethe of fury just as I can see the branding of Hell upon your skin. You are talking to one who possesses the sight."

The Devil clapped his hands and laughed with his croaky voice, laughing as if to clear an eternity of Hell-smoke from his lungs. "You do not have the sight, or do you think I am foolish? You are blind, child. Madam has not yet given you her most precious gift. A handful of people have ever been given the sight, and sadly, you are not one of them. I can offer it to you."

"Is that what you do? Peer into the heavens from your roost in Hell? Does it make you bitter knowing that you're banished, never to return to the place you once called home?"

She had tested his patience.

"I did not take you to be an insolent one," Lucifer spoke, his face sullen. "But regardless of your insolence, I have seen the extent of your power. The day you set fire to Salem, I was there in the crowd, relishing the flames. When you rendered Bridgewater fertile with your boon, I sensed the ampleness from afar. You are a most powerful witch; join me in my legion." The voice at the end became stern, aggressive, and serious.

"What makes you think that I will ever join your legion?"

"Oh? I should think you'd want to," Lucifer said, snapping his fingers. "They are down here with me." He started to cackle.

The sharpness of the snap transported her into a vision, one where she saw the same thing as she had in her dream. Her husband and child by her side at the dinner table, supping on roasted duck, laughing, talking to each other, Christoph's hand on her cheek as he patted her, David's plate filled with gravy because he was being cheeky.

The scene changed to another, where Lilly and Christoph danced in candlelight, somewhere far from the madness of Bridgewater and Salem. This was their honeymoon, and they were in Boston, seeing the big city and how modern it was becoming with each passing day. Dancing in each other's arms to the sound of music coming out from the window of their hotel.

In another moment, Lilly was between the sheets, her body naked, her husband with his brimming youth lying upon her, kissing her breasts.

A blink and she was in a hospital, holding David in her arms, Christoph kissing her forehead.

All the memories that she had suppressed came undone like water crashing from a broken levy, wetting her eyes, drawing sweat on her skin, and making her weak in the knees.

"Would you like to see them?" Lucifer said, snapping again and bringing her back to the hill. "Hear the laughter of your dear loved ones? Satan doesn't make ransom notes, my dear."

But this time Lilly had enough; the emotion of seeing her long gone family, her only chance at true love displayed before her started to send vibrations through her body. A vibration she felt at the dawn of her awakening in Salem.

"Who killed my son?" Lilly's body crackled with rage as the familiar electricity began coursing through her veins. She sat, her breasts heaving.

"Killed?" The Devil laughed. "Child, they simply chose to accept the offer I gave them when I appeared at their final breath. Where were you at that final moment? Conjuring more spells instead of nurturing your flock?" The Devil twisted in the rocking chair and brought his claw-like hand to his mouth, laughing immaturely, one dagger finger in its mouth.

Lilly's eyes shone with pure white light, her hair floating, her body charged with power. "You must think me some dawdling wench desperate for love. Was that all the bargain you'd come with? My husband is dead. So is my son. There is nothing anyone can do to bring them back. And you are most cruel and heartless for having rekindled that pain in me." Lilly ran to the lawn in front of the house and turned around. But Satan wasn't on the porch anymore, he was standing behind her. His body bigger, arms claw-like, the epitome of Hell on Earth.

"Witch, do not think that you can take me on. I do not lie when I tell you that your husband burns below. As does your son. An eternal consequence to pay for being related to the Bridgewater Witch. Deny me again, and I shall worsen their terror, deepen their torture," the Devil said slowly. "Join me, and I shall return them, both of them imbued with the same immortality as you. To live with you for the rest of your days. Memories of hellish torture forgotten. It will be like not a day has passed."

Lilly did not respond. Instead, she raised her arms into the sky and brought down lightning bolt after lightning bolt, each one jolting the Devil out of his stance.

"Enough!" Lucifer growled. "I bring you a bargain and you attack me? I came to you like I do every other witch, with a choice, and this is what you have to offer? You insult me."

It was Lucifer's turn to raise his hand and suspend Lilly in the air, her arms spread out like Jesus on the cross. He rose to match her height and reached out his hand, pointing toward her chest.

"I ought to claw your heart out and throw it to the dogs," Lucifer sneered, shedding his humanoid form and revealing himself to be the beast that he was. Much worse than what Lilly had perceived him to be. His red skin had hair growing off it, and those weren't just hooves, but the entire hindquarters of a ghastly animal. His horns curled like those of a ram, and the tail in question was broader than

Lilly's arm, longer than Lilly's height. It coiled itself around Lilly's body lecherously, almost as if the Devil was deriving sexual pleasure from it.

"Do it!" Lilly said, choking against the strain of the tail around her neck. She knew at that moment that if there was someone who could really kill her, it was Satan, despite what Mallory had said. And there would be no other opportunity as good as this. "End me!"

But instead of doing her bidding, Satan let go of her. She fell to the floor, hurting her body upon collision, and lay there. The Devil floated back down, his bat-like wingspan retracting, curiosity etched on his hideous face. His forked tongue sprawled out, tasting the air.

"A witch with a death wish? You make it too easy and not fun at all."

"I'm done playing your games. Either kill me or get lost," she said, spitting blood and getting up. "I'm not going to join your legion."

"If you are not with me, then you are against me. It is as simple as that, Frost," the Devil said, putting back his guise and producing his top hat out of thin hair. With his hands on his walking cane, he looked upon her with great disappointment. "You are a powerful one."

"And I have no one to thank for it. It's my power. My own."

"I can wait for as long as it takes for you to break. Just observe. And when you're broken, torn, and pathetic, I shall come to you again, and you will take what I give you, and in return, I shall have your soul."

Lilly wiped her lips with her thumb and looked at the Devil, showing him the blood he'd drawn. "Didn't anyone ever tell you not to make a witch bleed? Nothing good ever comes of it."

The blood on her thumb shone red, making the Devil wince and take immediate steps back.

"Blood magic?" he stuttered.

"Per sanguinem effusum, te in infernum Redigo," Lilly whispered. *By the blood that has been spilled, I banish you back to Hell.*

"You will join me, witch." Satan laughed as he turned and walked away with his cane, slowly disappearing into the night.

"No." Lilly shook her head. "Never."

NO MORE HELLISH RETRIBUTION. No infernal contracts.

Only silence, and Lilly, standing tired and bruised on the front lawn of her house, looking up at the moon, wondering if the reach of Hell extended to lunar provinces.

"Child."

Lilly scoffed. She did not want to turn around and face another celestial entity, be it God, Madam, or Mallory.

"What do you want?"

"I'm here to check up on you."

Bitter tears coursed down her face upon recollecting the past hour's events. The dark memories that she had been made to relive.

"Where are Christoph and David?" Lilly asked. "I never talked to you about them, because I always thought that you would disapprove of me taking a mortal as a husband and birthing a mortal as a child."

"I was never angry at you for that," Madam said. "In fact, I was happy for you. Most witches do."

Madam's hand fell upon her shoulder, and the matron of magic reached forward, hugging Lilly from behind. "You have been through so much, and tonight was..."

"A test?"

"No. It was a crossroads. You were either going to join forces with the Devil, as countless before you have, or you were going to stay steadfast. I knew that I'd made the right choice when I watched you banish him."

"Doesn't mean I'm aligned to your cause either. Maybe I'm a free agent from now on."

"What if I told you that the Devil has done nothing but lie in this entire conversation? I am not the cause of your magic, nor its source. You are magic incarnate. I could not take it away from you if I tried. As for your life...immortal though it is, it is still yours."

Lilly turned around, upset with Madam. She scorched her with her fiery gaze and screamed, "You can stop right about now. You know what I want to hear, are you fooling me too? I am nothing, I have no one, I am alone, cursed to wander this planet for the rest of time."

Madam, draped in crimson, her loose hair flowing down her shoulders, nodded, lips pursed.

"You mean to ask of your husband and child?"

"Are they in Hell?"

"No."

Lilly gasped, then scoffed and looked away, tears spilling from her eyes. "Of course you're pandering. Do you realize how damn stupid that is?"

"Your folk were folk of magic. Touched by it. Shaped by it. When your husband's life path crossed with yours, he became associated with the weave. Your child too. You really think I would let them go to Hell?"

"Then where are they?"

"Out there, far beyond Heaven, far beyond Hell, where there's true rest, where there's no test. The Axis Mundi. It's the same place where I come from, and the place where people of our kind go back to when they have passed away. An afterlife of magic. Magic shapes it. Magic keeps it. It is unaffected by dogma. Creed. Religion. All those of the craft are welcome to call it home. David and Christoph await you there. As does Bridget. As do all the women you once called sisters and lost along the way. You can relinquish your immortality and go there now, if you choose. I will not test you any further with the trials of the living. Or you can stay. Continue to do good. To be my vessel in this realm. And when all is said and done, there will come a time when you can be with them again."

Lilly wept inconsolably, and this time, she reached forward and hugged Madam with a ferocity that knocked Madam's wind out. But she put her arms around Lilly and patted the back of her head.

"So what happens now?"

"Your choice, child."

Lilly thought about it long and hard, still not letting go of Madam.

And when the flames of her enraged thoughts had died down, leaving calm ashes in their wake, Lilly made a choice.

She chose to stay here as the witch that she always was, to serve Madam, and to ensure the balance of this world.

"There will come a time when your watch ends, and I will deliver unto you all that I have promised," Madam said after hearing Lilly's renewed vow.

"And the Devil?"

"He'll appear again. Throughout your time on this Earth, you live in the spectral light of all realms," Madam said. "Now that you have faced it, you will be better prepared in the future."

Before Madam took her leave, she asked, "My child, do you want me to veil your mind and rid you of the painful memories the Devil unleashed today?"

"No." Lilly shook her head. "I want to feel the pain. I want to remember how it feels to have loved. To be loved. I will not be censoring my own mind from now on. If there's agony, I shall gladly bear it in hopes that one day, when all is said and done, I might find my way back to those I love. So long as they're not in Hell."

"My darling, they aren't. You have my word. And if that's not enough, here. I shall show you."

That night, Madam gave Lilly a gift that was greater than any magical ability or spell. She gave her a vision of her husband and her son out in a field, racing each other in strides of happiness. When they saw Lilly watching from beyond the veil Madam had conjured, they smiled at the same time and waved in her direction.

She wept, not out of longing but out of happiness. They were exactly as she had remembered. And seeing them thriving in the Axis Mundi gave her great peace.

"Thank you, Madam," Lilly whispered, wiping her tears as the veil disappeared.

"They are always with you."

"Just tell them that I love them," Lilly said. "And that I cannot wait to be with them."

"Hope and love, Lilly," Madam said, disappearing into the wind.

"They are a magic any human can cast. It is a gift from me unto all who aspire to be better, to do good. And Hell is bereft of all hope, all love. You really think I was going to let your family squander down there?"

That did it. It knocked what little strength she had left, and brought her to her knees, making her cry without anything holding her back. She let her tears cascade down her cheeks.

Tears of bliss. Of loss. Of sorrow. Of relief. Of hope.

Of love.

4

THE FLOATING FEATHER

The Diary

"You know what we should do?" Sophia had a piece of bacon at the end of her fork and she wagged it around the table to reinforce her point. The rest of the ladies looked at her vexedly, because she was taking too long to get to the point. They were all sitting around the largest table at Wick's, an up-market establishment in Bridgewater, mimosas in hands, plates filled with food, and minds hungry for gossip. The fog had cleared enough for them to drive to Main Street and enjoy a brunch; after all, it had been a while.

"What's that?" Linda asked.

"We make her a gift basket of our own," Sophia said, taking a sizable bite out of her bacon to cement her point. "And then we'll be on even footing with her."

"Even footing with the richest woman in town? We can't possibly pull something off like that," Nora said. "I mean, you're asking us to dig deep into our pockets."

"Nora," Maggie said. "It's not about the size of the gift as much as it's about the sentiment behind it. No one needs to dip into their bank accounts."

"It's about the sincerity," Jennifer, who knew nothing of sincerity, said. This was easier on the budget; if this was the direction the women were going in, she was all too eager to help them get there faster. "Who's going to be in charge of the basket then?"

"I'll do it," Evelyn said, draining her mimosa. "I think I know how to cater to her sensibilities."

"Huh?" Charlotte asked. "Do you think we won't be able to? Come on. Even you know there's something bizarre about how she just handed each of us the right gifts, which were almost custom-made for us."

"So, what do you suggest then?" Linda asked.

"We each buy her our own gift, and then put it in the basket. A collective effort is always better than an individual one," Charlotte said, finishing her French toast and looking around at the table for seconds. There were none. Those were the seconds that she had eaten, and if she needed more, she had to go to the banquet table. But she was so stuffed from eating that she did not have the strength to get up and walk over.

"Crude delivery, but valid point," Sophia said, handing Charlotte a napkin. "Wipe your mouth. You've got sauce all over your chins."

"Sophia, don't be mean," Linda said rather sternly.

"Sorry," Sophia said, her face flushing. "It's just...it was my idea and everyone's getting carried away with it."

"Tell you what, you'll get the final say in the matter," Jennifer said. "Does that help?"

"Yes, a little," Sophia said, and bit into her buttered toast.

"With that matter decided, let's move on to the next one," Linda said.

"There are more matters?" Maggie asked.

"Yes," Nora said. "I think we should at least discuss what it means to start a relationship with this mysterious woman. Who is she? Is she really who she says she is? I mean, it kinda makes me angry that she'd just strut down the hill and take one look at our street and go, 'Yeah, they'll do.'"

"I get you," Linda said. "But we're kind of her closest neighbors, I don't understand why we're all acting like she's some quack?"

"You buy into that whole shtick about her family being Puritans and all of this being passed down as generational wealth? It sounds really iffy," Jennifer added.

"She did tell us quite a bit about her background yesterday," Maggie said.

"And all of it could be lies; no one, and I mean no one, rocks up with gifts like that. Something is up!" Evelyn agreed.

"So...is anyone gonna say it, or am I going to have to spell it out?" Charlotte said.

"No...you eat your vegetables," Linda said, suppressing a smile. "Talking with one's mouth full is very unladylike."

"Now who's being rude?" Sophia was quick to chime in, earning Linda's ire.

Sophia, undeterred, carried on. "I think that if this woman's just going about telling lies, there's no reason why she's not one of those illegal businesspeople who do this, that, and the other. Cass has had to deal with them all his professional career." Cass was her husband, a financial lawyer who worked in Boston five out of seven days a week.

"And if she's lying about her history, she might be...bad news for Bridgewater. I'm just thinking of the people," Sophia said. "I mean, isn't it a little condescending that she'd just give us those gifts like no big deal? It looked more like charity."

"Yeah. So condescending to be giving seven women expensive gifts expecting nothing in return," Maggie said, shaking her head. She was tired of this brunch. Tired of the women around her. In fact, she was just too tired. She needed to go home and sleep off all this laziness that had crept up in her bones.

"Who's saying that she doesn't expect something in return? She's buying us, can't you see?" Nora scoffed.

"What I propose is going to be borderline—" Jennifer began, but Linda cut her off.

"Next time, don't preface it. Just say it. Fucking Christ."

"I thought your lot weren't supposed to take the Lord's name in vain," Charlotte laughed. The others joined in, laughing with her at Linda's expense.

"Bite me," Linda said.

"Don't tempt me. I might," Charlotte laughed, her heaving bosom and belly jiggling as she did so.

"Guys! We're seven women. We can distract her, break into her home, and snoop around to find anything incriminating!" Jennifer hissed.

"Oh, I'm sorry, could you be a bit louder? I don't think they heard you across the street," Evelyn snapped.

Jennifer shot an embarrassed look around the café, realizing she'd been too loud.

"She's not wrong," Linda said. "And we'd be justified in doing so. Preemptive safeguarding is still safeguarding. If she's bad news, we need to know what we're getting ourselves into."

"I'm loving how we're all just jumping right on board with this," Sophia said, making Nora giggle. Maggie just sighed. Charlotte, while no one was looking, slid the plate of bacon closer to her and was having at it in the wake of this conversational chaos.

"What are we thinking?" Jennifer asked. "MacBook? iPhone? Ye olde journal tucked away under her mattress?"

"People like her always leave a trail, and we're going to find it," Linda said. "Me and Jennifer are going to hold her off. Distract her when she's in town. Charlotte and Nora will keep watch. Maggie... Maggie? Are you there? Christ, woman. Pay attention. Maggie's going to go in the house."

"No," Maggie said, just about done with this conversation. "I'm not doing it. Besides, what if she has cameras?"

"Fine," Linda snapped. "You get to drive the getaway car. But she does have a point—if there's a whiff of a camera, we're out."

Maggie shrugged.

"And Evelyn..."

"If it means I get to hang with the big girls, sure thing. Count me in," Evelyn said, tapping her fingers together. "But I'm not going to break into her house. Evelyn's afraid Evelyn will steal more than just information from the house. And Evelyn doesn't want to do that."

"Evelyn should stop talking about herself in the third person," Jennifer snapped.

"Sophia?" Linda asked.

"I thought you'd never ask." Sophia sighed, moaning a little. It turned her on, the idea of breaking into Lilly's house and being in that big manor all by herself, picking things up, going through her belongings. She was so ready for this.

"That leaves Nora. What do you say, you wanna come with the big girls?" Jennifer asked. "Three heads are better than two."

"Not when one of them is such a hothead," Linda scoffed, giving Nora the side-eye. "She can keep Charlotte company in Sophia's minivan."

"A plan taketh shape, ladies," Sophia said, raising her mimosa flute.

They cheered in the quiet, desperate, pretentious little way that they had perfected in this very café over several years' worth of brunches, making heads turn in their direction when all seven flutes clinked and they burst out into carefully calculated laughter.

It turned out that planning a heist on a single woman's house was not as hard as they had initially thought it would be. With practically all of them staking out Lilly's house from the comfort of their own bedroom windows, it was only a matter of time before Linda and Jennifer gave the go-ahead for Operation Information Extraction.

The plan was simple. As soon as Lilly drove down the hill toward town, Jennifer, Linda, and Evelyn would drive a comfortable distance behind her. Later, they would happen to come across her naturally and say, "What are the odds? Small world, isn't it?" thereby wasting her time with a stalling routine they had all but perfected over the years. They would coax her to come with them and have a coffee at Starbucks, ensuring that she wouldn't go anywhere for the next twenty to thirty minutes.

While that was happening in town, Sophia, Charlotte, Nora, and Maggie were going to drive up the hill in Sophia's minivan. Charlotte and Nora would get out earlier so they could be lookouts. Maggie would wait in the car while Sophia broke into the house and searched for something valuable with information.

Once Sophia found something, she would make off with it along with Maggie, Charlotte, and Nora, and promptly give the signal to Linda via a quickly placed missed call that she had succeeded.

Linda, Jennifer, and Evelyn would then part ways with Lilly and regroup at Jennifer's home. Or maybe Linda's if they wanted to.

As far as plans were, it was a solid—yet not entirely foolproof—plan. They did not account for the fact that while in the car, Nora would get angry at Maggie for breathing through her mouth and the two would start fighting, wasting precious minutes.

They didn't account for the fact that when Sophia would go inside the house, she'd walk into every room and lounge on the living room sofa as if she owned the place, wasting more precious time.

They didn't account for the fact that Charlotte would find her way into Lilly's organic garden and start stealing heirloom tomatoes.

And, worst of all, the thing that ended up hindering their plan the most, was that none of them accounted for the fact that Lilly might not want to sit with the ladies. Tried as the three did to stall her, she left the coffee shop urgently, leaving no sign of where she'd gone.

As a result, the three had to ring up the others and tell them to call off the plan.

Maggie ended up being the voice of reason and dragged the other three women away from Lilly's house and into the minivan. And she'd only just driven down the hill when Lilly's car turned the corner and drove up the road leading up the hill.

"Close call!" Maggie panted.

"Stop breathing so loud!" Nora yelled and slammed her fist on the back of the headrest.

"Ouch!" Maggie whimpered.

"Did you at least get it?" Nora asked Sophia.

"Yeah, did you get it?" Charlotte asked, her pocket filled with fresh tomatoes.

"I got it," Sophia said, raising a diary in her hand.

The women squealed with glee and regrouped at Linda's house, where they met with the other three.

"What took you so long?!" Linda snapped angrily.

"Oh, come on. You don't know how hard it was to look through her entire house. Woman doesn't own a single gadget. No iPhones. No laptops. Nothing. This is all I found, and, girl, it is juicy," Sophia said, tossing the diary to Linda.

The women huddled around Linda at the dinner table, going through the contents of the diary, their eyes growing wide with disbelief after turning each page and reading the horrendousness within.

The Confrontation

It was nothing less than an impressive feat that they had orchestrated this whole thing in a day. Not any less remarkable was the fact that after they'd finished reading through the journal, they maintained their cool and acted like nothing had happened.

Whenever they saw Lilly coming down the hill, they'd just wave in response, and she'd wave back, apparently oblivious, a smile on her face.

It was only a matter of time before the ladies of Alameda Avenue would pounce on her from all sides and confront her, but little did they know that Lilly had other plans.

On the eve of Sunday, there came a rather official-looking invitation in each of the seven women's inboxes. Since it was such short notice, the ladies did not get a chance to consult amongst themselves other than what they would wear.

In another two hours, they were all in their cars, driving up the hill and parking in front of Lilly's house. Lilly awaited them on the porch, a smile plastered on her ageless face, her hands greeting them welcomingly as she received the women.

"Oh, I see you brought back my basket," Lilly said, nodding at the cloth-covered basket.

"You gave us such precious gifts, it was only fitting that we gave you something in return," Linda said, smiling so ominously that one might think she was in pain. Her perfect white teeth shone in the lantern light as she led the progression of women inside the house after Lilly.

"My, what vintage resplendence," Jennifer said, whistling as she looked around at the architecture, interior design, and furniture. "You live like a queen up in here, girl."

"Live like a queen? I am a queen," Lilly chortled, making the women join in with their high-pitched superficial laughter.

"Aren't we all?" Sophia laughed.

Maggie was the only one blushing uncomfortably in the group, but for now everyone ignored her demeanor. Lilly gave them a walking tour of the house, showing them the rooms, the library, the study, the rooms on the second floor, the attic, and finally the rest of the wraparound porch.

"And over there, you see that road leading down? My ranch is on the other side of the hill," Lilly said, pointing to the roof of the barn visible from her house.

"You own a ranch?" Charlotte asked in disbelief. "You have ponies?"

"Nah. Just horses. Three of them." Lilly grinned.

"Who even are you?!" Evelyn said, trying to mask the fact that she already knew exactly who Lilly was, just like the rest of them did.

This phoniness continued well after dinner, which was a three-course meal that began with an appetizer of mixed greens topped with pecans and crumbled goat cheese. It was slightly seasoned with pepper, oregano, and balsamic vinaigrette. The main course was succulent roasted pork, served with garlic mashed potatoes and a side of asparagus drizzled with lemon butter. Dessert was a decadent chocolate lava cake with a warm, gooey center, accompanied by scoops of vanilla ice cream.

The women talked politely throughout the conversation, commenting on the fog, the town, each other's hair, clothes, and jewelry, and what they thought each other's husband was up to. They did this while maintaining their façade of friendliness, hiding their true intentions beneath forced smiles.

Once dinner was over and done with, each woman sat with a cup of frothy coffee in their hands, all of them seated on the big sofa in the living room, looking at each other's faces in the wake of the sleepiness that good food and the warmth of the house had brought forth.

"What's in the basket?" Lilly asked, coming out of the kitchen with one last cup of coffee. Hers. She sat down on the rocking chair in front of the coffee table, the eyes of all seven women affixed on her.

"Well, what do you give a woman that already has everything?" Jennifer asked, running her hand through her hair.

"I don't have everything," Lilly said modestly.

"Come on now. Compared to us, you're like… I mean, Linda's the one who's old-money rich, but you're like ten steps beyond, know what I mean?" Evelyn said, looking around the house and all its splendor. "The things that you've got here…"

"So, what's in it?" Lilly asked. "I'm really intrigued."

"As were we when we picked your gift. It knocked our socks off," Charlotte said. "The things that we learned."

"The stories we read," Nora piled on.

"The rich history behind this gift is unlike anything we've ever seen before," Sophia capped it off.

Maggie wordlessly pushed the basket forward.

Lilly took the cloth off the basket and peered inside. She looked at all the women with an expressionless gaze and then took her diary out of the basket.

"Fascinating, isn't it?" Linda gleamed. There was no mercy on her face. "And to think that we thought you were the daughter of a baron. Hey, at least you weren't lying about your family being Puritans."

"You broke into my house," Lilly stated, rifling through her diary. "And stole my diary."

"Yes. And now we know everything there is to know about you," Jennifer spat. "Witch."

"You guys should have brought your torches," Lilly smiled, disappointment showing on her face. "Because what kind of a witch hunt is complete without torches and clubs and machetes?"

"Oh, please," Sophia cackled. "This is the twenty-first century, lady. We're straight-up going to cancel your ass. Expose you for the sham you are, and once your story and your face are out in the open, you won't even find a studio to lease in Harlem, let alone live in this palatial house!"

Promptly, the ladies took out their iPhones and Linda, leading them, waved her phone in Lilly's face, saying, "These are our torches. We just wanted to look at your face when we told you that your jig's up."

Other than Maggie, who did not bring her phone, the rest of the women started recording on their phones at the same time, Jennifer narrating the six recordings.

"Ladies and gentlemen, here we have in our midst a witch who claims she's been alive for four hundred years! We—"

Before she could so much as speak another word, Lilly casually moved her wrist and made their phones float in the air, their screens turning off. Flicking more of her hand, the phones flew across the room and hit the wall before dropping to the floor.

Lilly stood up slowly. "Now. What were you saying?" she asked, looking at the women. "You seriously thought that confronting a witch in her house was going to end well for you? Not to mention you earned my wrath by literally stealing my journal. Is that any way to repay my generosity?"

"Generosity?!" Linda snapped.

"Tut-tut, not while I'm talking." Lilly shook her hand, making Linda's mouth snap shut. "What did you think was going to happen?"

By now, all the women were so petrified at the display of magic that they didn't speak a word. No one even whimpered. They all sat frozen to their spots, not knowing what to say. It wasn't until Maggie spoke that the rest found their voices.

"We didn't come to bust you or anything," Maggie said. "We..."

"We were just so damn curious!" Sophia sputtered.

"Yeah. You don't know this, but random women don't bestow their kindness upon us like you did," Evelyn added, her tone on the verge of hysteria.

"Honestly! We were just playing with you just now," Charlotte said. "We're sorry about the phone thing."

"Is it true, all that's written in the diary? You're really a witch?" Linda asked.

"You've been alive for that long? There was that part about your husband and—" Jennifer said before being cut short by Lilly's loud boom.

She placed her coffee cup down and snapped, "ENOUGH!"

Silence befell the women, and they froze just as before.

"Whatever you were—curious, interested, bored, alone, or straight-up crazy—it doesn't justify you breaking into my house," Lilly said, her words charged with wrath. "But..." she added, her tone softening just a little. "You did it without me noticing. So, points for that. If I weren't so mad, I'd say I'm half-impressed."

"So," Jennifer whispered like a meek dormouse. "You're not going to murder us?"

Lilly laughed, clapping her hands, throwing her head back, and said, "Murder you? As I'm sure you've read, I wasn't born yesterday. Why would I murder you when I have good use for you?"

Fear replaced confusion on the faces of all the women as they stared at each other. What use did a witch have for seven women?

But Lilly's eyes traveled from one woman to the next, telling them that she had already planned something for them.

"What are you going to do to us?" Maggie asked really quietly.

"Turn us into frogs?" Nora added.

"Please. Don't insult me by listing all the stereotypes you might have heard about witches. I don't intend to harm you. I hope you don't intend to harm me either, because there's a way that we can let this slide. I can forgive and forget the fact that you barged into my house, if you all agree to one thing."

"What's that?" Linda asked, her haughty aura coming back to her now that she knew she was out of immediate danger.

"You're seven of the most prominent women in this town. As you all know my stories, so do I know yours. Trapped. Bored. Hanging in limbo, waiting for husbands to come back from their jobs in big cities, forced to raise kids that you'd rather stayed in daycare or school all day, having nothing to do other than carefully calculate just how much you can spend with your credit cards without your husbands getting angry or the cards getting maxed out. You're getting blunt, ladies. It's like I'm watching an episode of *Desperate Housewives: Bridgewater*. What do you say we all do something useful with our time? Something that's worth your attention and efforts?" Lilly asked, leaning back into her chair, her coffee in her hands.

"You're inviting us to join your coven?" Evelyn asked with a touch of intrigue.

"I don't have a coven. Never had one. I'm thinking it's about time I started one." Lilly nodded.

"Paganism," Linda scoffed. "What you're asking for is heresy."

"Not any more than what you're already doing. You take Yule from the Norse pagans; Santa's just St. Nicholas dressed in red; Samhain, what you know as Halloween, is a Celtic tradition. Easter's a pagan celebration of the spring equinox. And don't get me started on you worshipping one God. You're worshipping three. The Father, the Son, and the Holy Ghost. I'm not denying the existence of any of them, nor am I confirming it, but Christianity's a polytheistic religion, if anything. Pretty pagan, if you ask me."

Linda was shocked at the sudden barrage of insinuations coming her way, but it seemed as if she was the only one. The others were remarkably impressed by Lilly's grasp on this topic.

"But Jesus Christ," Linda began, only to be interrupted by Lilly once again.

"Oh, you mean the guy who literally turned water into wine, his own body into bread, and rose from the dead after three days? The same person who went around healing lepers and raising Lazarus? Remove the element of him being a Christian prophet, and you have a pretty powerful wizard."

"Christ was a servant of his Father, God," Linda snapped. "His was not magic but miracles!"

"Tomato, tomato! Do I commune with evil spirits to make my coffee hot? Do I conjure Satan to float in the air? No! I do it as naturally as he did. What you call miracle can be called magic, just as magic can be called miracle. Why are you all letting her be your collective mouthpiece? I didn't invite you to hold a pointless debate on religion, of all things. I'm not asking you to change yours. I'm just saying, you—"

"We'll do it!" Jennifer cut Lilly off. "I mean, I don't care about any of what Linda was saying, but you literally are a witch. I can't quite believe it, but I don't have my phone in my hand. I saw it fly away. You can do magic. And I want to learn how you do it."

"More coffee, anyone?" Lilly nodded at their empty coffee cups, and they all watched as coffee filled up in all of them. A collective "ooh" escaped from them, even from Linda's pursed lips.

"I'm sorry if I hurt your sentiments," Lilly said to Linda. "I didn't mean to, just as I am sure you didn't mean to hurt mine when you stole my diary."

Linda shook her head. "It's okay."

"Will you really teach us magic?" Maggie asked.

Lilly smiled at Maggie. "Yes, dear. I most certainly will."

"Those things in your diary," Nora asked. "They all happen for real?"

"Yeah," Lilly said, nodding solemnly.

"Poor girl, the literal shit that you've been through," Charlotte said, coming over to Lilly and giving her a rather awkward hug. "I don't know why I just did that."

Lilly patted her back as she returned to her place on the sofa.

"I have one question," Evelyn asked. She had been quiet for some time, thinking hard. "Can this magic that you'll teach us make us rich?"

"Rich, famous, powerful, whatever you want," Lilly said. "But you know what would surprise me? If you actually put it to some good use."

"Oh, come on. Like you're gender-swapped Dumbledore and this is *Harry Potter*? What are you gonna do next, sort us into houses based on our inclinations?" Jennifer asked, cracking her knuckles. "What's putting magic to good use going to do for us anyway?"

"Well, do you like Bridgewater?" Lilly asked.

"It ain't Hollywood, but it's home," Nora nodded.

"I've been raising this entire city for centuries. Wouldn't you say that that's putting magic to good use?" Lilly asked.

"Not everyone's got altruism on their mind, Ms. Frost, or is it Ms. Thurman? Or, what's your real name anyway?" Sophia asked.

"Does it matter? Call me Lilly," Lilly said, shrugging.

"Lilly the witch," Linda said.

"The Bridgewater Witch." Maggie smiled.

"Shush now. I've got the perfect name for her," Sophia said, grinning wildly. "Sugar mommy."

Lilly was so caught off guard by that remark that she didn't laugh. But the rest of the women all laughed, and not in the calculated way that they did. This was sincere laughter, one where they showed their teeth, guffawed loudly, snorted, and clapped each other on the shoulder.

"Sugar mommy's gonna teach us fricking magic!" Jennifer said, wiping her eyes.

It took Lilly a second to realize that they weren't making fun of her. Which was when she joined in with their laughter.

Once the laughter subsided, Maggie was the first to speak. "Hey, Lilly?"

"Yes?"

"All that stuff we read in the diary... I don't think you've ever told it to anyone in person," she said.

"What are you getting at, Mags?" Nora asked.

"I'm just saying that it must be lonely being an immortal witch, you know?" Maggie stated.

"Duh," Evelyn said. "Why do you think she's invited us?"

"I mean, we're all here, and we have nothing to do for the rest of the night. You wanna tell us your tale in your own words?" Maggie was meek in asking this question, her tone indicating that the rest of the women didn't often let her speak.

"You really want me to?" Lilly asked, taken aback yet another time. It was the first time in her life someone had asked her to do that.

"Yeah, I mean, if you break out some of the harder stuff in your wine cellar," Linda said. "We could do with some story time."

"Oh, you meant this?" Lilly asked, conjuring a bottle of '32 Macallan out of thin air.

"Now we're talking!" Jennifer said.

Lilly's magical floating bottle poured shots into the spontaneously appeared crystal glasses, each glass floating toward one of the women.

"Where to begin?" Lilly asked herself.

"How about when they caught you in Salem? I mean, we've only read about that stuff. What was it actually like?" Charlotte asked.

"But first," Linda said, establishing her authority once more. "A toast."

"Yes! A toast to this newfound bond of...witch-hood? Sisterhood? Covenliness? What's the right vernacular, Lilly?"

"A toast to the Bridgewater Coven," Lilly said, raising her glass. "Simple and classy."

"Hear, hear!" the women said, clinking their shot glasses in the air, saying cheers, and downing their shots.

As the night grew older, Lilly told them her tale once more, this time giving them more details than she'd written in her diary. By the time she was done with her story, a story that also heavily featured a writer named Joseph Banbury, the night was getting late.

Tired, drunk, and sleepy, the women walked out of the house.

"Hey, Lill..." Maggie slurred. "Did you cause this fog?"

"Believe it or not, I have nothing to do with it," Lilly said, waving as the women walked out of her house and toward their cars.

"Ladies. Thank you for your time," Lilly continued. "A parting gift, if I may."

She clapped her hands and performed a spell that took care of their drunkenness and tiredness. She needed them around, not crashing their cars into trees as they drunkenly descended the hill.

"Whoa! What did you do?" Jennifer asked. "And can I have some more of that?"

"A simple rejuvenation charm to take the edge off," Lilly said, standing on her porch, watching the women get into their cars, their faces no longer tired, no longer all that guilt-ridden. Instead, there was promise on their faces. For once, they had something monumental to look forward to.

They had all already decided they would meet at Lilly's house the next day for their first lesson in magic.

The Test

The very next day was a Monday, which meant that the kids were off to their schools and the husbands were where the husbands should be—working away in the big cities, living their weekdays in their apartments in Boston, Philly, New York. This left the ladies with ample time on their hands, and more importantly, allowed them to prepare for the day that awaited them.

The ladies were ready promptly at 9am, convening outside of Linda's house, surprised to see the Christ-follower waiting and ready.

"I thought Lilly hurt your delicate sensibilities," Nora chided.

"Eh," Linda shrugged. "She's certainly a character. And I suppose if you live long enough, you become either crazy or super skeptical. I can give her the benefit of the doubt if she's genuinely willing to teach us what she claims she's going to teach us."

"You doubt her?" Jennifer asked, dressed in a tight top that revealed plenty of her surgically enhanced cleavage, her hair done in a high ponytail.

"Don't you? I shouldn't be dealing with this Devil worshipper!" Linda stated.

"We're going to be late," Maggie said, walking toward Sophia's minivan. Sophia was already behind the wheel, tapping at it impatiently.

"You're one to talk, lazy bones," Evelyn said, cutting Maggie off and getting in the car before anyone else could.

"Guys, I'm genuinely scared," Charlotte said.

"Are you sure it's not just your stomach grumbling because you're hungry?" Nora said.

"No," Charlotte said. "What if something goes awry?"

"Awry? You've been reading *Pride and Prejudice* again?" Sophia laughed.

The women got in the car and drove up the hill. As they climbed out of the van, the ladies admired the tall, handsome, stately home.

"What if there's a secret contract that she asks us to sign, pledging our souls to the Devil?" Linda whispered.

"Listen, Linda, I'm surprised you're even joining us at all. Shouldn't your religion be keeping you away from all this?" Maggie chimed in.

"If there's a Devil, then Jesus will be there to protect me!" she responded. "And besides, maybe Jesus wants me to be here, to help me better my life!"

"I can assure you there will be no secret contracts," Lilly said, appearing suddenly from behind, catching them all off-guard. She took off her gardening gloves and threw them in the wheelbarrow she had been pushing. "But if you steal any more of my tomatoes, I'll sic some hellhounds on you."

The others chuckled uncomfortably before Lilly smiled and said, "Just ask next time. Why you gotta damage the vines, girl?"

"I'm sorry. I hadn't eaten anything all day, and..." Charlotte didn't know what more to say. There was an eeriness about the house, especially with the mist rolling all around it. Lilly stood taller than all of the women. And with her hair loose and her loose gown, she really looked like the witch she said she was. All that was missing was a crooked hat.

"I've got a potion with your name on it," Lilly said, taking Charlotte's arm and taking her inside. The rest of the women followed.

"Is that what we're doing today?" Linda asked. "Potions?"

"Nothing so advanced just yet. Today, I just want to initiate you to magic and see how that goes."

"What does that potion do, the one with my name on it?" Charlotte asked.

"Well, you have a propensity for food and drink. That potion quells it by tackling the underlying trauma that's causing you to binge-eat. It's a healing potion that will subdue your hunger without affecting you in any other way. Does that sound like something you'd be interested in?"

"Hell yeah!" Charlotte said. As she stepped inside the house, she caught sight of her pudgy body in the foyer mirror. What she wouldn't give to have a figure like the rest of the ladies in her group. That potion could be a start.

Lilly procured the bottle of red liquid from thin air and handed it to Charlotte.

"A drop a day in water, and you'll feel the effects in a week," Lilly said, patting Charlotte's back.

"Hey, not fair, what do we get?" Jennifer asked in a faux-whiny tone.

"This," Lilly said, pressing her thumb into Jennifer's forehead.

"Ouch!" Jennifer gasped, stepping back, touching her suddenly hot forehead. "What did you do?"

The rest of the women stood around her defensively.

"I just bestowed you with some of my magic," Lilly said. "So that you can perform your first spell. Come now. The rest of you. Form a line. Get touched by Aunt Lilly. She won't tell nobody," Lilly joked, the joke falling flat, but not her command. The women lined up in front of her. She touched their foreheads with her thumb, imbuing them all with her magic, making each of them able to perform and understand sorcery itself.

"Hang on," Linda said, her turn being the last. "Isn't it like... I guess what I'm trying to ask is, don't you have to be a magical person inherently to be able to do magic?"

"You're thinking of Harry Potter again, dear," Lilly said. "Anyone can do magic as long as they have a teacher who initiates them to its ways. Fortunately for you, I am her." Lilly was feeding the women a white lie; not just anyone could perform magic, she was instilling the powers in them for a purpose.

"Cool. And just so we're clear, there's no blasphemy or profane shit going on underhand?" Linda asked, still cautious.

"I promise," Lilly said, and then pushed her thumb onto Linda's forehead.

The seven women stood there, looking at their hands and staring around at each other. Finally, the brief spell of confusion was over, and they all looked to Lilly to see what she had planned.

"Now that your latent magic has been activated," Lilly began, but Jennifer raised her finger.

"Yes?"

"Explain."

"Okay, I see that this is going to take much longer than I anticipated." Lilly sighed. "Your bodies have their mechanisms. Metabolism. Peristalsis. Respiration. Heartbeat. Yes?"

They all nodded in unison, standing around the dinner table in the dining room, wondering what the feathers on the table were all about.

"Magic is a latent function of the body, if you want to look at it like that. It's like when mothers toss their newborns into swimming pools and they suddenly remember how to swim because they'd been swimming in the womb for nine months."

"Nice," Charlotte grinned.

"So, sugar mommy just threw us into the pool?" Evelyn joked.

"Sugar mommy did exactly that," Lilly responded. "And now, I'm going to see if your bodies have activated its dormant magical system. We shall begin with the simplest of exercises. Telekinesis."

"Like Charles Xavier?"

"Close, but this is about lifting things with magic. You're thinking telepathy. I can teach you that too, in a later lesson, but first things first. This is the most basic of lessons. And it has to do with these feathers laid before you. I'm going to show you how to make them float, and then you will try to do it yourselves. We clear?"

"I'm sorry to be such a pain in your delicious derriere, but what are you getting out of this?" Sophia asked, looking at Lilly's ample buttocks with a strange hunger in her eyes. "Why teach us? Like, is that even worth your time?"

"You mean is it worth my time to finally have a coven of my own after all these years?" Lilly asked.

"Fair enough," Sophia nodded, still looking at Lilly's pelvis. She shook her head and drove out the thought of burying her face in there so she could focus on the lesson better. She had, as they said, "experimented" in college, and had found those experiments successful. There was a way about women that men just didn't have. A delicateness that begged to be explored. Sophia wondered if Lilly was into that, but then, looking at Lilly's stern face, she realized that while the rest of them didn't know any magic yet, Lilly probably already knew telepathy and had just gotten a read on Sophia's lustful thoughts. She blushed and looked away.

"Right," Lilly said, looking at the rest of them. "The spell for levitation is, Levicantate!"

"That's it?" Evelyn asked, scoffing at the end of her question.

"Yes. That's pretty much it. But try to repeat the word and you'll see that the word alone won't do anything. You have to add the will behind the word. The intent. You must really want to make this feather float. And then, when your focus is deepened and fixed on your goal, you'll whisper the magic word, and watch the magic happen."

Maggie, who was normally slow to pick on these sorts of things, closed her eyes, hovered her hand over the feather, and whispered, "Levicantate!" Much to everyone's surprise, the feather began to float in the air, and reached up to Maggie's palm.

"All right, Maggie!" Lilly clapped.

Maggie opened her eyes, breaking her concentration, and watched the feather fall back onto the table.

"As far as beginnings go, that was splendid. You succeeded on your first attempt. Now, Jennifer?"

"Okay. Here goes," Jennifer whispered, and then repeated the spell. Nothing happened. Her feather did not so much as budge, let alone float.

"You're doing it wrong," Nora said impatiently, came forward, and yelled, "Levicantate!" She did it with such aggression that everything flew off the table. The candles, tablecloth, and feathers crashed into the ceiling.

"Jesus Christ," Evelyn gasped, stepping to her side to avoid the candleholder. "Calm yourself, will you?"

Nora had a sheepish grin on her face.

"That's putting a little too much will in there, Nora," Lilly said. "But that's to be expected." With a wave of her hand, she rearranged all the fallen things on the table. "Let's do over. Jennifer?"

"Why can't I do it?" Jennifer asked, looking at Lilly with envious desperation. Two of her friends had already done it.

"Because you're not finding your inner balance. You must believe that you can do it, and then utter the spell. If there's doubt, it will hinder you from performing any magic. Comparison, as they say, is the thief of joy. Just track your own progress and get back to me when you can make it float." Lilly handed Jennifer her feather and told her to go into the living room so she could practice on her own. "Maggie, go with her."

Next up, she taught Linda how to do the spell. Following that, Evelyn, Charlotte, and finally Sophia. It took them each several minutes to learn it, and not all of them had the level of success that Maggie did.

After an hour of trying to make feathers float in the air, Jennifer came rushing from the living room, her face red with glee. "I made it happen!"

"Show me."

"I'm gonna brag, okay?" Jennifer said, with Maggie turning up behind her. "Look."

Jennifer pointed her palm at the basket of apples on the shelf and said, "Levicantate!"

To everyone's surprise, including Lilly's, all the dozen apples in the basket floated in the air, hanging suspended.

"Wow," Lilly said, clapping. "That was impressive."

"Come on! More impressive than me flinging all the things off the table?" Nora asked, frustrated.

"Yes, because Jennifer somehow found her inner balance. How did you find it?" Lilly asked.

"Maggie told me how to do it," Jennifer said, focusing on bringing the apples down into the basket without them falling.

"And how do you know?" Lilly asked Maggie.

"It's like what you said. There has to be will behind it," Maggie said. "I just thought to myself, what if I were that feather? Would I want to float to the command of someone's voice? I sort of empathized with a non-living thing, if that makes sense."

"You became the very feather you were trying to float," Lilly said, her hand on Maggie's shoulder. "That's quantum-level thinking, Mags."

"Thanks," Maggie said, blushing.

"When it comes to spells, finding your inner balance is all about connecting the source of your magic to the object you are performing magic upon. It's empathy, is what it is."

"So...when you burned all those people in Salem, were they the empathetic objects that you're talking about?" Linda asked this question so ruthlessly that several of the women gasped at the audacity.

"Linda!" Maggie hissed.

"It's okay. It's a fair question," Lilly said, suppressing her real emotions. "When I was wrongfully charged for..."

"You weren't wrongfully charged. They found you guilty of being a witch," Linda said.

"What's your deal?" Sophia whispered, elbowing Linda. Linda ignored her.

Lilly smiled painstakingly.

"No witch should ever be burned at the stake. And no people should ever turn an eye so blind with hatred that they cannot see that they are sentencing someone innocent to death. I had already seen my friend, my teacher, Bridget, get consumed by the flames on the stake. I had no empathy in me at that moment. All I had was wrath. Rage. Vengeance. You can harness magic with all kinds of emotions. When I scorched all those people to their deaths, I did so out of rage. It was why my magic was so chaotic. Every single one of the people I set fire to had betrayed me. Testified against me. Stood there idly as they let an innocent woman burn. Empathy? Fuck, yes, I did it out of empathy. Empathy for Bridget, who had been burnt to a crisp. Empathy for Sarah, who wasn't even a witch, yet was tied up next to me, next in line to burn. But most importantly, empathy for myself. Whatever my 'sin,' I knew I did not deserve such a humiliating and painful death. Do with that information what you will," Lilly finished speaking.

An awkward and dense silence hung in the room as the women watched Lilly head over to the bar and pour herself a drink.

"Hey," Linda began. "I didn't mean it like that."

"If there's one thing I hate, it's a hypocrite. Own the fact that you meant it like that. I'll respect you all the more for it. Don't deny that you tried to sting me. You succeeded. Some of the people I killed that day, I called them friends. It's not a memory I am fond of reliving. But that's okay."

"Say sorry, Linda, for God's sake," Jennifer spoke.

"I'm sorry, Lilly," Linda said, swallowing her pride.

"It's okay," Lilly said, downing another shot of whiskey. "A little trigger warning would be appreciated next time."

Deep down, Lilly knew what it was. Yesterday, she had hurt Linda's sentiments with her talk of paganism and the phoniness of Christianity. Linda had been waiting for this opportunity. She wasn't one to let things go. Even though it was exactly the kind of behavior that she had expected from her, it didn't soften the blow.

"You're not expelling us, are you?" Jennifer asked. "I mean..."

"Oh, no." Lilly shook her head. "I'm actually going to teach you the next spell next week. For this week, I'll leave you girls be and let you practice what you have learned. I am eager to see how far you go with one spell, and just what you can do."

"Are you going somewhere?" Evelyn asked.

"Yes. There's some business I need to take care of elsewhere. I'll be back before Sunday," Lilly said.

~

As the ladies walked out of the house, Lilly closed the door behind them, not waving goodbye nor saying it with her words.

"Nice going, Linda," Nora raged. "The woman's genuinely trying to teach us something, and you go and pull that."

"Zip it, will you? No one asked for your opinion," Linda said, getting into the passenger side of Sophia's minivan.

"That was not cool what you did," Sophia chimed in.

"Need I remind you all this is a witch we're dealing with?" Linda snapped, glaring at them all through the rearview mirror.

"Yeah, but, Linds," Jennifer said quietly. "So are we now."

"And the least we can do is look after one of our own," Maggie voiced her opinion.

"Fine," Linda said. "I'll be less of a bitch next time. Thanks for the guilt trip. I'm going straight to Hell for this."

~

For the entirety of the next week, the ladies tried to forget the note on which their first lesson had ended and instead focused on practicing their magic.

Linda practiced it the least, as she wasn't entirely sure if she wanted to continue with her lessons. In fact, she was not really sure why the rest of the women had drunk Lilly's Kool-Aid with such eagerness. She felt a power shift, a threat rising in the form of the witch on the hill. If she let her, Lilly would take the rest of the women for her own, leaving Linda all by herself. The first lesson was a demonstration of that.

Lilly had something that Linda didn't. Magic. It was only natural that the rest of the women gravitated toward her. She had to think about her next steps. Carefully.

As for Jennifer, she couldn't stop making everything float in her house. Clothes fresh from the wash floated in neat stacks and piled themselves in her cabinet. Toys that the kids had left in the living room flew in the air and into their baskets. She even made her bed with just one spell.

The rest of the women got up to their own things with the spell. Charlotte, Nora, Maggie, and Evelyn got together at Sophia's and practiced every evening, having fun while they were at it.

But for all the women, one thing could be said with great certainty.

Their thirst for this knowledge had been kindled, and after three days of practicing the same spell, they wondered what other kind of magic they could perform.

That entire week, they did not see Lilly, and they wondered if the Bridgewater Witch had ditched for good. But come Sunday, they all saw her Range Rover roll down the road and drive up the hill, which allayed the worries in their hearts.

All except Linda, who had decided over the course of the week that she was going to put on a charade. Act polite. Be super nice to everyone. Make up for her brash behavior. And learn while she was at it. Learn until she was self-sufficient.

And then, if she wanted, she would make her move. A power play that would set all balances right, both inner and outer.

For now, all she had to do was bear Lilly.

PERHAPS THE STRANGEST of all things to happen happened to Charlotte. She had taken heed of Lilly's advice. A drop of the potion mixed in a glass of water. At first, the potion had done nothing for her, and she had continued eating the way she always did.

But on the seventh day, just as Lilly had promised, she woke up to a strange sensation. Suddenly, she did not want to gorge on pancakes and waffles first thing in the morning. She wanted to go on a run. She did not want to consume anything sugary. Water was good enough.

On Sunday night, after they had all observed Lilly drive up the hill, they gathered at Brischetto's Bistro on Main for dinner. To everyone's surprise, Charlotte ordered a Caesar salad and nothing else.

"What's gotten into you?" Linda asked. "Don't you like their steak?"

"I'll pass," Charlotte said, completely dismayed by the sight of all the food in front of her. "There's the kind of magic that she's teaching us, and there's the kind of magic that she's keeping for herself. I mean... This potion she gave me. I literally don't feel like eating. And you all know just how big of a problem I had."

"I don't think she's keeping any of it for herself in the long run. That is, if Linda doesn't upset her any further. If we keep on learning, I think Lilly will teach us all there is to teach," Maggie said, digging into her steak.

"Sometimes it baffles me just how dense you can be, Maggie," Linda scoffed. "What good will it do her to teach us all she knows? How will she maintain her position as the head honcho of the coven? She's never going to teach us all she knows. And what's with all that talk about doing magic for good?"

"I think you're the kind of person who thinks people cannot improve or evolve over time," Charlotte said. "And you'd be fair in making that assessment. Most people don't. It's what explains them getting canceled in the long run. But give someone a long enough timeline, and they change. Lilly's had a long time to live. Why are you so adamant in believing that she's not evolved for the better?"

"Because with that much power, you simply don't evolve for the better!" Linda stated. "She's hiding something."

"What could she be hiding? We literally read her entire diary, remember?" Jennifer asked, not touching her ratatouille. She didn't even know why she'd ordered it.

"I don't know. I just don't sit well with this whole thing, it's against Christ" Linda said; deep down, her greed overthrew her love for the man upstairs.

"Someone's feeling threatened," Nora said, her eyes on the stack of empty plates that the waiter was carrying on a big tray from a vacant table to the kitchen.

"Please. Me? Threatened? As if," Linda said.

"All right. Listen. I'm bored of this conversation," Nora said. "If you have a problem with Lilly, don't show up at the next meeting."

"So you're the one calling the shots now?" Linda rolled her eyes, but no one was listening. They were all intently focused on what Nora was doing.

Nora made all the plates in the tray float just a teeny bit to the left without anyone in the bistro noticing, least of all the waiter lugging the whole stack to the kitchen. In a split second, all the plates spilled from the tray and began clattering and crashing on the marble floor, causing a cacophony of noise.

The ladies held back their laughter as they watched several waiters come forth with brooms and mops to clean the mess in the packed diner.

As far as their first lesson was concerned, it was evident that they had all mastered it.

Even Linda.

5

THE WAYS OF MAGIC

The Consequences of Marriage

Even though they met every day, talked about their troubles at length, and spent a sizable chunk of their time together complaining about the things that were askew in their lives, the women of Alameda Avenue had mastered the craft of zoning out two of the most important aspects of their lives.

Their children and their husbands.

When you were as unsatisfied and unhappy in your life as these women were, it became second nature for you to block the very things from your mind that were making you unhappy. The children were a tether, the husbands were a leash. Even though each of the seven ladies claimed that they were freer than most, they were trapped in Bridgewater and had no way of circumventing this situation.

So, the children became background noise, and the husbands became a human-sized hole in their lives that would fill itself on the weekend when they'd come back from the big cities to spend some time with their families.

The ladies had figured they only had a select few hours during which they had to fake their roles as mothers and wives. For the rest of the time, the children were off at school, after-school soccer practice, hanging out with friends on playdates, or playing on their phones and consoles in their own rooms. As for the husbands, it was the same deal. Whether they worked out of town or in, they were gone for nine hours during the day, came home tired, had dinner, enjoyed a beer or two in front of the living room TV with the game on, and then went to bed.

Besides those little windows of feigning duty, the women were free to be who they wanted to be, and it was because they all shared this sentiment so deeply and inherently that they all hung out so religiously.

It was a deed—this zoning out—that took a lot of practice, and lately, for these women, it was as if their husbands and kids did not exist at all. Whenever they did exist, the wives went on autopilot mode for however long, escaping into the realms they'd so carefully crafted in their minds.

On the following Monday, after Lilly had come back from wherever she had mysteriously disappeared to, the ladies awaited messages on their phones. They waited all day, each of the women watching the mist roll in from the windows of their bedrooms, wondering what was taking her so long, and if Lilly was still upset about the way Linda had confronted her.

But in the evening, Lilly messaged them all in a chat group she'd created.

"Eight o'clock. Be there."

Intrigued, a little afraid, and mostly anticipative, the ladies braced themselves for the next lesson, not knowing why it was scheduled for eight in the evening.

When it finally came time for them to convene, each of the seven crept out of their houses in parkas and jackets. Despite it being a summer month, the fog had turned the night air cold—yet another inexplicable phenomenon. There were no rains, no El Nino winter, no hurricane, and yet fog and cold.

Given the density of the vapor surrounding them, the ladies decided that it would be better if they walked up the hill instead of driving in the dark, especially seeing how their cars would no doubt disturb their children. Sneakers and boots clomped and thumped on the asphalt as the congregation made their way up the road, past their ordinary, identical, banal houses, and toward the grandiose estate up the hill.

Jennifer's heart twinged with envy as her mind did meaningless calculations, wondering how much it would take for her husband to afford such a house. Even if he was making a million a year (which he was not), it'd take them around six, seven years to save enough money to buy such a house. Not an exact one. God no. That one was too expensive and too high maintenance as it was.

Linda was the kind of person who humbly stated that her parents were rich, not her. She was going to inherit all that money upon their death, being the only child, but dear God, her parents were resilient about not croaking. Both of them in their late eighties, both of them active and fit. She hated herself for the fact that she prayed for their deaths, but not all that much. She hated herself just the right amount. When her parents would finally die, she would have her lawyers do their thing. Divorce her husband. Take her kids. Take the money. Leave.

However, for others in the group, leaving was not an option, especially when they were tied to their husbands in more than just material ways. Maggie, for instance, lived perpetually in the shadow and fear of her husband. Gregory was a man with hairline patience, and each of Maggie's mistakes, if you could call them mistakes, earned her creative abuse ranging from belt slaps on her backside to punches in her gut. Her last miscarriage was a result of being tardy thanks to her morning sickness and overdoing her husband's fried eggs. When he saw that the yolk had been over-cooked, he slammed the plate on the table, cracking it, and delivered a right hook to her stomach.

As she lay there, bleeding, whimpering, knowing that there would be no more kicks, no more ultrasounds, her husband, who had since regained his composure, sat beside her on the carpet, patting her head, whispering, "We will have another baby."

Jennifer had come from a white trash family in Missouri. She'd realized early on that she was not meant to live in trailer parks for the rest of her life, washing plates in cheap diners where the patrons harassed you every time you passed them by. Not particularly academically inclined, she put herself through college despite the added difficulty of not doing quite well in her studies. But she had one thing working for her. Her looks. Of all the ladies on Alameda Avenue, Jennifer's deep green eyes, freckled face, and brunette hair was empirically the prettiest. It was this same natural beauty that drew the attention of her to-be-husband toward her when she was doing a sales rep job right after college. She did not right away believe that another sales rep from another company was going to offer her the world on a silver platter, but her husband did exactly that. He worked his way up the ladder, and within a few years found himself in the position of regional manager at Westchester Pharmaceuticals located in Bridgewater.

These days, he was VP of R&D and doing quite handsomely in terms of making money, but now that Jennifer was living (relatively) large, she was doing so amongst peers who had been living well for quite some time. It drove her envious to see Charlotte, Maggie, Nora, Sophia, Evelyn, and most importantly, Linda thriving in the Bridgewater bubble, and nothing that she could do would change it. Her husband wouldn't get any more promotions, and Westchester was not Pfizer where they paid the VPs the big bucks. These were aggressively medium bucks, if anything. So here she was, stuck in a limbo where she had just enough to maintain herself in society yet not enough to rise higher than it. Like Linda. Or Lilly Frost, for that matter.

In Charlotte's case, it was quite egregious in its own way. Her husband was the guy who was known in kink subreddits as a chubby chaser. She resisted for the first few years of her marriage, but once she got pregnant, she noticed how much her husband's attitude toward her changed for the better. She did not get rid of the post-pregnancy weight (couldn't, as a matter of fact, thanks to a C-section), and instead, started to eat whatever he sent her way. And he made sure to plump her up like a pig for slaughter. Within the next year, this ninety-pound woman had gained a hundred and twenty pounds and was, in her own eyes, disgusting, but in the eyes of her husband, she was a sexual marvel worth fucking from behind every night. The fatter she got, the hornier he got. The more she ate, the more she hated herself, and the more she hated herself, the more she ate to compensate for the guilt and shame.

A truly evil cycle, if there ever was one.

Not more evil than Nora's, who was diagnosed with bipolar disorder at the age of thirty-two. Nearly six years ago. Nora's cycle was one of mania and depression. And in the lull between, she would be angry. Plain, straight-up resentful on the hand life had dealt her. Her manic phase saw to it that she wrote "schizo-mathematics" on the walls of the bathroom all the while throwing salt upon her body to combat the demons that were trying to hone in on her. When the mania subsided, and the bathroom was a mess of linear algebra colliding with differential equations, she would sink into a deep depression wherein she'd just sleep, weep, and wish for a swift death. Thanks to mood stabilizers and antidepressants, she was much better now, but occasionally she forgot to take her pills. And when she did take her pills regularly, the side effects ranged from palpitations to severe irritability. They'd prescribed her Haldol for the irritability, and while she did not know this, her husband often crushed Haldol pills and mixed them in her fruit smoothies so she would be less angry.

As for Evelyn, it was her husband who was in a deep depression as opposed to her. Knowing that he'd earn and earn and earn and it still wouldn't be enough to pay off the credit card debt his wife had amassed buying shoes, clothes, and jewelry online. The man had taken out a second mortgage on his home so he could pay off some of that debt, but what he didn't know was, she had taken out a couple more credit cards and was in the process of maxing them out without him knowing. The day she would confide in him about those cards would be the day he'd have a third cardiac episode.

Or perhaps it was Sophia who had it worse. Hers was the childhood sweetheart blossoming into a full-blown love kind of marriage. And for the first five to ten years of their relationship—two of those years as a married couple—they enjoyed each other. Matt and Sophia were the kind of couple everyone idolized and envied. He was a gym owner, eye candy for the ladies, a source of inspiration and guidance for the men. Sophia had often confessed to her college friends that the reason she'd married him was because he was so damn hot, that if it were between John Cena and Matt Shaw, she'd pick Matt Shaw eight times out of ten. The other two, well, she wanted to see what John Cena felt like. After the flame of their marriage fizzled out sometime later, Sophia tried her best to understand what had happened.

She couldn't wrap her head around the fact that the same man who fucked her seven ways to Sunday thrice a day had now stopped doing so, and the only time they'd ever make average love was once a month.

She still loved him. Could not think of cheating on him. He was her friend, after all. Friend first, husband later. Once, after a long fight, they had discussed the possibility of making their marriage open, only for Matt to end up weeping and confessing that he could not imagine the thought of another man touching her.

But he did not say anything about her touching herself.

Something quite amazing happened after that fight. The mood around the house lightened and things seemed to be going better than okay. Matt kept on pumping his body full of steroids that made his testicles shrink and his testosterone level increase, and Sophia took the responsibility of satisfying her unmet needs into her own hands.

As the women converged on the road leading up the hill, they looked at each other with gazes, identifying and acknowledging each other's not-so-perfect history, a history filled with misery, compromise, and deep-rooted sadness.

Even the most belligerent amongst them hoped that somewhere, something that Lilly would end up teaching them would bring meaning to their lives. Like it had Charlotte's.

Whether it was selfishness or curiosity, one thing was certain: They were all of them bewitched, unable to resist the pull of the Bridgewater Witch.

The Witching Hour

"Good evening, ladies," Lilly said, her smile impersonal at best. She was standing outside of her house, awaiting the women.

"Why are we meeting again?" Linda asked, looking at her watch.

"Because I have someone I want you to meet. Now, I'd have dragged you all here during the witching hour, but since you all have children, three in the morning wouldn't be ideal for you. It's also coincidentally the right time to conduct magical trials because that's when..."

"Magic is at its strongest," repeated Evelyn, Sophia, and Nora in unison.

"Good! And just for that, you get extra points," Lilly said, winking at them.

"I did not know there were points," Jennifer said, stuttering.

"They're just brownie points, girl, give yourself as many. Here, have ten for showing up," Lilly said, chuckling. "And I want you to have this."

Jennifer held onto the stick that Lilly gave her, looking at it with awe.

"How come she gets one and we don't?" Linda asked with cerebral indignation. She had a look in her eyes that suggested she was going to yank the stick out of Jennifer's hand. But Jennifer was clinging fiercely to it, thinking it was a special wand that would allow her to do a more powerful brand of magic than the others. For just a brief spell, her envy dispelled into nothingness. Finally, someone saw her true potential.

"Because none of the rest of you have insomnia," Lilly said, looking around the semi-circle of ladies standing under the half-moon. "She does. This is nothing but magically enhanced Valerian root. I believe you know how to take it, Jenn?"

"Jennifer," Jennifer said, her face turning to stone, all that envy coming gushing back. "And yes. I do know how to take it. I just thought..."

"What? That this would be a wand? Come on, ladies. Real witches can do magic with just about anything, and in most cases, our fingers suffice," Lilly said, winking at Sophia, who blushed for a reason she could not immediately understand. In the morning, when she'd be beat and tired, she'd revisit this conversation, eyes closed, her fingers sufficing, and she'd laugh to herself at Lilly's secret wit, not at all worried about the fact that the witch knew about her lust. Some part of her wanted Lilly to know. Wanted Lilly to do something about it.

"I have all that, and you should not undermine the efficacy of those devices. They each work, if one possesses the sight. Tonight, I am not going to impart any more devices or tools or potions to anyone. Tonight, I'm going to do something different. Something that hasn't been done in the history of recent witchcraft."

"Pray tell, what is it?" Linda asked, vexed.

"Follow me down the hill, if you please," Lilly said, ignoring Linda's attitude.

The women followed Lilly down the dirt path that led down the other side of the hill. They saw the ranch, barn, and farm buildings for the first time, amazed by the grandeur of this hidden place. And, Jennifer thought, her heart scorching, it touched the lake! None of their houses touched the lake, even though they were sold as lake-front properties.

The night was beautiful all around them. The fog, seemingly sentient, trailed away from the clearing, leaving the silhouettes of the trees to stand with mosaic moonlight falling upon them. A gentle wind caused ripples on the surface of the blue lake. The grass in the field waved to and fro, and from inside the barn, the gentle coos of hens and bleats of goats could be heard as they rested. It evoked a sense of great calm in the ladies, making them want to stay here longer.

"You've still got animals down there?" Maggie asked, peeking in through the stables and looking at the horses.

"There are always animals down here. I've got a stablemaster to see to the horses, and a farmhand who comes to take care of the hens, the goats, and the pigs. It's my own little ecosystem. Every witch should have one, no matter how small," Lilly said.

"Like rooftop gardens or those terrariums?" Maggie asked.

"You're bang on the money. It's not about abundance. It's about appreciation. My family were farmers from the beginning, and I have just a tiny portion of what we once had. We had acres back in a time when acres in this land were as good as free."

"Modesty does not suit you," Linda said, stepping past Maggie and joining Lilly's stride. "Those are million-dollar properties, both the house and this entire farm."

"All right," Lilly said, taking them to the center of the ground. "This will do. We're going to make what's known as a witch's circle."

The ladies listened closely. This stuff sounded like it meant business. Lilly asked each of them to stand equidistant from each other, and came to stand at the center of them when she was done arranging them in the right order.

"There are eight disciplines of magic," Lilly said. "And I intend to do something a little risky, but I have confidence in all of you that you will do what's right."

"Eight disciplines?" Sophia whistled. "Surely we don't have enough time to learn all of them, do we?"

"The magic will call to you," Lilly stated.

As the seven of them sat in a circle, Lilly walked around the back of each of the ladies. They tried not to giggle like schoolgirls in class as they sat down with crossed legs.

She started to chant, invoking the spirit of the Axis Mundi realm, and bent down to scrape dirt from the ground. She held it above her head as grains of dirt started to filter through. She then quickly threw it into the middle of the women, igniting a fire that blazed from the wood she had placed there earlier.

Linda started to look uneasy, shifting in her seat.

"I'm...I'm not sure I can do this," she started to say anxiously. Maggie grabbed her arm to calm her down, and it seemed to do the trick.

Lilly then stepped into the middle of the circle. "Each of you has a connection to the magic that pervades our world, unique and waiting to be understood," she began, her voice a soft murmur against the rustling of the hay. "Tonight, let the magic find you. Open your minds and hearts. Let it fill you, let it reveal your true potential."

Clouds above them started to form as Lilly waved her hands in the air, chanting. The women started to look altogether uncomfortable, wondering what they might have gotten themselves in for.

Then, silence.

Lilly stood stationary for a moment, before kneeling down and looking into the flames.

"Per me venias et magiam ad animas destinatum liberes." Which meant, *Come through to me and deliver your magic to its intended soul.*

Then it appeared. A spirit from the Axis Mundi appeared from the flames, its form smoke rising up like a dragon. The women were mesmerized. Lilly continued her chant and danced around the fire, summoning more of the smoke. It momentarily retreated back into the flames, as if unsure that it wanted to be there, unsure that it wanted to bestow any power to the women sitting before it. Lilly ushered it back out, chanting and singing in a language the women didn't understand.

Flickers of lightning in the distance and thunder gave way to an already uneasy scene.

The smoke was now ten feet in the air and forming a face, a face that was staring at each of the women. It softly descended and moved around the circle, as if assessing each of them, peering into their souls and understanding their darkest secrets.

It stopped at Nora, who was trembling but ready, whispering under her breath, "*What the fuck is happening?*"

Lilly, who could not hear her, was still chanting at the angel who appeared from the Mundi.

The angel moved on from Nora and the smoke swirled around the necks, bodies, and faces of everyone before rising above the flames once more. Lilly was still chanting, clapping her hands in a rhythmic tone. Lightning was clashing above them, and then the smoke started to howl as it swirled around the circle, eventually unleashing its power in all seven directions, entering the mouths of the women, knocking them on their backs.

Lilly looked astonished. She stood, mouth agape, staring at the women.

"It chose all of you, you have all been chosen!"

THE FIRE WAS EXTINGUISHED and the women were slowly raising themselves from the ground, static in the air, on their fingers and clothes. They looked at each other rejuvenated, as if a life force had entered them and taken twenty years off them.

"I feel...I feel strong," Nora said. The others nodded and smiled as they looked at their hands.

"What just happened? What the hell was that thing?" Linda stated with her usual flair.

"That, my dears, was a spirit from the Axis Mundi. It knows you now, it has seen your darkest fears, your secrets, your desires. It chose each of you; sometimes it doesn't—" Lilly was interrupted by Charlotte.

"It may not have chosen all of us?"

"Indeed, my dear, it uses its power at its own discretion, it knows why you might need it, what you will need it for, and how you are going to wield it."

Nora touched Jennifer's shoulder. "How are you feeling?" And in doing so, she was able to read into Jennifer's mind, an image of Jennifer having sex with someone who was not her husband flashed into her mind, prompting an immediate pull away reaction.

"I feel great, normal, not sure I feel that different," she replied.

"Oh, but you will," Lilly interrupted. "For you all will." She began to chant again and the storm slowly crept closer, rain started to drip, falling on the women as if they had been baptized by the spirit of the Mundi. As the rain picked up, soaking the women, laughter and joy erupted, their clothes soaked. The ecstasy of ethereal magic had them running their hands through their hair, faces to the sky screaming.

It took Maggie no time at all to notice that Lilly was no longer in the circle, and as she peered off to the edge of the hill, she saw her floating in the sky, the moon illuminating her presence, casting a shadow on her body.

"Join me," Lilly seductively ordered. She spoke softly, but the voice traveled up the hill.

The women jumped up and ran toward the hill's edge. Maggie looked worried and didn't jump up with the same gusto, but she followed nonetheless. Laughter and elation filled the women as they ran to Lilly, looking up in amazement as she hovered above them.

Super terram ascende, me flutuare sine, dignitatem meam novi.

Rise above the Earth, let me float, I know my worth.

Super terram ascende, me flutuare sine, dignitatem meam novi.

Rise above the Earth, let me float, I know my worth.

Lilly chanted the spell, and the women slowly began to lose their footing. A force slowly pulled them up from the Earth as if gravity had been reversed, the feeling akin to floating underwater but being able to breathe.

Their faces were alight with the thrill of levitation, their bodies swaying gently in the night breeze. Laughing and cooing in awe. But Lilly's expression was somber, her eyes piercing each of them with a seriousness that stilled them.

"Ladies," Lilly began, her voice steady yet tinged with an undeniable gravity, "tonight, you've all touched the ether of ancient magic, a force that binds the very fabric of our existence. This power now flows through you, an indelible part of your being. But heed this warning: With such power comes a burden, heavy and demanding."

She paused, letting her words sink into the depths of their newfound exhilaration. The wind seemed to carry her solemn tone across the open hill, whispering through the grass beneath them.

"Magic is not merely a tool; it is a living, breathing essence that chooses its bearers wisely. Each of you will discover strengths—talents that may seem as natural as breathing. Yet, within those strengths lie potential weaknesses, hidden snares that could grab your soul if left unchecked."

Lilly's gaze softened slightly, but her voice retained its firmness. "Remember, the brightest light casts the darkest shadow. What you choose to do with your abilities can illuminate the world or shroud it in darkness. Some of you may find that your powers are potent, intoxicating even. This allure can lead to a path fraught with peril, where the temptation to dominate or coerce will beckon."

Raising her hand, she let a small orb of light flicker to life, floating up toward the starry sky before dissolving into nothingness. "Just as this light vanishes into the night, so, too, can your essence dissolve if you misuse the gifts you've been granted. Beware the seduction of power, for it can corrupt the noblest of intentions."

She let her gaze traverse the circle of women, each absorbed in her warning. "Strive to balance your powers with wisdom and humility. Protect each other, and guard against the darkness that inevitably follows unchecked might. If you fail to respect this balance, the consequences will be eternal."

"Tell us in English," Nora mocked while spinning around mid-air.

Lilly simply smirked back. "Be careful what you conjure."

"I FEEL A SENSE OF ABJURATION?" Maggie asked timidly, taking Lilly to the side as the women walked back up the hill. The rest of the women were busy exploring the ranch, playing with their new power, talking to each other, or simply lying on the grass and staring at the moon.

"Pardon?" Lilly asked.

"Like... Did you see something in my life that made you want to teach me protective spells? Did you tell that angel to protect me?" Maggie asked, thinking about the most recent beating she'd gotten from her husband.

Not that long ago. The bruises from it were still purple on her back. He'd wanted to find out where the TV remote was, and Maggie happened to be sleeping on her stomach in the bedroom. It was a series of three powerfully delivered fists on her back that woke her up crying. She whimpered and told him that she had no idea where the remote was. Maybe one of the kids had gotten their hands on it and misplaced it, but her husband wasn't willing to listen to that. He slapped her face and held her by the chin, screaming at her.

"After a long fucking day of licking people's boots and kissing asses, I come home and cannot fucking find the remote, you useless bitch!"

Another slap, this time on her other cheek.

Meanwhile, Tommy, their son, stood in the doorway holding the remote, witnessing the domestic violence unfold before his eyes. "S-sorry, Papa. I was playing with it. He's a Transformer."

The reason she bore her husband was because while he beat the shit out of her, he never laid a hand on his children. Never on Tommy and never on Tammy. He just snatched the remote out of Tommy's hand and went downstairs to catch the game or whatever it was that he'd wanted to.

Maggie hadn't slept that entire night because of the pain.

Not even when he'd come back in the room in his boxers, apologizing for losing it as he applied some balm on her aching back.

And yet, her life was so displaced and stagnated that, try as she did to leave it, she couldn't. Who would take care of Tommy and Tammy in her absence? Both her own mother and father were dead, so there was no place where she could go rushing off to for sanctuary. If she went to a women's shelter, she'd be the laughingstock of Bridgewater.

Fresh tears spilled out of her eyes and onto her cheeks, making her lower her face and wipe the wetness with the palms of her hands.

"Hey, hey," Lilly said, holding Maggie's hands. "I didn't prod into your life or anything. If you think that I'm onto something or that I know something, well, rest easy. It doesn't work like that. The magic you've all been granted tonight...it's a reflection, a mirror of your innermost selves. For some, it will manifest as goodness, amplifying the light within. For others, it might draw out the evil, the parts of you that lurk in the recesses of your intentions. The smoke knows what you need, and what you don't."

"LINDA! LINDA! LINDA!" Lilly and Maggie turned around to see the women cheering on Linda as she conjured lightning out of the sky. The bolts angrily flew to earth and connected with her fingertips.

"Linda, NO. This is too soon," Lilly screamed. "Linda, be CAREFUL!"

The lightning that had been pulled from the sky had connected with Linda like a conduit and refused to let go, her power surging. The women stepped back in a panic. "Lilly, what the hell is happening?" Linda shrieked.

A bolt of white lightning shot from her hand and traveled across the field toward Maggie.

"Maggie! Watch out!" Lilly screamed, knowing that she had made a mistake. But it was too late. The lightning bolt was accelerating through the air toward her.

Maggie hit the ground before the bolt could reach her, and it crashed into the stables. A painful shriek came from one of the horses.

"Bella," Lilly whispered. She cast a freezing spell on Linda so that she wouldn't do any harm in the meantime, then ran toward the stables.

"What the hell was that? It was uncalled for," Maggie said, running behind Lilly.

"I'll deal with her in a minute."

As Lilly went inside the stables, the rest of the women, except for

Linda (who was still stuck to the same spot where she was), followed her inside to the sight of a chestnut mare.

"Oh no," Sophia whimpered, covering her face with her hands as she saw the giant gash along the horse's torso where the lightning had hit. The rest of the horses were neighing uncontrollably, kicking against their enclosures.

Evelyn and Charlotte, who both had taken horse-riding lessons in their free time, rushed to their enclosures and calmed them down, all the while keeping an eye on what Lilly was doing.

Lilly knelt beside Bella and placed her hand on the horse's unmoving body.

She recited a spell none of them could overhear.

The gashes on the horse's body started to close up. Bella neighed, shook her head, and slowly got off the ground.

"Necromancy," Jennifer said.

"Yes," Lilly said. "A necessary evil. One that I never want to use. You okay, baby girl?" she asked Bella.

Bella looked at her with hurt eyes, but then nodded and neighed, brushing her mane against Lilly's head.

Lilly patted the horse one more time before exiting the stables. The rest of the women followed suit, then approached Linda.

"Unfreeze me now!" Linda spat at Lilly.

"You killed my horse," Lilly said, her eyes dripping with fury. "It goes to show that you're not equipped to be a witch. If you think that I'm going to teach you anything further, you're sorely mistaken."

"I'm so so sorry," Linda yelped, the pain in her eyes genuine and sincere. "I got carried away and didn't realize what I was doing."

"This was the first and final strike," Lilly said, removing the stationary hold she had on Linda. "If you pull anything like that again, I won't be so kind."

"Is...is your horse okay?" Linda asked. "I didn't mean to kill her."

"Save it," Lilly said. "Now, all of you, go and practice something smaller, try and read each other's minds for a start."

~

"Are you okay?" Nora asked. After the debacle, Lilly had taken her to the side, and while Nora was just standing there, Lilly was watching the other women.

"Yes. It's just...seven is quite a handful, and there's always that one student," Lilly said.

"Yep. That's Linda for you. Drives me nuts every time," Nora said.

"Yes," Lilly said. "Sometimes our emotions get the better of us, and we need to step outside of our bodies and take a look at things objectively."

"God. That's like my entire life summed up." Nora chuckled. "So, you're saying there's a spell for that?"

"A magical technique called astral projection, as a matter of fact," Lilly said. "How would you like to step out of your body and into the spirit realm?"

"What will it do to me?"

"Give you clarity. Allow you to see things that are normally invisible to the human eye. You can travel anywhere you want in the world without a visa, how does that sound? Ever taken mushrooms?"

"A ton in college." Nora chuckled.

"Well, it's like taking mushrooms, but you're sober. Does that make any sense?" Lilly asked, rubbing her temples.

"Not at all, but don't let that stop you from teaching me. I learn better on the fly anyway; I'm not academic!"

"Let's not dwell on the flaws of each other," Lilly said. "Everyone's flawed. It's what makes us human. Even Linda. It's what we do with our flaws that decides if we possess the capacity for good or not."

"How will astral projection help me, exactly?"

"Has it ever happened in your life that you're feeling extremely angry or extremely hurt? Do you fear that you might lash out at those close to you?" Lilly asked, opening the upper three buttons of her shirt, revealing just a little bit of her cleavage. Her entire body was covered in sweat. That necromancy spell had taken a lot out of her. She wasn't sure if she had it in her to teach the rest of the girls their spells.

"Yes. All the time. I lose control when I…err… Can you keep a secret?"

"Always," Lilly said, giving Nora a gentle smile.

"The rest of the girls don't know this, but I'm… I've been diagnosed with… I have bipolar, okay?!" Nora said, ashamed, her face strained with emotion.

"That's nothing to be ashamed of," Lilly said, putting her hand on Nora's shoulder. "In fact—"

"Don't. Please. You don't know how insulting it is when people try to make it out to be a good thing. No. The 'giftedness' of it isn't enough to cancel out all the bad that it's done in my life. I've got to take pills for the rest of my life. And even then, it's not enough. I'm always afraid. I'm afraid that I'm going to do something terrible one day and everyone's going to make fun of me. Like, back when I was in college, and I was manic, I'd streak across the quad. There's literal videos of me doing so on the internet. I cannot take that shit back, so I got to own it. I hope that's not what you were trying to do. Pander to me, you know," Nora said, wiping her eyes.

"No. I was going to say that astral projection during your manic or depressive phase can take you out of your body and give you immediate relief from your disorder. It's all chemical, right? Dopamine imbalance? Serotonin runs wild? That's why you take those SSRIs and SNRIs? Venlafaxine? Yes? All those pills, they affect the chemicals in your body. In the astral realm, your soul is free from its bodily restraints. No more chemical imbalance. You can take refuge in the astral realm's safe space. Come on. I've been around for centuries. You think I'd pander? Bipolar fucking sucks. No way around it. And you're tough for dealing with it. That's all the pandering I'm going to do," Lilly said.

Nora put her arm around Lilly and pulled her close, hugging her.

"You're the first person who hasn't spewed bullshit when it comes to my bipolar, witch. So teach me your magic. I'm ready," Nora sobbed.

"Close your eyes, sister. Repeat after me. Igna cosma matta veritas liberum."

"Quite a mouthful, isn't it?" Nora said, her eyes closed.

"It means, out of fire, out of the universe, out of the drunkenness that comes from the wine of one's soul, I free myself with truth absolute," Lilly said, her body slipping into the astral realm.

Nora repeated the words, and upon immediately feeling the weightlessness, fell back, but instead of landing on her behind, she floated alongside Lilly in a universe so brilliantly lit with effervescent colors, iridescence of purple, green, blue, and green hues. Vapors of colored wind blew through them, past them, around them.

She could see as much of Bridgewater as she wanted to. It seemed each neighborhood was just an arm's throw from each other.

"All this brilliance," Nora whispered, looking at the town and the rainbow colors around her.

"This is your first time," Lilly said. "As you practice this spell, you'll get better at it. It won't be as overwhelming as whatever you're seeing right now."

"Reminds me of the first time I did LSD, ha!" Nora gleamed, looking at her see-through hands.

"Look below." Lilly pointed at their vacant bodies standing in front of each other in the clearing. "Those are our bodies."

"And you were right. I don't feel...fucked in the head, for want of a better phrase." Nora chuckled. "I feel like I did when I was a kid. So free. So full of possibilities."

"Go, then, there are other worlds than these. Explore them at your leisure and at your own discretion. There are some realms that are welcoming to spirits, while others are malevolent. You would do better to stay away from those."

Lilly decided there had been enough action for one evening, and herded the women back to her porch for one last hurrah.

"That reminds me. Ladies. One last bit of magic before we part ways for the night. Everyone, put your hand on mine," she said, bringing her hand forward.

Each of the women brought forth their hands, Maggie the first to do so, Linda the last. Once all hands were placed upon Lilly's, she whispered, "Fortior una, debilior sola."

Their hands started to glow in unison as energy surged from the source of convergence to each of their bodies, rejuvenating them, charging them with power.

"Stronger together, weaker alone," Lilly said, retracting her hand. "I just bound our fates together."

"What does that even mean?" Jennifer asked.

"It means," Lilly said, looking approvingly at all of them, "we're officially a coven now."

6

THE FALL OF THE BRIDGEWATER WITCH

The Torture Vault

After the events of that night, Lilly gave the women ample time to practice the spells she had taught them, citing that she had to go out of town on urgent business as the reason for her unavailability for the next month.

"When I come back, nothing would please me more than seeing that you've all learned the spells well and taught each other too. Sharing is caring, ladies." That was the last message from her in the group chat.

No one heeded it.

While they each practiced their own spells to damn near perfection, they did not share their spells with each other.

At least not at first.

And the longer they went about practicing their solitary spells, the longer Lilly remained out of the picture.

But soon, bored of their own spells, they turned to one another, bartering. Jennifer was the first one to teach Linda how to fly, but only on the condition that Linda teach her how to shoot lightning bolts out of her fingers. Charlotte teamed up with Evelyn, one teaching the other how to conjure things out of thin air, and the other teaching how to freeze people where they stood. It wasn't much fun that they only had each other to practice on, so they asked Sophia to join them.

And thus, the coven was a little bit stronger.

No one really asked Maggie or Nora about their spells, and for that matter, no one really cared. Maggie kept calmly practicing her own spell, and when she did go to other members of the coven to teach her theirs, they laughed her off. It was as if all the sincerity they summoned in the presence of Lilly was for her benefit alone. When out of earshot and eyesight, they reverted back to the people they were. Maggie, not so much, because she genuinely wanted to improve herself, but the rest did not think of Lilly's instructions as more than casual guidelines.

~

LEAST OF ALL NORA.

Lilly had asked her not to astral project too far from her body and most certainly not to visit another realm. Nora, on the verge of a manic episode, dismissed Lilly's directive right at the time September rolled around. It had been two months since Lilly had absconded somewhere. Surely that "advice" wasn't all that important.

On the last day of September, right around when the leaves turned crisp and the air became chilly, Nora lay in bed, trying to reason with her manic mind if she should astral project to one of the captivating realms she had seen or not. Her husband, Jimmy, was away at the Goose and Gander for his evening beer, leaving her alone in the house.

She closed her eyes after a long deliberation, and pushed her astral form outside of her body. Greeted by the resplendence of the vivid colors that were the quintessence of this dimension, the colors of the rainbow danced around her.

"I'll stay on this planet," she convinced herself, and found it easy to talk some sense into herself now that she was free from her manic mind.

Where to go?

Lately, it had felt that she'd ignored her husband for quite a long time. That was okay. This was in their wedding vows. He'd promised to give her a wide berth when she'd be having one of her episodes, and she had promised to always trust him to do the right thing whenever she'd be going through one of her episodes. Then they'd kissed and the officiant had declared them man and wife.

Driven by nostalgia, her astral body floated toward the Goose and Gander in downtown Bridgewater. She could sit with him without him knowing, watch him chase a beer down with a shot of vodka, or whatever his poison of choice was.

A smile crossed upon her face, borne of gratitude. There weren't many people, at least not in Jimmy's age range, who were all too understanding about mental health issues. The stigma in the Gen-Xers and baby boomers around mental disorders was still appalling, even though the millennials and the Gen-Zers had become really appreciative and supportive of the mental health movement. But not her Jimmy. Jimmy wasn't your average Gen-Xer. He was, however, your typical All-American guy. Tall, dark-haired, handsome. He'd rock up a bar dressed in a sack and still have people clambering over him.

But Nora trusted him.

She knew that her man was not vapid. Not shallow. He had proven that to her time and again during their marriage, even when she had been the one to test the durability of their vows.

She figured that checking up on her husband in the same town in which she was doing astral projection was not going against Lilly's rule. Besides, the man worked ten hours every day as one of the town's top realtors. He deserved his little breaks. It was only an hour at Goose and Gander. And it was good that she wasn't actually there. Her being actually there would mean that she would have to face him, and that would come with its share of blame and shame. She would have to ask for forgiveness for what she had done in one of her episodes, and he would have to put on an understanding and sympathetic face that was not his genuine face. He wasn't quick to anger like Nora was. In fact, the reason why their marriage worked well—as per Nora—was because Jimmy never resorted to anger. But she was tired of the charades. Tired of always being embarrassed in front of him and tired of him always being his sympathetic self. Looking at her with pity. She could not stand it.

She wanted to go back to a time when the husband and wife could talk freely without the burden of the bipolar beast weighing down their relationship.

And this was as close as it was going to get. She was sitting next to him on the barstool, there and yet not there. Him, doing his own thing.

The bartender was not there. Jimmy just sat there in his plaid shirt and his blue jeans, sleeves folded up to the elbows, looking as handsome as ever. She wanted to scream, "That's my man, y'all," but to what effect? She wasn't actually there, and no one cared that he wore that wedding ring on his finger.

The bartender, a brown-skinned girl with a slim figure and curly hair, came out of the back, "You're a lucky bastard," she said with a wide grin on her face. "I'd hid it in the back before one of those hipsters showed up last night. Bridgewater County Stout. Your favorite."

"Well, ain't you a doll, Candy," Jimmy said, his hand reaching for the beer, and holding onto Candy's hand. Candy didn't draw her hand back but instead leaned forward, giving him the full view of her luscious brown breasts wanting to slip out of the deep neck of her t-shirt.

"Your doll," she said, winking at him.

Nora felt like she was having a heart attack, and then realized that she'd left her heart along with the rest of her body. This...this was a pain in her soul. Seeing her husband here in the bar flirting with a woman who knew him on a first-name basis.

"Why you early today, boo?" Candy asked, leaning closer and taking a whiff of Jimmy.

"Rough day today, Candy. A couple on Benevida won't sell for anything less than four hundred thousand. Took two hours to get them down to three fifty. And then the fucking buyer bailed because it was still too expensive."

"Sounds rough," Candy said, squeezing his hand and playing with the ring on his finger.

Nora looked around the bar, her astral face wet with tears, to see if anyone else was noticing this. But the bar, it seemed, was empty now. Strange. When she'd entered it, there were a couple patrons. Where had they gone now?

"What are we doing today?" Jimmy asked, making Nora's heart sink even further. Not her heart. Whatever was the soul-adjacent to the organ that pumped blood. Her heart chakra? It just hurt when she looked at him, eying her pink G-string when she bent over and picked up the bottle cap of the beer he'd just opened. It hurt even more when she heard him moan at the sight of her big ass.

"Anything you want, baby," Candy said, winking at him in the mirror behind the bar.

"Nurse my beer for me, will you? I gotta hit the john. You know what they say, you don't buy alcohol," Jimmy said, heading over to the bathroom.

"Yeah, yeah, you rent it," Candy said, giggling at him, taking a sip out of his beer for him to see. He blew her a kiss as he went inside the bathroom, and what choice did Nora have other than to follow?

It appeared that her husband really did need to urinate. She floated over to him, standing in the stall, and saw that he was sporting a massive erection. Eyes closed, he was doing that thing he used to do to get rid of his hard-on back in the day.

While he was standing there, eyes closed, Candy crept inside the bathroom.

"Stay away from him!" Nora yelled. She could either go back to her body, wake herself up, and drive all the way downtown to confront the two of them, or she could watch. Watch the ways in which her husband was being pleased. The ways in which she could not please him because she was no longer a petite, tight-assed, big-breasted young woman but a pudgy, dead-skinned, depressed one. This Candy, though, was the living symbol of sex and eroticism with her ribbed crop top, her lithe body, and her dark skin exuding exuberance.

She reached a hand around and grabbed his cock, stroking it while planting kisses on the back of his neck. Her free hand busied itself exploring the topography of Jimmy's beefy hairy torso, slipping inside the shirt, feeling his dad bod, feeling his hair.

Jimmy moaned, his cock growing stiffer, but he was always one about control. Control was more pleasurable to him than pleasure itself. He wheeled around, freeing himself from Candy's grasp, and pinned her to the adjacent wall, kissing her lips, her cheeks, her neck ravenously, his hand shooting down her jeans, resting itself between her thighs, feeling the warmth, the wetness.

Nora stared helplessly as he got down to his knees, never minding that it was the floor of a dive bar, and pulled down her jeans. She hoped that at any given moment someone would barge in through the bathroom door and put a stop to this extramarital madness.

No one came. And even if they did, the door was locked from the inside.

Jimmy turned Candy around and pinned her to the wall. With her jeans down by her knees, he had his hands on her ass, squeezing it, gently pulling it apart, and inserting his face in between, sniffing her panties, breathing between her thighs. He slowly pushed his tongue inside, flicking it against the string of her thong. Candy moaned, her legs quivering as Jimmy's hands found her breasts and pulled them out of her ribbed crop top. Then his hands traveled back to her supple cheeks and pulled them apart so he could taste her better.

Now that he was done with her rear, he turned her over again and pulled her panties to the side, sinking his mouth into her vagina.

"Fucking...sweet...pussy," Jimmy moaned between breaths, and then dove back in, licking ravenously, sticking his tongue against the clitoral hood, and then lowering it to her vulva, gently probing.

Candy was now moaning louder with pleasure, her thighs shaking as she came. Jimmy kept kissing her inner thigh as she came, and then, right before the big fireworks, he stuck his finger inside and watched her eyes turn white with blind pleasure.

Nora flew out of the bar, the pain, the sorrow, and the jealousy all too much for her to bear.

"Okay, that was fuckin' hot," Jimmy mused to Candy as they sat back at the bar. "Y'know, obviously, I got a wife, and I can't be—" But Candy cut him off.

"Listen, buddy, you're a hot sweet piece of ass, and that dick is all I'm interested in. No need to be tellin' me all about ya bizniss."

"Sweet, real sweet," Jimmy replied, smiling while putting the bottle back to his lips.

"Now, if ya wanna ever shoot the shit with me, tell me about your woes; that's what a three-clock beer in an empty bar is for, and, honey, I'm always here." Candy felt like she had upset him with her non-emotional response, and she wanted Jimmy to know that she really did like him, she just wasn't interested in ruining his marriage.

"Well now, ain't that nice." Jimmy looked sheepishly up at Candy. "I dunno, man, it's tough. She ain't the woman I married. She's changed, and I get blamed for having an expectation and a standard. I'm just not attracted to her anymore. The body stuff, that I could deal with; sure, I like smaller women, but ain't like I couldn't deal with it. It's her mind, her mind has shifted in a different direction. I wake up and wonder what personality I'm gon' be dealin' with today!"

Jimmy spilled more than he had intended to, but he'd been drinking at Candy's bar for months now, and he felt somewhat acquainted.

"Well, look, people change, things change, and lives change. This is normal, and to be honest, honey, I'd do the same thing! My man wasn't givin' me the attention I deserved, so I left him." Jimmy started to feel more relaxed; he wasn't expecting Candy to react in this way or even say much at all to him after their bathroom encounter.

Nora had exited the bar from the front door, but instead of exiting into the street, she appeared at their second home on Brandt Street. It was always meant to be the retirement plan. Jimmy had bought the Alameda home so that its value would appreciate over time, and when it ripened, they'd sell it and shift to the one on Brandt, which was bigger, better, and had an amazing view of the countryside. Just on the edge of town and yet close enough to downtown for a quick grocery run. It was also a fixer-upper, so there was no reason to ever go there, and Nora couldn't stand construction work.

It also housed infidelity.

The street was foggy and dark. Nora stood across from her home, streetlamps illuminated the other homes that looked lifeless and empty.

As she stared at her house on Brandt, the front door slowly opened, beckoning her inside.

She was terrified. Looking around, she could see nothing other than bleak, dark, empty homes, each terrifying and intimidating in their own measure.

She walked cautiously across the street and stopped at the gate. Inside, blackness, and as much as a witch she was, this was new territory. Her powers were useless down here; after all, she was already using one of them, and conjuring during astral projection was not something she had mastered.

She turned around and stepped back from the open door, not daring to step inside. But behind her, something was coming. She turned back toward the door, peering into the blackness, taking a gulp.

The fog in the street moved faster down here, and the streetlamps that glared through them offered a window into any shapes that may appear.

One such shape was walking slowly in the middle of the street, its large bulging eyes and dagger smile could be seen cutting through the mist. Its claws scratching the concrete below it. The shape became more apparent.

The beast was like nothing Nora had ever witnessed, its large body covered in black fur. It strolled slowly, confidently, with malice. A bob in its step indicated it was in no rush to chase its prey, for if it needed to, no one could escape its chase.

It was looking at Nora as it was getting closer to the house, whispering her name. "Norrrrra, come back to the street, Nora." It was smiling, teasing her.

Nora let out a cry and ran inside the house, slamming the door shut.

The windows to the side of the front door allowed a limited view outside, and as Nora frantically looked out, the beast was nowhere to be seen.

Scurrying down the hallway, she looked behind her, and as she reached the door to the basement, she saw it. The creature was looking through the window, smiling at her.

She gripped the doorknob in a panic and pulled it open, jumping inside and slamming the door shut behind her, collapsing to the floor in tears.

Please, help, get me out of here. Lilly, if you are there, please help me.

The front door to the house started to open, and it prompted Nora to run farther down the stairs into the dark, bleak basement.

The house was dark, it creaked, and everything was covered in dust sheets. The basement of this house was typical Americana from the eighties: wood-clad walls, a green carpet, and a dark elusive nature from the lack of natural sunlight coming in.

And the red room.

Red because the light that shone from under the door whenever she visited that house was always the color of blood, and when she asked her husband about the room, he said that it was a surprise and he did not want to ruin it.

"Trust me, babe," he'd said during one of the house tours. And trust him she had.

Nora turned on the light hanging from the ceiling, which quickly relieved the darkness she had endured on the surface. She walked toward the basement hallway, a rare hallway that housed various rooms on each side and spanned the entire length of the house. Whoever built this thing did so for some apocalyptic purpose!

As she walked farther, she heard a new noise which momentarily suspended her fear of the animal upstairs that had followed her.

Why did it chase me into the basement? she thought.

The noise was undoubtedly Jimmy; he was huffing, moaning, and slapping.

Nora slowly walked toward the room, looking up and behind her for any reference to the beast. The noise from the room became louder with each footstep, and as she got to the room, she slowly opened the door. And there inside, Jimmy was fucking Candy, her body tied down to a pommel horse-type equipment, her pants down to her ankles, and a ball gag in her mouth.

"You like that? You fucking whore!" Jimmy grunted.

Candy moaned in approval.

Whimpering and sobbing, Nora ran out and up the stairs. She didn't care about the beast that was waiting for her outside anymore. This was all too real. Not to mention the taste of puke in her mouth. What was the point of being in her astral body, she wondered amidst the cacophony blaring in her mind.

The beast was gone, and she ran back to the street, screaming, hoping someone would hear her. For now, she wasn't sure where she was trapped. Was it Jimmy's mind, or her own?

There had to be a reason why Nora was here. Why was she now in town in a gray expanse? A town filled with fog, with no people?

Then it ran past her.

"Hello?" Nora spun around, hearing the scuttering of it across the street. Tears had filled her eye sockets, fear almost paralyzing her.

Above her, the flapping of wings. *A bird? That was too big to be a bird.*

At this very moment, being back in the basement would have been a reprieve from wherever she was. For wherever she was wasn't home.

More flapping above her.

Something was wrong, very wrong, and Nora had left herself believing that this couldn't be real. *Is this Lilly's doing?* Whatever was happening right now only happened after Lilly had cursed her with this gift.

Nora started to run softly, as to not let anyone hear her. But before she could pick up speed, she saw the creature that was scuttling earlier, waiting in a doorway of another house.

She froze.

It looked in Nora's direction and smiled menacingly at her once more.

A step to the right, Nora tried to conjure any magic available to her, but nothing worked.

The creature mimicked her with each step she took, its gaze following. Smiling as if to let her know she was about to be devoured.

The noise above caught her off guard, and she stumbled to the ground. She looked up, but they weren't wings, dragons, or anything that she imagined. The Collectors were flying around her frantically, their robes mimicking the noise of something flapping.

What in the fuck is going on? she said to herself.

Swoosh, one flew over her. Swoosh, another, swoosh, then another.

Nora had no idea what these beings were, but the Collectors only called when death was near or when they wanted something, and she was in a realm that was in between. It wasn't the Axis Mundi, it was a realm of torture and evil.

She looked back to the doorway where the creature was standing, but it wasn't there anymore. And as she got up to her feet, she felt the heavy breathing on her neck.

She turned around to see the demon.

Screaming, she ran as fast as she could, leaving the demon for dust. She ran so fast and so quick that she could barely comprehend what was happening. Given her larger size of late, she wondered how she did it all. Her magic was returning.

She ran all the way, two miles, to Alameda Avenue and her house, where a different woman and different children ran outside the front door, waiving off a different man of the house for the day. *Who is this family?*

Ignoring the commotion in front of her, she ran into the house, turning left into her living room. The beast that was chasing her was gone. Instead, a new fear greeted her. A man in a suit was sitting down in the armchair by the fire.

"Well, hello, Nora. I've been expecting you. My name is Lucifer."

THERE IS a level of fear beyond screaming, beyond wetting yourself. It's when your body jams up and renders you unable to move, your skin turns pale, and your vocal cords turn to stone. Try as you might to fathom that scale of fear, but there is nothing that can be done about it other than staring into the unending abyss of madness.

Thrown back into her body, Nora lay drenched in sweat, unmoving, unbreathing, her heart rate jacked to a hundred, noticing her husband lying beside her, sleeping, snoring.

For most people suffering from bipolar disorder, there is always that one tipping point, that one thing that breaks the camel's back and sends them into a manic episode.

For Nora, it was coming face to face with the Devil in the astral realm.

Not to mention, it made no sense to her that when she woke, the very husband whom she had seen anally penetrate the bartender was lying oblivious beside her, as deeply asleep as he could be.

Was it just a dream? Or was that astral journey real?

With the onset of mania, you could never tell. Least of all, if the Devil who came to greet you was as real as death or just another figment of your chemically imbalanced mind.

Witches' Sabbath

"I'm telling you!" Nora spoke sharply, her face covered in sweat and tears. "The witch has brought the Devil here."

"I knew it!" Linda snapped. "I had the craziest dream last night too."

All the other women who listened to her account did so with pursed lips and pin-drop silence, deferring to their de-facto leader's judgment; after all, who knew the Devil better than the woman who was a staunch Christian, the woman who had told them time and again to refrain from learning magic from the witch?

Each of the women had been busy using their newfound magic since they had been blessed (or cursed) with the ability, and it was usually for more selfish reasons. The fog had started to lift from the town, and it prompted the women to get out and do things and, of course, to test their magic.

A MAJOR GRIPE of Evelyn's was bad drivers. She would aggressively honk at anyone who broke the speed limit, even by ten miles an hour. "*Children play in this fucking street!*" she would holler after them, them being oblivious to her anger.

Driving down the 495 freeway one afternoon brought on such rage, when a driver who thought the HOV lane meant *I can go however fast the fuck I want* was riding Evelyn's tail. The F150 truck tailed her aggressively because she wouldn't move out of the way, flashing his lights. When Evelyn refused to budge, the truck sped up around to move in front of her, slamming his brakes to check her, almost causing her to crash.

Her car slammed on her breaks for her, making it veer violently from left to right.

But the truck driver had another thing coming. For with a mere wave of her hand, Evelyn steered the driver out of her way and to the right of her on the freeway. As she slowed the truck down, she came face to face with the driver. He looked at her in shock as he was trying to figure out why his truck was driving itself.

Evelyn's Tesla took over the driving for her and she turned to stare at the aggressive driver to her right. As they locked eyes, she held up her hands and then scrunched them into fists, simultaneously watching as the truck driver's fingers broke in several places.

The driver screamed, but his truck kept moving.

Then, with another wave of her hand, the driver's face smashed against his steering wheel, not once, not twice, but three times, shattering his nose and sending blood splattering across his dash.

Evelyn released her hold; the man's hands, now badly mangled, couldn't steer. The F150 rocketed forward at breakneck speed, losing its course, and in the rearview mirror Evelyn saw the chaos unfold like a nightmare vision—vehicles swerving violently, trying to avoid the uncontrollable truck. It was futile; the truck clipped a sedan, triggering a catastrophic chain reaction.

Metal crunched and glass shattered, filling the air with the terror of the unexpected. A fuel tank burst, flames erupted, painting the night sky with orange fury. Screams pierced the air, a chilling symphony of horror, as the inferno consumed everything in its path. Evelyn drove on, the screams echoing in her mind, a haunting reminder of the devastation left behind.

LINDA HAD an air of haughtiness about her as she sat at the head of the table, listening to Nora's account about her husband's cheating and the appearance of the beast, Lucifer, and the Collectors. The way Nora had described everything, Linda was inclined to believe her. And yet, Nora, while in one of her moods, was never one to be trusted blindly. They all knew this as plain as day.

"Goes to show how much Lilly knows," Linda scoffed. "Teaching astral magic to the hothead in the group. Of course you're going to end up seeing the Devil. It's the Devil who imposes anger upon us. Or have you never read the Bible?"

"I have!" Nora snapped. "You fucking lunatic, are you listening to what I'm saying?"

Linda shook her head.

"There is an easy solution to all of this. Your husband built that depraved space within the basement of that house. Or so you say. If we want to ascertain the truth behind your statements, we need only go visit that house, see that room. If it's indeed a torture vault, as you so called it, it means that your visions were factual. Astral or not. And if it's just an ordinary room, then it was just a dream. Make note, Nora, that you mentioned your husband was asleep with you in bed when you woke up. It's not above you to make an attention play. After all, after Maggie's, yours is the most mundane magic trick that Lilly taught. Perhaps this is your way of tempting us to learn some astral projection in exchange for teaching you one of our spells?"

If Nora wasn't sitting at the other end of the table, she might have leaped forward and slapped Linda across the face, but she kept herself calm through deliberation. Linda was right. The only way to make sure that it was real was to head down to Brandt, go into the basement of that house, and see for herself.

"Tonight then," Nora said. "Jim went there in the evening. All this time, I used to think that he was going for a drink. I see now that he's going for the bartender." It hurt her threefold now that she was in her body, a body capable of feeling betrayed, torn, alone.

"I can't believe you don't have his location on your phone!" Sophia chimed in.

"You know, since this damn fog, none of our locations have been working, woman!" Nora responded.

"You want us to catch him in the act?" Jennifer asked, suppressing her pleasure.

Nora nodded, her mania taking over.

"And then what?" Linda asked.

"Kill that cunt whore woman and that son of a bitch," Nora spoke, but these were not her words. She had finally given in to the rage that had consumed her all her life. Only now, there was something she could do about it other than suppress it.

Evelyn smirked.

~

Seven women dressed in black walked in a line down Brandt Street, the waning sun casting long silhouettes in the animated fog all around them. Linda led them down the street, knowing that this was as good a time as any to gain the favor of the rest of the women and get them to see things her way. But it all hinged on the accuracy of Nora's account.

Why was the Devil here? Linda wondered, then thought, *What does it matter why? The fact is, if Nora's right, then the Devil is here, and we've all been deceived by the witch to think that our magic is benign. If she's working with the Devil, and if the Devil's dropping hints that he's been expecting us, then she has us in her lure, and we're not just coven members to her. We might be a sacrifice, an offering to the fallen prince, ripe for the plucking.*

Her first instinct about Lilly had been correct, and hopefully it was not too late to make the others see sense.

The women stepped inside the house one by one, Sophia nodding at the garage, indicating with whispers that Jimmy's car was parked inside. As they entered the home, all seven of them tiptoed so as not to make a sound. Evelyn pointed below, to the sounds coming from the basement, and mouthed, *Oh my fucking god, it's true!* Dull thumps and the muffled sound of screams. The basement wasn't as soundproof as Jim thought it was.

Nora's heart wasn't one to sink any longer. There was just billowing rage waiting to be let out. She slowly opened the door to the basement and led the coven down the stairs; so as not to disturb them in the act and give way for any excuses, they quickly pranced to the red room and kicked open the door.

"Versatile little fuck, aren't you?" Nora seethed, stepping into the room, the rest of the women following suit.

Before either of them could budge, before Jim could remove his cock from Candy's mouth, Charlotte cast a petrification spell upon them both, freezing them in this position. Their eyes could still move, terrified eyes studying the faces of the vengeful witches gathered in the room, but the rest of their bodies were frozen in the middle of the act. Candy's eyes bulged with the length of Jim's cock still inside her mouth, her face growing redder as she could not draw breath. She was strapped to the pommel horse as it was, and the spell did nothing but further cement her to the equipment. The expression of fear, shame, and how-do-I-get-out-of-this was still smattered across Jim's face.

"That means one thing," Linda said, ignoring the two and walking around the room, looking at all the perverted items hanging from the wall. "You weren't lying, Nora."

"The question remains, what do we do about your husband?" Jennifer asked, walking over to Jim, placing a hand on the nape of his neck.

"He's no husband to me. He stopped being my husband the day he broke our vows," Nora said, her tone dry, her mind numb.

She watched as Candy's face turned from red to purple, and from purple to a deep maroon. Nora walked over to her and bent down to meet her face to face. Candy was struggling and trying to move; the panic had set in, and tears were streaming from her eyes, her throat making any noise it could in an attempt to scream for help. But it was no use. Candy's eyes rolled back in her head, and vomit started to protrude from her mouth, soaking Jimmy's appendage.

Jimmy screamed any noise he could at the women to stop, but it was too late, the vomit went back down into Candy's lungs and she passed out from the suffocation. A suffocation that would lead to her death.

She stopped moving, and Charlotte did not lift her spell.

Not for another ten whole minutes, until Evelyn and Linda had gotten a hold of enough cuffs and leashes and had set up a chair to subdue Jimmy.

Charlotte snapped her fingers and let them go.

Candy collapsed on the pommel horse, breathless, lifeless, the last few minutes of her existence spent desecrating her body, first voluntarily, then involuntarily.

Jimmy screamed as he, naked from the waist down, was propelled backward.

"Candy!" he gasped.

Sophia, Linda, and Evelyn tied him to the chair, while the others stood around him.

"Still Candy after all this?!" Nora shouted, putting her heel on Jim's chest and digging. "Who is Candy to you that I couldn't be? Your cute little twisted fuck that you could plow behind my back?"

He wanted to speak, but the fear stopped him from making anything other than muffled groans and grunts, tears streaking down his face.

"I trusted you, motherfucker!" Nora yelled, digging her heel deep into Jimmy's chest, drawing blood. "Trusted you to take care of me, and this is how you repay me?"

Linda stepped forward and started to conjure static from her fingers.

There was great pleading in Jimmy's eyes as Nora, enraptured by a mix of wrath and mania, stepped back and allowed Linda to send a bolt of electricity into his body.

Jimmy shook violently, surging from the thousands of volts that coursed through his body. He shook one final time, and then, while the blood was still spouting from his orifices, lay dead in the chair.

"Thank God the carpet was already red," Linda remarked.

"What have you done?!" Maggie, who had been standing in the back, too meek to say something, too outnumbered to do anything, gasped upon the finality of the act the group had committed.

"Shut up," Nora said, looking at Maggie. "Or you're next."

"Enough. Not one of our own," Jennifer said, taking Nora's hand and pushing it down to her side.

"Then who?" Nora groaned, her voice coming out twisted from her throat. She fell into the hug that Jennifer had ready for her. Jennifer patted her back as she stood beside the corpse of her husband and the whore he'd been fucking all this time.

"I believe it's time to pay the witch on the hill a visit," Linda said, and the rest, all but Maggie, nodded.

"What's the point? She's not even there," Sophia said. Sophia, who had, in the course of the last month alone, added several zeroes to her bank account with the spell she had been taught. Sophia, who now had more gold in her dresser than all of Bridgewater combined. Sophia, who wondered where the real good spellbooks were that Lilly was hiding, and what magic was written in there, waiting to be learned.

It was time to take magic into their own hands.

"I saw her drive up last night," Jennifer said.

"Enough of this trickle-down witch economy. We're going to take what's ours and confront her about what she's doing to this town, bringing the Devil in our midst," Linda said.

"This stopped being about the Devil when you all decided to murder two people," Maggie said quietly, standing in the doorway. "You're going to kill her, aren't you?"

"What are you still doing here?!" Linda snapped, sending a lightning bolt at Maggie. Maggie conjured forth a shield and avoided getting hit, but hit herself against the doorframe. She fell unconscious and slumped to the floor.

"Leave her. We've got more important things to deal with," Jennifer said before Linda could cast one final spell on Maggie to make sure she was dead.

"Are you the one calling the shots?" Linda asked, her hand crackling with lightning.

"Enough," Charlotte said, freezing the both of them. "If we're turning on each other, we're no better than that bitch who burned all her townsfolk. We do not harm one of our own."

She let the two women go, who lowered their hands and deepened their breaths, calming themselves down. They promptly left the basement, leaving Maggie lying there unconscious along with the dead bodies.

It wasn't until they had all gotten out of the house that they heard the Collectors.

"This is what I was telling you about!" Nora squealed, pointing at the shadow of the shrouded being beyond the clouds, lurking, weaving in and out of the fog and the clouds as cover, circling them, eyeing them.

"You're not alone this time, Nor," Jennifer said, holding her hand. "We're all in this together."

THEY DROVE, aware of the presence tailing them, and came to a halt at Jennifer's place. Linda's basement was a no-go. It served as storage for all her old stuff. Jennifer, on the other hand, had an empty basement which her husband had forever been meaning to turn into some sort of a man cave, a desperate cry for help from a man experiencing the agony of midlife crisis. But as with all agonizing things and one's resolution to resolve them, her husband hadn't gotten around to building the basement.

It was entirely empty, lit by four bulbs on each wall. The air in there was damp and cold, but lately, what wasn't damp and cold given all this fog?

"Why are we here?" Charlotte asked, looking around at the eerie basement with the concrete walls and the opaque egress windows.

"It's been expecting Nora, hasn't it?" Linda said, thinking hard. "What's to say that it hasn't been expecting the rest of us?"

"Who are we talking about?!" Evelyn wailed. Clearly, they could not mean the Devil. Things had taken a very exponential turn, and now it felt like everything was out of her hands. But she was complicit. Just like every other woman in the basement. For all it mattered, they had murdered Nora's husband and the whore he was breeding.

"Shut it, Eve. Shut it, Charlotte," Nora said, sweat on her forehead, her hands shaking, and her face pale. "What do we do?

"I think...we summon him," Jennifer said, an understanding dawning on her face.

"Summon the Devil in Bridgewater?" Linda asked incredulously.

Outside, the fog rolled and turned this poor impression of a day into an even darker shade, making it hard for them to discern what time it was. They had left the scene of the crime in the evening, and yet the haze outside suggested that it could be anywhere between twilight and dawn.

All of the women suddenly got a serious sense of vertigo, as if this reality was distorting, making them remember details from their lives that they had no recollection of. Their husbands weeping. The faces of their children sullen with grief. Not memories, but visions of darkness and gloom.

In each of their hearts, the ladies felt such misery as they had never felt before. And before they could so much as join hands and form a circle, the presence that had been lurking outside, peering through the egress windows with its infernal gaze, manifested itself in the basement.

"Where else would you summon me?" the Devil asked, a great beast of a thing covered in a dark coat of fur, his form that of a blend of man and animal. The head, that of a goat, bore massive curling horns spiraling toward the heavens, their black texture gleaming in the dim light of the basement.

Abysmal eyes peered at them, glowing with the ancient malevolence of loss and knowledge, reflecting the void of time itself.

His body was bare, revealing sinewy muscles under the fur. His arms ended in claws that glistened like obsidian, sharp enough to tear flesh.

Below the waist, his form was more animalistic, legs ending in cloven hooves clacking against the floor.

He looked at them with a deep and charged gaze, looking around the room with amusement on his face.

"Summon? No need to summon me. I am already here," he spoke, dousing the basement in darkness, drawing the black abyss of nothingness outside the windows until the only light that remained in the room was his deep red aura shining on the haunted faces of each of the women standing around him. "And I come bearing alms."

"Wha..." Jennifer couldn't begin to speak.

"Why are you here?" Linda, trying to summon her love for Christ and the Lord Father, failed in the face of the Devil, realizing that if there were a Christ and God in her heart, they had long since ditched it when she had trespassed. Murdered. Usurped.

"You're my favorite!" Satan said, his forked tongue rolling out of his ghastly mouth.

"What do you want from us?" Evelyn asked.

"Want? I want nothing. I am only here to guide you. Help you, even." The Devil chuckled, a sound that sent chills down their spines.

"Guide us to what?" Sophia asked.

"You'd like to know, wouldn't you?" The Devil licked his lips. "And I will tell you. Power. The power that you all crave. The power that you deserve. I can tell you how to grasp it. It's yours for the taking. But there is one holding you back. Someone who's preventing you from becoming the witches you're meant to be."

"Lilly," Charlotte whispered, the realization sinking in.

"Yes," the Devil sneered. "The Bridgewater Witch. She's been lying to you. Withholding the truth about yourselves. She is not all that she seems, and intelligent women that you are, you're already beginning to see it."

"Yes," whispered Jennifer.

"What would happen if we killed her? Can we even kill her? She's too powerful," Linda said.

"That's why you're my favorite. Asking the right questions," the Devil said admiringly, then placed his arm upon her shoulder, drawing her close. He whispered in her ear, "You can kill her. All six of you combined can take down that whore. And once you do, you shall feel the power of magic surge into your bodies. Unstoppable, each and every one of you. No longer will you feel the need for spells, nor will you have to memorize magic like schoolgirls. You will wish it, and it shall happen. It is yours for the taking, if you only do what is needed."

Linda's eyes had gone blank, as had all their eyes. The Devil was showing them a vision where they were each as powerful as Lilly

Frost herself, harnessing the elements, weaving magic as they pleased.

As swiftly as he had arrived, the Devil disappeared, leaving fumes of sulfur in the wake of his absence. The room fell silent again, the weight of the choice looming over them as thickly as the fog outside.

"You've already taken the first step. Now, finish what you started." His voice lingered in the cold basement, making them all realize that there was no turning back now.

Until The End

A storm crackled overhead, bringing on the chariot of the blackest clouds, rolling on thunder, the wind blowing every tree slanted, the crimson leaves of fall blowing in the havoc that ensued. The fog, sentient, snaked along every street of Bridgewater, holding its own despite the storm. It acted in accordance with the tempest weaving itself around Bridgewater, weaving, hazing everything out as the six witches of Alameda Avenue embarked up the hill for the last time, their eyes dark, their minds fractured with power.

Linda raised an authoritative hand in the air, commanding the storm to do her bidding. A streak of lightning came crashing through the dark sky, falling with fire and fury upon the witch's house, setting it aflame. Walls came crumbling down as the house imploded upon contact with the lightning.

"Come out, come out, witch!" Linda yelled, laughing maniacally.

Jennifer rose into the air and scouted the surroundings. The severity of the storm made it impossible to see anything, but the silhouette of the woman coming out of the burning wreckage of her house was hard to miss, seeing as how that woman was protected by an orb of light around her.

"She's here," Jennifer said.

"You are a woman short," Lilly said matter-of-factly, as if she was taking a stroll in a park and had come across her college clique instead of six women adamant on killing her.

"We're thinning the herd," Evelyn said. "The weak get culled."

"You have all come undone," Lilly said, casting a powerful spell to bring Jennifer back down from the sky. She stood facing the six women in the same place where she had first met them. "In Wiccan laws, there is no blasphemy greater than turning upon your own coven."

"Save your precious laws for yourself," Charlotte spat, casting her magic with both her hands, putting all her will and strength behind it, rooting Lilly to her spot on the front lawn. Behind her, her house burned. Around them, the storm raged on. The surface of the lake resembled a boiling cauldron, the water boiling, the waves roiling. "We've come to take what's rightfully ours."

"Thank you, Charlotte," Linda said, circling the unmoving witch. "We have decided that we're not going to do things your way. Not when you're inviting the Devil in our midst."

"What?" Lilly asked, effortlessly breaking free from Charlotte's spell.

Linda gasped and stepped back, shooting an angry glare at Charlotte. Charlotte cast her magic again, but to no avail. This made the women reconsider what they were about to do.

"You brought Satan in our midst. Nora saw her in her astral visions," Linda said. "What do you intend to do with Bridgewater? Barter the souls of its residents for eternal fame and glory?"

"Nora? Did you see the Devil?" Lilly asked, walking over to her.

"STAY AWAY FROM ME!" Nora yelled, and performed the first spell Lilly had taught, levitating her and throwing her against the wreckage of her burning home.

"You think that you can tame us like we're your horses," Jennifer said, lifting herself off the ground once again. "That you'll divide and conquer, give us a spell each like we're unruly children in a class and you're trying to teach us something about ourselves. Hell no. We kill you, we get your magic for ourselves. We become unstoppable."

"All that power, and you're so greedily hoarding it without sharing it with us," Evelyn said. Together, the women stepped forward, their clothes flailing in the torrential wind, their bodies wet with the downpour. They surrounded Lilly once more, leaving no room to escape.

"You don't understand," Lilly coughed, wiping blood from her face. She helped herself to her feet, but Linda reached forward, delivered a powerful kick to her face, and made her fall back down.

"No, *you* don't understand. This is not your town. Bridgewater is ours. You do not get to strut about, you do not get to be some mystical sage imparting magical wisdom at your whim. You should have been burned the day they tied you to the stake," Linda said, spitting on Lilly's face. "Oh well, no time better than the present."

"You don't have to do this," Lilly whispered, her nose broken, her teeth shattered. "This was just a test."

"Yeah, right. Another in the long list of Lilly Frost's great and unquestionable teaching methods? Was it a test when Nora saw her husband fucking that bartender whore? What was the test, Lilly?" Linda screamed in a high pitch, her face utterly deranged. And she was not alone. The rest of the coven—if it could still be called that at this point—was just as unhinged, standing atop Lilly with their malevolent faces.

"Kill her," Sophia said, drenched in rain, consumed by the flames of her depraved desire.

"Kill her, and we get her powers for our own," Evelyn concurred.

"The coven's called a vote, Ms. Frost," Jennifer sneered.

"And you're not going to be leading us anymore." Charlotte stomped on Lilly's hand, crunching her bones. "Enough with your slow-burn magic, your whimsy."

"And what?" Lilly laughed, spitting blood and wincing in pain. "She's going to lead you?"

They all looked to Linda, who did not hesitate in delivering another kick to Lilly's battered face.

"Who says we need anyone to lead us?" Linda yelled. "We'll teach ourselves magic. We'll ransack your house. We'll get our hands on the books you've got."

"That house?" Lilly pointed the fingers of her broken hand at the house burning behind her. "Good luck."

"Fuck you!" Linda yelled, and brought forth three angry red bolts of lightning from the sky, each of them striking Lilly with brute ferocity, charring her body, smiting her deeper and deeper into the burned ground. And the lightning did not stop. The bolts came flying from the sky and crashed into Lilly's blackened body.

The ground where she lay was now a four-foot-deep crater marked by the smoke and flames where the lighting had hit, and the corpse of the Bridgewater witch.

"Is she dead?" Nora asked.

"What do you think?" Charlotte laughed.

"I think we can't take any risks. Eve," Jennifer said.

"I'm on it."

Evelyn summoned six pairs of sharp daggers while Linda and Sophia dragged Lilly's soot-blackened body out of the crater.

Together, the women began hacking away at her body, ripping away limbs, slashing away at her unbeating, unbreathing organs, cutting her down into smaller pieces.

"Do you feel it?" Linda asked, stepping back, her hands covered in ash, blood, and viscera. "Do you feel more powerful already?!"

"I do!" Evelyn laughed, and laughed so hard that she began to cry.

As did the rest of the women as they became enraptured in the ecstasy of unbridled magical power coursing through their bodies. They took their gore-covered hands and rubbed them on their faces, ran them down their necks, touched each other with the tainted remains of the dead witch.

"Burn what remains of her," Linda commanded, and to her surprise, Charlotte, who was still weeping with joy and frenzied madness, made flames appear out of thin air, realizing—like the rest of them—the true extent of her powers. They no longer needed spell-work to perform magic. Such was the power that they had siphoned from the dead witch that they only needed to think, and it was happening.

They formed a circle around the cut-up remains of the witch and set her appendages on fire.

"Enough of this," Jennifer yelled as she waved a domineering hand above her, causing the storm to end abruptly, no more wind blowing, no more clouds on the horizon, the night becoming still, wet, the remnants of the fog retreating away from the hill.

With the storm subdued, the women once again performed their intuitive magic, setting her tattered corpse on fire.

They stood around her for the longest time, watching the flames turn into embers until nothing but ash remained.

"Spread her ashes at the lake," Linda commanded, and Nora was the first one to oblige. She raised her hand, manipulating all the ash to rise in the air like a swarm of bats, and directed it toward the lake.

The women, with their senses heightened and their magic uninhibited, watched the ashes soar across the slopes of the hill and down toward the lake until they came into contact with the water.

And here they sank, the last vestiges of Lilly Frost.

7

THE AFTERMATH

The Aftermath

Jennifer never enjoyed a tardy libation.

Neither did the rest of the group when it came to day drinking.

The women sat in Linda's living room three days after the events at the house atop the hill. The town, with all its stores, houses, diners, restaurants, and streets, was still enveloped in fog.

"Can't you do something about it?" Linda asked casually, bringing the '32 Macallan bottle out from the shelf. This was not the one her father had given her. This was the one Lilly had given her as part of her bequeathing.

"I tried," Jennifer said. "But the fog doesn't budge."

"No matter," Linda said, nodding at all the books on the table that they had salvaged from Lilly's house. The ones that the fire didn't touch. "There's got to be a spell somewhere in there, and together, we'll find it. No more fog in Bridgewater for the rest of our days."

She poured doubles in each of the women's glasses, even Maggie's, who was sitting at the edge of the table, frozen stiff by Charlotte's spell. Charlotte had granted Maggie a bit of leeway in that she could move her head and talk and breathe, but no more than that.

“Cheers,” Linda said, raising her glass.

“Why aren’t you joining, Maggie?” Nora asked, and then burst out laughing.

“You are all reprehensible, each one more than the other,” Maggie sobbed. “Why am I here?!”

“Because whether you like it or not, you’re a part of our coven. And stop with your whining. Don’t tell me you don’t feel stronger now that she’s dead,” Jennifer said, downing her shot and feeling nothing. The rest of the women also felt none of the scalding that they’d anticipated when they drank the shot.

“Hmm, guess she wasn’t all that rich, was she?” Linda said, looking at the bottle. “This feels like honey water.”

“Why did you kill her?!” Maggie sobbed.

“You want to join her?” Charlotte asked, cracking her knuckles.

“Come now, Charlotte. She’s just upset,” Evelyn said. “Give her a couple days, and then she’ll be fine. Barring that, nothing like a beating from her husband to get her back in line.”

“Ooh,” Nora said. “Do you know she’s sworn off magic? Won’t use a spell to save her hide.”

“Maggie,” Linda said, shaking her head. “Why do we even keep you around?”

“Come on, guys,” Sophia said. “Leave her be.”

“What’s with this weak whiskey?” Linda took another sip from the bottle and spat it on the table.

“Hey! I’m sitting here!” Jennifer yelled. “You ruined my top. Great.”

The bottle turned to ash in Linda’s hands, ash that fell in great clumps upon the table.

Startled, Linda stepped back, looking around at the table.

The rest of the women shook their heads. This was not their doing. No tricks were being played by any of them.

Maggie laughed.

“What’s so funny?!” Linda snapped.

"Serves you right," Maggie said. "You kill a witch, you get cursed."

"Jenn, show me that ring," Linda said, pointing at the ruby ring Jennifer was wearing, the one Lilly had gifted to her.

"Why? It's mine," Jennifer said, pulling her hand away.

"You can have it, just let me take a look at it!" Linda said impatiently.

"I don't think I want to," Jennifer said, and before she could say anything else, the ring, like the bottle of whiskey, turned to dust and slipped off her finger.

"What the hell?" Evelyn cried out, standing up. The Mughal Era bracelets she was wearing—gifts from Lilly—turned into black dust, that dust trailing off her wrists.

"What kind of trick is this?" Charlotte asked, worried.

"One that she's playing from beyond the grave. Don't you see? She bought our allegiance with fake gifts!" Linda remarked, dusting her hands free of the ash and soot on her fingers. "Goes to show we made the right choice."

"And what of the Devil?" Nora asked, looking worried and afraid.

"We didn't make any deals with him. With Lilly dead, I don't think he's going to bother us," Linda said.

"Or maybe it would incentivize him to seek us out again," Evelyn said, stepping back from the table, forgetting what she was saying as all of them saw what was unfolding before their eyes.

All the books they had taken from Lilly's house started to implode into dust and ash one by one, all that soot falling off the table and onto the immaculate hardwood floor.

"No!" Linda said, kneeling and trying to pick up the dust. "Those were all the spellbooks. They couldn't have been fake, could they?"

"Err..." Jennifer said. "I...I can't fly."

"What?! You're thinking of flying at this time? We got bigger concerns!" Nora grunted.

"I mean I can't do my magic anymore," Jennifer said with great desperation in her voice.

The rest of the women tried to do their bits of magic. Evelyn tried to conjure something but failed. Sophia's illusion spell did not work either. Charlotte's spell on Maggie broke, and now the seventh member of their group was getting up from the chair. Charlotte tried to bind her again, but Maggie just stepped away from the chair where she was bound and looked at all of them with great satisfaction. Nora cast her spell and attempted to descend into the astral dimension, but found herself stuck inside her body. Linda, sneering, raised her hand to create lightning, and came up empty.

"What is happening?" Linda whimpered.

Before anyone could answer her, there was a knock at the door.

All the women turned to look at the door, but Maggie was the only one who went toward it.

"Where do you think you're going?!" Linda asked. "Don't you open that door."

Maggie didn't listen to Linda. Instead, she went to the door and opened it.

~

"Hello, ladies." Lilly smiled at the women standing in the hallway, dressed in a peach-colored sundress.

"Oh, come now, don't act so surprised," she said, smiling as she stepped inside the house.

"But they killed you," Maggie said quietly, tears streaming from her eyes.

"Come now, darling," Lilly said, placing a hand on Maggie's wet cheek. "You really thought that?"

"I don't know," Maggie cried.

The rest of the women didn't dare move or speak. They stood around the table, ash, soot, and dust on their hands and on the floor, pieces of the home turning to ash one by one. Everything was crumbling around them.

"It takes quite a lot and then some to kill a witch," Lilly said, shaking her head and letting her hair flow down her back. "Many have tried so far. None have succeeded."

"How..." Linda's throat had gone very dry all of a sudden. Urine trailed down her skirt as the strength in her legs and pelvis gave away.

Lilly smirked and walked over to the table, touching the pile of dust at its center, the table then turning to dust itself. "Didn't I tell you it was a test? You thought I was lying?"

"We killed you, burned you, and spread your ashes on the lake," Nora whimpered in fear, her disbelief overshadowed by the anticipation of what was going to happen to her.

"And you would have done a lot worse if you were more capable," Lilly said, scowling at Nora. "I was sent here, ladies, to help you. And I tried to. By my way of magic and the universe's will, I tried to help you grow as people. It was my understanding that if I taught you how to harness your power, you would look past your weaknesses and try to move toward your virtues, but you failed me. All but one of you."

She gave Maggie an approving look, but that was it. Then she turned her attention to the rest of the women, still standing there like culprits.

"I saw so much promise in you, Charlotte. I really thought we connected, Nora. Some of you have disappointed me more than others," Lilly said.

"Enough with your riddles! Tell us what is happening right now," Linda said, her quivering voice betraying her and revealing just how petrified she was. The walls of the home started to crumble, exposing the fog outside.

"Look outside. Do you see that fog? Have you not wondered where it's coming from? Why won't it go away for months? Take a look at your own lives. Where are your husbands? Where are your children? You can ignore them and block them out, but do you see them anywhere? Have any of you seen your husbands and children in the past few months? I'm not talking about you, Nora. That was its own thing. Part of the test. And my, my, how pathetically you failed. Didn't I tell you to wait before you astral-projected yourself into the realm of dreams and thoughts? What did you think you were going to find there?"

"I don't understand," Charlotte said, wiping away the fresh slew of tears trailing down her face.

"Then maybe this will help you," Lilly said, raising her hand and lifting the mind-veil off all of them.

~

THERE USED to be an eighth house on the street, one that was so dilapidated that it was an eyesore on Alameda. The seven women, whose husbands had worked hard to earn their esteemed spots on this street, were livid upon the resident's resistance in the face of gentrification.

They had tried everything.

Payoffs. Talking to her. Threats.

In the end, what ended up working in their favor was a lawsuit. Armed with the best lawyers in town, the Alameda ladies made a case, first in front of the HOA, and then in front of a judge whose pockets had been lined well in advance to make a judgment in their favor.

And the woman, who had been living hand to mouth, had no means to pay for an expensive lawyer and had instead to make do with one provided to her free of cost, had to stand there in the court red-eyed and sunken-faced as the judge, much to everyone's surprise, deemed that the house should be demolished, citing health code violations and jarring municipal codes that prohibited the existence of dilapidated residences. The woman was paid for the land that her house was built upon, and despite how many times she pleaded that the house had been in her family for four generations, and that she did not know what she was going to do with the meager sum that she had been paid, the judge banged his gavel, and later that evening, the seven ladies celebrated with martinis at Nora's house, not knowing that the woman they'd won the case against was busy tying a noose around her neck in a last bid to die in the same place as her mother, and her mother before her.

Right around the time Laura McFarlane hung herself, the women sought it fit to take their celebration to Lake Nip. They took Nora's boat to the lake, not knowing that her husband had forgotten to tinker with the motor, forgotten to apply the marine sealant to the leak at the bottom. Instead, he had covered it with a shoddy resin job, and had hoped that the next time he visited the store, he'd buy a coat of marine sealant for the boat. But he hadn't. And the ladies did not know this.

Drunk, relieved, and ecstatic, they got into the boat, their wireless Bluetooth remote speaker blaring, the women, too drunk and high from their vape pens, ignoring the fog that was creeping over the lake.

The resin used to plug the hole in the boat did a marvelous job of staying put until it reached the middle of the water.

And then, unable to bear the pressure of the water and speed, it popped like a cork, filling the boat up.

In their elation, the ladies had forgotten to pack in life jackets. And since the shoreline was half a mile away in every direction, they couldn't swim that far while inebriated. In their desperation, they tried as best as they could to plug the leak, but by then it was too late. The boat was already supporting more weight than it could hold, and now that it was half-filled with water, there was nothing that any of the women could do about it.

It's perhaps one of the worst and most painful deaths that anyone can have, knowing that they are going to die in a matter of minutes, knowing that there's nothing to be done about it. And yet, these women tried. They tried to swim, even though none of them knew how, least of all in a lake that was as deep as Lake Nip. The fog crept farther, blocking the view from the shore.

Maggie died first, wondering why on earth she had chosen to party with the ladies and then agree to the boat ride. She died with a heart filled with remorse and pain.

Charlotte was the second to go. Evelyn quickly after her. Sophia stood no chance, having drank more than the others, forgetting how to move her hands and legs. Nora, still in denial that her husband's boat had betrayed them like that, drowned close to where the boat had sunk.

Jennifer made it quite far, but after a quarter-mile, she could swim no longer. Her arms felt like lead, and her lungs were on fire. She was not willing to die this easily. But there was nothing to do. Slowly she sank, legs thrashing, arms flailing, mouth and lungs filling with water. And then, like the rest of the dead, her corpse bobbed on the surface of the lake.

But it was Linda who outlived her friends, Linda who cautiously swam as far as she could, weeping, coughing, arms and legs giving up so far, yet so close to the shore. She could see the house. The eighth house that was to be demolished next Monday. It was a pity none of them were going to live to see next week.

But before she drowned, Linda did see one thing. She was close enough to see the hideous house with the peeling paint and the rotting woodwork. She could also see the light on in the bedroom.

The silhouette of a woman hanging from the rafters.

It quelled the final moments of desperation brought on by her death, knowing that even if they wouldn't live to see the fruit of their judicial labor, at least she had seen Laura hang.

And then, once the sickest part of her heart and her body exhausted, Linda, too, sank to her death.

"YOU HAVE all been dead since June of this year, your souls trapped in limbo because of the great karmic imbalance your pathetic act created. You all died right after that woman, whom you sued, committed suicide. I knew her great-grandmother. I knew her grandmother, and I also knew her mother. They were good people. And you couldn't let her live on your prestigious street, could you? Your aggression caused her to lose her life out of desperation. And in that moment, right before she died, she cursed you. It doesn't take a lot of magic and spellbooks to make a witch. Any woman hurt, scorned, defeated, when she utters a curse through her lips is a witch, and her words are magic," Lilly said, grief in her voice. "Your cursed souls were not willing to comprehend the fact that you had all died, and so they were trapped in the inevitable place where all souls refusing to let go are banished.

"The Axis Mundi sent me here to guide your lost souls from limbo to the next realm, if I deemed you worthy of it. That fog isn't some weather phenomenon. It is the very air of the limbo that traps you in this place," Lilly revealed at long last. "And I was the one sent to help you, but what did you do? Kill the messenger."

"If we're dead, how did we go about town? How did we learn magic? Stop listening to her, she's just lying more to cover up for herself," Jennifer said, but no one, not even herself, listened to what she was saying.

"Do you remember the day you all went boating in the lake?" Lilly asked, sighing with disappointment. "Your boat sank in the middle of the lake because of a leak. They recovered your bodies, but by that time, you were all lifeless corpses. Your bodies were sent to the morgues, and later to the funeral homes and crematoriums. Your souls, trapped in this place because of your unresolved business." Lilly walked in their midst, looking at each of them, watching the disbelief descend upon their faces in one perplexing emotion after the other. A quick slideshow of the various stages of grief.

"Your husbands mourned you, your children visited your graves, yet your souls linger here, oblivious of the fact that you are all dead. When I was sent here, I was given a task. Guide you to the shores of the afterlife in hopes that you would be saved a fate of eternal Hellfire. For all of you were headed there anyway," Lilly said.

"I'm a Christian!" Linda wailed.

"And what a pathetic one you are," Lilly boomed. "You embody the greatest sin amongst this group. Pride! You cannot fathom that there are people better than you. You crush them with your stature, undermine authority, liken yourself to a baroness of the olden days with your wealth. Wealth that you don't even have yet. I really hoped that you would outgrow your pride, learn to work with others, and become a better person for it. That way, I would have taken your soul to the shores of the Axis Mundi myself. Redeemed you from a fate of eternal fire. But you let me down the worst.

"And you. Don't think she's the only sinner here," Lilly said, pointing a finger at Jennifer. "Always so envious of others. You were as bad as Linda yourself. Yet you showed no remorse for how you bitterly think of others and wish failure and strife upon them. A shallow woman with a void in her heart."

Jennifer cried, hiding her face in her hands, knowing that it was already too late. Each of them could now recall the event that had taken their lives.

"Charlotte's sin was gluttony. I thought I'd made some headway with her, but it shows that what you think you know and what actually is are two different things. You became ravenous for more power, didn't you? Isn't that why you were so quick to join the mutiny?"

Charlotte shook her head, mortified, but Lilly had no time for her. No time for any of them. What time they had was up.

"Evelyn, with her greed of things. No amount of conjuring wealth really satisfied you, did it? You had to come after my wealth in the end, and not to mention you let your anger get the better of you," Lilly said, putting a stern hand on Evelyn's shoulder and giving it a painful squeeze.

"Sophia, driven to the depths of lecherous depravity at the hands of lust. It was your lust for power, for more, for a world where you had everything and everyone to do with as you pleased. You did not hesitate in smiting me. The least you could have done was stop them. But you didn't," Lilly said, making her way around the table.

"But it was you who disappointed me the most," she said to Nora. "I thought that I had bettered you. Helped you. I thought that you were sincere with me. But when the opportunity arose, you murdered your husband? It's a good thing that you are already dead; otherwise, imagine the scandal of two dead bodies found in your Brandt home!"

Now that she had made her rounds at the table, she went to the one woman who stood as far apart from the rest of the women as she could.

"Your sin, if you're wondering, was sloth. You did not do anything in your life to change your situation. Never should a woman live in fear of another man," Lilly said, a gentle hand resting on Maggie's shoulder. "In life you were what you were, but I am glad to see that in death, you gave yourself a chance to grow. You were the only one who stood up for me, weren't you?"

"Yes," Maggie wept. "I tried to stop them from—"

"I know. I saw it all," Lilly said, patting Maggie on the back before turning her attention to the rest of the group.

"Get the fuck up here, Lucifer," Lilly said.

I thought you would never ask, Satan hissed back in Lilly's mind only.

The house had fallen down like ash from the end of a cigarette, and Alameda Avenue was crumbling with it. Outside, the fog had enveloped the entire street. Everything was gray, from the trees to the bricks that built the homes. And it was all imploding before their very eyes.

Footsteps approached the group, but the fog was too dense to see beyond the street. Lilly placed her hand behind Maggie's back and pointed toward the door of her home, the only thing still standing.

"Walk through that door, to salvation," she told her. As the rest of the women attempted to follow, a tall man in a black suit, loafers, and slick black hair greeted them.

"You're a few hundred years late," Lucifer said to Lilly.

"Consider this my response," she replied.

Satan smirked back and, with the clasp of his hands, turned toward the women and dragged them to Hell.

Lilly's story continues in Interview with the Devil: Epoch

www.ingramcontent.com/pod-product-compliance
Lightning Source LLC
Chambersburg PA
CBHW060541310726
48982CB00009B/1341/J
* 9 7 9 8 9 9 0 4 0 2 8 9 8 *